D0429269

THE
FEROS

ALSO BY WESLEY KING:

THE FEROS

WESLEY KING

G. P. PUTNAM'S SONS · AN IMPRINT OF PENGUIN GROUP (USA) INC.

G. P. PUTNAM'S SONS • An imprint of Penguin Young Readers Group.
Published by The Penguin Group.
Penguin Group (USA) Inc., 375 Hudson Street, New York, NY 10014, USA.
Penguin Group (Canada), 90 Eglinton Avenue East, Suite 700, Toronto,
Ontario M4P 2Y3, Canada (a division of Pearson Penguin Canada Inc.).
Penguin Books Ltd, 80 Strand, London WC2R 0RL, England.
Penguin Ireland, 25 St. Stephen's Green, Dublin 2, Ireland (a division of Penguin Books Ltd).
Penguin Group (Australia), 707 Collins Street, Melbourne, Victoria 3008, Australia
(a division of Pearson Australia Group Pty Ltd).
Penguin Books India Pvt Ltd, 11 Community Centre, Panchsheel Park,
New Delhi—110 017, India.
Penguin Group (NZ), 67 Apollo Drive, Rosedale, Auckland 0632, New Zealand
(a division of Pearson New Zealand Ltd).
Penguin Books South Africa, Rosebank Office Park, 181 Jan Smuts Avenue,
Parktown North 2193, South Africa.
Penguin China, B7 Jiaming Center, 27 East Third Ring Road North,
Chaoyang District, Beijing 100020, China.
Penguin Books Ltd, Registered Offices: 80 Strand, London WC2R 0RL, England.

Published simultaneously in Canada. Printed in the United States of America.
Design by Annie Ericsson. Text set in Scherzo Std.
Library of Congress Cataloging-in-Publication Data
King, Wesley.

The Feros / Wesley King. pages cm
Sequel to: The Vindico.
Summary: "James, Hayden, Lana, Sam and Emily use their new superpowers to
try to save abducted members of the League of Heroes, and when Emily disappears,
they must find their friend before it's too late"—Provided by publisher.
[1. Superheroes—Fiction. 2. Supervillains—Fiction. 3. Good and evil—Fiction.
4. Kidnapping—Fiction. 5. Science fiction.] I. Title.
PZ7.K58922Fe 2013 [Fic]—dc23 2012048222
ISBN 978-0-399-25655-4
1 3 5 7 9 10 8 6 4 2

For Juliana

"JUST ONE TRYOUT," COACH THOMPSON SAID, JOGGING TO KEEP UP WITH James. "No, not even. You're a walk-on. Just show up tomorrow for the team's preseason workout and you're in."

"No," James replied firmly. He picked up his pace. He had been walking down the hallway after class when the coach appeared beside him. This was not the first time he'd asked. It had been an ongoing argument for almost two weeks now.

"Just think about it," he said.

"I did. Still no."

The coach scurried in front of James and proceeded to walk backward so he could stare directly into James's eyes. His tight yellow sweater, embroidered with a big C, was straining against his muscular arms. "Can I ask why?"

James sighed and glanced at his friends Dennis and Pete for support. They were both pointedly looking away.

"Because I don't like football," James explained. "I don't get the point."

"The point is to score points and win the game! What don't you get?"

James rolled his eyes. "Yes, I figured that much out. But why would I want to do that?"

The other students were all staring at James as he walked down the hall, whispering among themselves, but he barely even noticed. He was used to that by now.

His return to Cambilsford High had been a source of gossip and debate for four months now, and the interest still hadn't subsided. The League's official story, the one they'd reported to the media, was that James, Hayden, Lana, Emily, and Sam had been taken hostage by the Vindico as a scare tactic. They were allegedly held in a small prison compound in the Wisconsin wilderness, unharmed, in an attempt to distract the League and the public at large as they tried to take down Thunderbolt.

But that story didn't explain how a pale, skinny kid had managed to come back with bulging muscles in the space of a month. How and why that happened was a question asked in the hallways at least forty-five times a day. And then there was the story from Mark Dilson, who claimed that he'd had a conversation with James shortly before being tossed out of a bus by a giant assailant.

"Why?" Coach Thompson exclaimed. "*Why?* Because football is more than a game, James! It's an opportunity! I saw you in the weight room with my own eyes. You bench-pressed six hundred pounds and you didn't even break a sweat! You could be a defensive tackle! The best. Don't you want a scholarship?"

"No thanks," James said. "I'm good."

The coach threw his hands up in the air. "You don't want to go to college?"

James shook his head. "I'm going to go a different route, I think. Thank you, Coach, but I'm going to have to say no. Again."

"All right," he muttered. "You know where to find me if you change your mind."

James watched Coach Thompson storm off and noticed several younger girls hastily turn away giggling from where they'd been watching the conversation.

"I wish he'd stop bothering me," James said to Dennis and Pete.

"I wish I had your problems," Dennis replied sourly. "Oh no! The football coach is begging me to be on the team—what a tragedy! Life is a struggle!"

"What is with you lately?" James said. "Your sarcasm has escalated to whining."

Dennis turned to face him. "Do you know how badly I want to be on that team? Do you understand what it means? Girls, popularity, friends. And yeah, most of those things would be for you. But we'll come along for the ride!"

James scowled. "I'm not playing football."

"Come on," Dennis pleaded. "I'll even memorize the plays for you."

"How would that help?" Pete asked.

James started walking again and they both scrambled

to catch up. *I can't play because the League would arrest me for abusing my powers,* he thought. Not to mention the fact that he'd already be living in League headquarters before the season started. But he couldn't tell that to Dennis and Pete. Thunderbolt's instructions to the five former protégés had been clear: they were not to use their powers, and they were not to speak about what happened to them. James just had to stay patient. In two months, he would finally be able to join the League of Heroes and become the superhero he always dreamed of being.

"I don't want to—end of story," he said aloud. "And stop asking me. I get enough grief from Thompson."

"Uh-oh . . . look who it is," Pete murmured as they rounded the corner.

Up ahead, James's ex-girlfriend, Sara, was standing beside his locker, fidgeting with her shirt. Her chestnut hair was streaked with a few blond highlights and artfully swept over her shoulder. When they'd first started dating, she'd worn jeans and graphic tees of League members to school; now it was always skirts and tank tops and expensive purses. At the sight of James, she perked up and gave him a shy wave.

"Not this again," Dennis said. "She just doesn't quit."

"That seems to be a theme lately," James agreed, and continued to his locker.

Sara smiled. "Hey, James. I was just walking by . . . thought I'd say hi."

"Hi," James said, undoing his lock. "How's everything going?"

"Fine . . . " she replied airily. "Well . . . Mark and I broke up."

James piled his textbooks on the shelf. "Oh yeah?"

"Wasn't the same, I guess." She leaned against another locker and played with a strand of her hair. "I also wanted to say sorry again for everything that happened . . ."

"Don't worry about it," James said, throwing on his jacket. "I keep telling you, it worked out fine."

He'd had to buy all new clothes over the last two months since everything else had ripped when he'd tried to squeeze into them. He noticed that Sara was staring at his arms, where the brown leather coat was straining to hold in his biceps. *I suppose I still went a bit tight with the new stuff,* he thought.

"Hi, Sara," Dennis said finally. "No, you're not imagining us. We're really here."

Sara frowned. "Hey, guys," she replied distractedly, and then shifted back to James. "I know you keep saying that, but still. I acted so stupidly, and you didn't deserve it—"

"It's fine," James repeated. "Trust me. I'll see you tomorrow."

With that, he started for the front doors, and Dennis and Pete hurried after him.

"Nice," Pete said, grinning.

"Very abrupt," Dennis agreed. "She looked stunned."

James glanced at them. "Do you have to comment on everything?"

Dennis nodded. "Yes."

Pushing through the front doors, James stepped outside

into the cool winter air. The trees surrounding the school were bare and covered with a light dusting of snow, and the sky was a clear blue. Tucking his hands into his jacket pockets, he hurried down the steps.

"Now, about football—" Dennis started again.

"Enough!" James said to him sharply.

Across the parking lot, a small boy carrying a pile of textbooks was being pushed around by a few older kids, who were laughing as he tried to get past them. One of them knocked the books out of his hand, and as he bent down, another boy pushed him to the ground.

"Maybe we should go call a teacher," Pete said, glancing at James and Dennis.

James narrowed his eyes. "I'll go."

He jogged down the steps, as Dennis and Pete ran after him.

"I know you have muscles now," Dennis called, "but that doesn't make you a superhero!"

James slowed down just as he reached the group of boys and walked up to them. He couldn't use his powers, of course, but he was hoping he could at least scare them off.

"Leave him alone," James said in his most authoritative voice.

The older boys looked over in surprise.

"What did you say?" one of them asked; Phil, a burly kid with shaggy black hair that was a year older than James.

James met his eyes. "I said leave him alone. I've already called the principal."

Phil scanned behind James. "That's funny. I just see two little nerds."

"I resent that," Dennis said, breathing heavily as he arrived.

The smaller boy was looking up at James from the ground warily, maybe wondering if his rescuer was about to be pummeled. If there was a fight, James would be in trouble. He couldn't beat them up, even though it would require as much effort as combing his hair. Thunderbolt would definitely find out, and that would not be good.

"He'll be here soon enough," James said. "So how about you get moving?"

"He's a cocky one, isn't he?" Phil said to his two friends, who snickered. "Thinks he's tough because he got captured by the Vindico. Very scary."

He stepped toward James, holding his gaze.

"I don't care how famous you are, Renwick. I'll take you down."

James really wanted to punch him. He could have thrown him across the parking lot. Or picked him up by his collar and let him dangle for a minute. Instead he just looked at Phil and smiled. "Maybe another time. But for now, just let the kid go."

There was a tense moment when James thought Phil was going to hit him. But he just looked around, saw that a small crowd had gathered, and then glared at James.

"Watch your back, Renwick," he snarled. "Let's go," he said to his friends.

The three older boys took off, and James helped the younger kid up from the ground.

"Thanks, James," he said gratefully.

"No problem," James replied. "See you around."

The boy started for the bus, and James was left with Dennis and Pete.

"Maybe you are a superhero . . . " Dennis said thoughtfully as they walked across the parking lot.

"Pass the potatoes, please," James's father said from the head of the table.

James reached out and grabbed the heavy bowl with two outstretched fingers, handing it over without even straining. He saw his mother raise an eyebrow, but he just smiled innocently and kept eating.

"Did you hear the news today?" James's father asked, shoveling down his mashed potatoes. "A League member is missing."

James immediately perked up. "Really? Who?"

"Renda. They didn't release much information, but apparently there are signs that she was abducted from one of their bases. The weird thing is, Thunderbolt said that all the Villains are still locked up in the Perch, so it couldn't have been them."

James sat back, disturbed. Was there another Vindico member out there?

"I hope they stay locked up forever," his mother said quietly, looking at James in concern. "Just the idea of them gives me the creeps."

"They did get rid of James for a month," his sister Ally pointed out.

"Ally!" their mother said. "Not funny."

"It was a little funny," his other sister Jen whispered to her.

"Are you all packed yet, Jen?" their mother asked. "You only have three days."

James looked up in alarm. "What do you mean three days? I thought you were going next weekend."

His mother frowned. "No. This weekend. I told you months ago."

"But I'm going to the reunion this weekend!" James said.

"No, you're not," she replied sharply. "*You* said the reunion was next week. And you agreed a long time ago to watch your sister this weekend. We can't bring her, James. We only have two seats for the spelling bee, and I won't leave Ally alone in that city."

"She's twelve!" James said.

"Exactly," his mother replied. "Too young. Jen will probably get to the finals. We could be in there for hours."

"No pressure . . . " Jen muttered.

"I'm just as unhappy about this, if it's any consolation," Ally added.

"No, it isn't. I haven't seen my friends in four months, and this was my one chance." James had suddenly lost his appetite. He couldn't stand to think of his friends having fun without him. He had been especially excited to see Lana. Even though he had come to terms with the fact that she was dating Hayden, he still missed her.

He was just about to ask to be excused when his father wiped his mouth with a napkin. "So bring her," he said.

"What?" James, Ally, and his mother all asked at the same time.

His father shrugged. "Bring Ally with you. I'll pay for the ticket."

James looked at his sister. He didn't like the idea of bringing her, but it was still better than missing the reunion altogether. Not by much, though.

Ally smiled sweetly. "I would like to meet the others. Especially Hayden. I've been reading all about him in the papers."

"Problem solved," his father said. "You'll take your sister."

"Great," James muttered. "This should be fun."

LANA SPRINTED DOWN THE LONG HALLWAY, HER LEGS PUMPING BENEATH HER.
A large hole had been blown into the wall up ahead and clouds of dust still hung in the air around it.

When she approached the opening, she burst through.

Inside, Avaria and Septer were locked in combat, both wielding deadly weapons. They attacked in complex, weaving patterns, and the sound of clashing steel filled the air. Suddenly, Septer's hand moved to his belt, and he withdrew a silver knife. Without warning, he turned and threw it straight at Lana.

"Watch out!" Avaria shouted.

Lana jumped to the side, and the gleaming knife passed an inch left of her arm, where it stuck into the wall. Avaria pressed the attack again, but the two superpowered foes were perfectly matched.

Lana knew it was up to her to end the fight. "Get down!" she screamed to Avaria.

Her mentor instantly dropped onto her stomach. Septer tried to dive out of the way, but he was a second too late. Lana pulled the trigger.

The red blast caught him in the chest. She saw his eyes widen in shock, and then he fell backward, lifeless. Smoke rose from the wound.

Avaria climbed back to her feet, smiling. "Well done," she said. "Your first kill."

Lana jolted upright. Her sheets were soaked with sweat. Even though Septer had lived, Lana still had constant nightmares. She knew she had almost killed him.

She lay down again, staring up at the ceiling and telling herself that it was over. She doubted she would sleep any more that night.

At seven thirty, Lana's mom came into the bedroom to wake her and found Lana sitting up in bed, reading. She shook her head. "You didn't sleep again."

"Nope," Lana said quietly.

Her mother sat down on the edge of the bed. "Was it the same dream?"

Lana nodded.

Because of Lana's attempted escape from the Vindico, her mother knew more about what had actually happened at the Baron's mansion than any of the other protégés' parents. So Thunderbolt had sworn her to the same code of secrecy that the kids themselves had taken, with punishment of a life sentence in the Perch if broken.

Her mother rubbed her back. "Septer's okay, remember? Everything's all right."

"I still pulled the trigger," Lana said, getting up and heading for the bathroom.

She inspected herself in the mirror. Her blond hair was tangled and matted from rolling around all night. Combined with the dark circles under her blue eyes, she looked exhausted. Grimacing, she combed the knots out of her hair and applied some makeup around her eyes. After she was finished, she threw on jeans and a sweatshirt and headed downstairs for breakfast.

Her father was already sitting at the kitchen table. He smiled hopefully when he saw her, but Lana just grabbed a granola bar and headed back to her room.

A few months ago she'd confronted him about his affair with the woman from his office that the Vindico had told her about during her training. Their goal had been to make her angry enough to forget about her family and become a Vindico member. And it had almost worked.

But despite the fact that her father admitted to the affair, her mother had chosen to forgive him. Lana was still coming to terms with that decision. She loved her father, but she was furious with him. They had barely spoken since she'd been home.

She passed her mother on the way up the stairs.

"Lana," she said. "You have to forgive him eventually."

"Maybe," Lana replied, and continued walking.

She checked her emails as she ate the granola bar.

Then she brushed her teeth, put on shoes and a jacket, and opened the front door.

"Have a good—" her father started.

Lana was already out the door before he could finish.

"Does my butt look good in these?" Alisha asked, looking over her shoulder.

Lana rolled her eyes. "Yeah, great."

Alisha grinned. "I love this sport. I mean, I wear these spandex shorts under my skirt all the time. But I love being able to just wear them on their own. You think there's a coed team?"

"I've seen you play volleyball," Lana said. "You won't be playing on any team."

They were standing in the school gym, waiting for their gym teacher, Coach Reater, to finish adjusting the volleyball net. Girls were standing in little knots all around them, talking. Once, Lana might have wondered what the day's gossip was. But now she couldn't care less.

Alisha laughed. "Probably not. Look who's talking, though. You're not any better."

Lana fought back a scowl. She'd been holding back in every sport for months now, and not just because of the League's sentence. The last thing she wanted was for the rest of the school to know what she could do. She got enough attention now already.

Despite the official report, rumors about the bonfire and Kyle's unconscious body in the woods were still raising questions around school. Lana didn't hang out with Tasha anymore. She was afraid that she might run into Kyle, and she didn't think she could stop herself from putting him through a wall.

"Yep," Lana muttered. "I suck too."

"All right, gather up!" Coach Reater called. She was a tall, thick woman and along with being one of their gym teachers, she was also the very strict coach of the girls' volleyball team. She didn't take any nonsense, and the gym class instantly stopped talking and hurried over. "Eight to a side!"

Lana went with Alisha to the far side of the court, where they took up positions in the back row.

"How are things with the BF?" Alisha asked. "Excited for this weekend?"

Lana smiled. "Yeah. It's been a month since I saw him last."

"Look at you. You're in love," Alisha said teasingly.

"I am not in love," Lana snapped. "I just—"

"Quiet, girls!" Coach Reater shouted, glaring at them. "Pay attention or you're gonna end up with a volleyball to the face. We're going to scrimmage today. Lana, your serve."

She rolled the ball to Lana, who scooped it up and backed up behind the line. *Lightly now,* she told herself. Holding the ball out with her left hand, she gingerly hit it with her right. The ball didn't even make it to the net before it dropped to the ground and bounced to the other side. Giggles echoed around the gym and Lana flushed.

"Put some meat on it, Lana!" Coach Reater shook her head. "Give the ball back to her."

Lana hit another overly gentle serve, and the ball hit the floor several feet before the net again. The giggles grew louder.

"Definitely not making the team," Alisha whispered.

Lana felt her temper steadily rising.

"You're hitting the weights after this!" Coach Reater called. She marched onto the court, snatched the ball with one hand, and forcibly threw it back at Lana. "My four-year-old can serve it over the net!"

Now everyone was outright laughing. Narrowing her eyes, Lana caught the ball. Her fingers tightened into an iron grip and she felt the ball's material straining. She wanted to show them what she could do. If she served it at Coach Reater, the woman would probably fly through the far wall. But she couldn't do that. Thunderbolt had been very clear: *use your powers and risk going to the Perch.*

Lana didn't want to be within one hundred miles of Avaria, never mind locked up next to her.

So she slowly released her grip, smiled, and hit the ball just hard enough that it made it over the net. But it took all of her restraint not to spike that ball into the floor every time it came her way. Just for a moment, it would have been nice to show what she could really do. *Two more months,* she told herself. *Then I can stop pretending.*

. . .

As soon as she got home, Lana tossed her backpack in the corner and grabbed the cordless phone off the base, dialing as she walked upstairs.

A bleary voice answered. "Hello?"

"Can you go online?" she asked. "My mom's making me pay the long-distance charges now."

"Yeah, just a sec."

Lana hung up as she entered her bedroom and then dropped into her computer chair. She signed on to video chat and a few seconds later, Hayden appeared on the screen. His messy brown hair was standing on end and his blue eyes were only partly open. Patchy stubble lined his cheeks.

"What's up, babe?" he mumbled.

"Stop calling me that," Lana told him. "I just got home from school. I almost cracked today. The teacher was giving me a hard time in gym, and I almost popped the ball right in my hands. If I'd served that ball like I wanted to, I think I might have killed someone." She shook her head. "It's so hard holding back all the time."

"I wouldn't worry about using your powers," Hayden said casually, rubbing his eyes.

Lana frowned. "Why not?"

"The League has bigger problems," he said. "Didn't you hear the news? Renda was abducted out of one of their bases. Emily told me last night."

"Really?" Lana said. "No, I didn't hear that. That's terrible."

"I know."

"They're still locked up, right?" she asked quietly, glancing at the window. The thought of Avaria on the loose made her forget all about gym class.

He nodded. "Yeah, they're still in the Perch, thankfully. Besides, they'd probably come straight for us. They do know where we all live, after all."

"That's comforting," Lana muttered. "Did you skip school again today?"

Hayden hesitated for a moment. "No."

"Then why were you asleep when I called?"

"I wasn't," he said. She continued to stare at him, and he shrugged. "Okay, maybe a little. But it's a different time zone. No school here today."

Lana sighed. "We're two hours apart. It's one thirty there, and it's Thursday."

"It's Thursday already? Nice. Only one more day!"

She cracked a smile. "Yeah, I'll be at the airport around seven. Do you know when James and Sam are coming?"

"Sam comes in an hour later, so we'll just wait for him at the airport. James is coming in on a later flight, so he'll take a cab to my house. He called last night to tell me he was bringing his 'very annoying' younger sister, so that should be fun."

"Great," Lana said sarcastically. But the excitement of seeing them all again was starting to bubble up now. "Is Emily there?"

"Yeah, I think she's asleep, though."

"Well, tell her I say hi when she gets up and that I can't wait to see her."

Lana leaned back, already feeling better. Hayden always seemed to have that effect on her. Maybe she did love him.

"So," he said, with a sly grin, "what are you wearing? I can only see your head."

Lana sighed. Sometimes.

HAYDEN SWITCHED OFF THE COMPUTER AND TIREDLY CLIMBED TO HIS FEET, stretching his arms over his head.

Guess it's about that time, he thought, and with a flick of his hand yanked the curtains apart. Light spilled across his computer desk, glinting off an old picture frame. In the picture, a three-year-old Hayden was sitting in his mother's arms at the park. Some passerby had taken it for them. He took a moment to look at it.

His mom had showed up at his house about a week after his return. It had been over a year since he'd seen her, and she looked different. She was wearing expensive-looking clothes, her hair was done up, and there was a diamond ring on her hand. But her blue eyes were watering when he opened the door.

"Hey," she said quietly.

"Hey," he replied, not meeting her eyes. He wanted to

ask her where she'd been. Why she hadn't called. But he couldn't even bring himself to speak.

She looked at him, her lip quivering. "I saw you in the news. A few days after you were taken. I thought . . . I thought you were gone."

Hayden looked at her coolly. "I *was* gone."

She obviously sensed the venom in his tone. "I know," she murmured. "I never said I was perfect, Hayden. I was just so desperate . . . for someone to finally take care of me. When your father left, I felt abandoned. I needed somebody, and when George came along, I couldn't pass up the chance. And I was scared that he might not want me if I told him about you." The tears were pouring down her face now.

"So you abandoned me," he said. "Thanks for checking in, Mom. I'm fine. I will be fine. Do me a favor—abandon me for good this time."

He'd closed the door on her. And then, for the first time in a long time, he'd cried.

Turning away from the picture, Hayden stumbled toward his bedroom door, which flew open before he reached it. He traipsed to Emily's room and poked his head in.

"Rise and shine!"

Her bedroom window was completely blocked by an overlarge shade, so no light of any kind could get in. Something stirred in the darkness.

"What time is it?" a muffled voice asked.

"One thirty. Didn't you say you had to do something today?"

"Yes. School."

Hayden smiled. "Oh yeah. Well, no one ever said playing video games until three in the morning on a Wednesday was a good idea."

"You did. Last night." Emily emerged from the shadows, not even bothering to brush aside the black hair that was matted across her face. "Are we having people over again tonight?" she asked, shuffling to the bathroom.

"Of course. We always have people over on Thursday. It's tradition."

"No school tomorrow either then," she said resignedly.

"Not likely. You know, moving in was probably the end of your academic career. You're lucky you already have a job waiting for you."

"Which is still two months away," Emily complained. "I wish the League would just let us in now." She closed the bathroom door. "I want to be a member already!"

"I don't know how I feel about talking to you while you're peeing," Hayden said.

"You talk to me while you're peeing all the time," she replied.

"Yeah, but I'm a barbarian."

She opened the door again, drying her hands on her shirt. There was a hand towel in there, but it hadn't been washed in about two years. "True. What time are people coming?"

"The usual. Eight or so." He stretched his arms again, blinking sleepily. "Well, I suppose I'll put on some pants."

A pair of faded jeans flew out of his room, rounded the corner, and landed in his outstretched hand.

"You're lucky the League hasn't caught you yet," Emily said. "You use your powers for everything. I still think that girl saw you float a bag of chips across the room last weekend."

"She was practically asleep on the couch!" Hayden protested.

"Her eyes were still open," Emily said. "You have to be more careful. You don't want to do anything to mess it up when we're this close to joining."

"Pssh," Hayden scoffed. "I'm always careful."

He lifted his right leg and the jeans started to pull themselves on. But they tugged just a little too hard, and he toppled over, smacking into the wall and landing flat on his back.

"Don't even say it," he muttered.

Emily just sighed and pulled him up again.

"Lana called earlier. She told me she almost used her powers today."

"What?" Emily asked. "Why?"

"A teacher was giving her a hard time. Apparently Lana wanted to make the world's greatest volleyball serve and probably kill one of her classmates," Hayden told her, rubbing his back. "That kind of hurt. We should get some carpet."

"We're moving to League headquarters in two months," Emily reminded him. "Well, I'm glad she's holding back, at least. If Thunderbolt ever hears that you're using your powers to put your jeans on—"

"Speaking of Thunderbolt, did you look into Renda's disappearance any more?"

Emily had broken into the League's network so frequently over the last few months that Thunderbolt had finally just sent her a pass code.

She nodded. "Still no leads. Renda was alone at the base, and she never even sounded the alarm. Whoever it was, they must have gotten in very quietly."

Hayden lifted his arms as the jeans pulled into place and zipped themselves up.

"Do you think we're targets?" he said.

"Possibly. They could have easily accessed the network from the base. Our files are on there, so they would know what really happened with the Vindico. If so, they might want to take us out before we can join the League."

Hayden glanced at the hall window. "Super."

"We'll just have to keep our eyes open," Emily said, heading downstairs. "And stop using your powers! I would like for *all* of us to get into the League!"

She stopped at the bottom of the stairs and glared up at him. "Hayden, why is there a frying pan floating toward the stove?"

He smiled. "Sunny-side or scrambled?"

THE NEXT MORNING, EMILY STROLLED DOWN A TRAMPLED DIRT PATH THAT CUT through a grassy meadow on her way to the woods. She plunged beneath the oak leaves and smiled as a breeze swept along after her.

Emily came here often, sometimes straying from the path and finding her own way among the knotted trunks. Some days she would just sit on a tree stump and listen to the leaves rustling in the wind. But today she had come for a different reason, as she did every Friday.

She heard water bubbling and picked her way toward the sound. Gently pushing the overhanging branches out of her way, she emerged at the bank of a creek. It was mostly lined with long grass, but a few trees strayed right up to the bank, their tangled roots exposed as the ground abruptly dipped away. At one of those roots lay a bouquet of wilted flowers.

Emily wandered over and removed a package from

under her arm. She crouched at the base of the tree and pulled off the wrapping, revealing a fresh bouquet of brilliant summer flowers. Placing the new bouquet under the tree, she tossed the previous bouquet's wilted flowers into the creek and watched as they were swiftly carried away by the current.

Since she wasn't able to visit the cemetery where her grandpa was buried now that she lived with Hayden on the other side of the country, Emily had made her own memorial here instead. She sat down and leaned against the knotted trunk.

"Well, Grandpa, it's been another week," she said. "They go faster here, it seems. It's fun, but there's not much purpose, I guess. I still haven't been going to school regularly. I know you'd want me to, but it's hard to motivate myself. I'll be joining the League soon, so it seems that school is less pressing now. I'll be fighting crime instead, so I think you'd be just as proud." She looked at the water. "I have to admit . . . I'm a little nervous. Not about the danger or anything, just about fitting in. The others all actually have superpowers—they're real superheroes. What if the other League members don't think I belong? If they wouldn't let the Baron in, why would they want a nerdy high-school girl just because she's good with computers? What if they send me home? I can't go back there. Not without you."

She sighed, playing with one of the petals of a flower on the ground next to her. "I know I say this a lot, but I keep having dreams. I just want to say I'm sorry again. I'm sorry I couldn't find a way to tell you I was all right. You might be alive now if I had. I wish you were."

She rested her head against the trunk and gazed up at the clouds moving across the blue sky.

"It's so beautiful here," she said. "Do you remember when we used to walk in the forest behind your house? I loved it there too. There were so many more birds there than there are here. Remember how we used to sit on that old log and watch them? Grandma always told you to come in, but you never listened." She smiled. "You'd wait until it was so dark we couldn't spot them anymore, and sometimes we'd still wait for owls."

Emily paused for a moment.

"You were my only family, Grandpa, you know that? Now Hayden is family, I guess, like a brother. But it's still lonely sometimes."

It hadn't been hard to leave her parents behind. When Emily came home after the battle at the Baron's mansion, they'd merely said, "You're back." They'd almost sounded disappointed. And when she told them she wanted to move in with Hayden, they agreed without hesitation. Now that she understood a little more about why they were so cold toward her, she didn't even care about winning their affection anymore. If they were still too hurt or angry about her mother's infidelity to treat Emily like a daughter, then that was their problem. She would be fine without them.

But leaving her parents behind was one thing. Losing her grandpa was another.

After an hour or so, the breeze became cool, and Emily pulled herself up from the ground.

"Good-bye, Grandpa," she whispered.

Emily started back through the woods, listening to the creek fade away. But as she walked, she felt a growing unease in the back of her mind: a sensation she knew very well. Someone was watching her again.

Her eyes darted around the forest, every sense on alert. Then, in the corner of her vision, she saw a flicker of motion.

A shadowy figure stepped out from behind a tree and ran in the other direction. Emily took off after it. She sprinted through the woods, jumping over divots and weaving around trees. But the figure was too fast, and it soon disappeared from view.

She considered possible explanations as she started back for the path. It was a good thing the others were coming tonight. There wasn't a group of people she felt safer with.

"Are you sure it wasn't a squirrel?" Hayden asked as he floated some dishes into the cupboard. He was sitting at the table with his feet propped up on another chair.

"No, it was humanoid," Emily answered. "And those dishes are dirty."

"Yeah, I know."

"So you're the one who keeps doing that."

"Yeah," Hayden said. "Can't have them on the counter. I think Lana almost threw up last time she came into the kitchen."

Emily sat down at the table. It was disturbingly sticky. "Yeah, most girls are sickened by this place." She stared at the wall. "I wonder what was watching me in the forest. It was very quick. I chased it."

Hayden glanced at her. "You chased it? You should have come to get me first. What if you were attacked?"

Emily held back a scowl. She knew Hayden meant well, but she couldn't help but be annoyed by his overprotectiveness. Needing constant protection was exactly the kind of issue that would hold her back from becoming a full League member. The last thing she wanted was to be babied by the others.

"I can take care of myself," Emily said curtly. "The Vindico are in prison, so it couldn't have been them. Unless one of them escaped from the Perch? I know Thunderbolt said they were still there in that news conference, but maybe he just didn't want the public to panic."

Hayden shook his head, and a dirt-stained rag started rubbing the counter behind him. "I doubt it. He would have told us, at least. Maybe it was the League?"

Emily frowned. "Why would the League be watching us?"

"To make sure we're behaving ourselves."

"In the forest?" she said. "Unlikely. And if they are, you certainly would have been reprimanded by now."

"This is true."

An old broom started sweeping the floor and piled all the dirt, plastic cups, and crumpled paper towels into the corner. Then the entire mass floated into the air and started down the hallway toward the back door.

"And I don't know why Thunderbolt still hasn't contacted us about Renda's disappearance," Emily continued. "You'd think he'd be keeping us informed. What if whoever was watching me is the same person who took her?"

"Well, we'll just have to keep our eyes open," Hayden said. "Whoever it was, they would be pretty dumb to try anything. We'd give them a royal butt kicking."

Emily smiled. "I guess. We do have experience in that field."

"Exactly. You know, I kind of miss the Vindico sometimes. Apart from the constant threats and beatings, they were pretty fun. There was no shortage of excitement when we were in supervillain school."

"Yeah," she said. "Well, this weekend should be good. We'll finally all be under one roof again."

"I know. I can't believe it's been four months since we've seen them. Speaking of which, we should probably get to the airport." He jumped to his feet. "To the Haydenmobile!"

"Are you sure that van is going to make it to the airport?" Emily asked skeptically. "It almost broke down yesterday on the way to the convenience store."

"Of course the Haydenmobile will make it," he said. "If not, I'll just roll it along with my mind. We'd save on gas that way, anyway."

As they climbed into Hayden's rusted, beat-up van, Emily scanned over the neighborhood. She felt it again. Obviously whoever was watching her in the forest had followed her home.

"I'll be happy when Sam is here," she muttered. "No one can sneak up on us when he's around."

"Yeah," Hayden said. "We just have to hope his mom lets him get on the plane."

He flicked on the radio and a deep voice filled the van. Emily and Hayden glanced at each other. It was Thunderbolt.

". . . doing everything we can to figure out who is responsible for these disappearances."

"There's been another one," Emily whispered.

"We don't know how they managed to get into our bases," Thunderbolt said, answering a flurry of background questions. "But I can assure you, we will find Renda and Peregrine, and we will bring the perpetrators to justice."

Hayden shook his head. "We had *really* better keep our eyes open."

"Yeah," Emily said. "Let's go get the others."

5

"CAN'T THESE FRIENDS COME TO SEE YOU INSTEAD?" SAM'S MOTHER ASKED
again. Her hands were fidgeting nervously at her side.

"The reunion's at Hayden's house," Sam told her for the
fifth time. "I'll be fine."

He could tell she was fighting back tears.

"What if they come after you?" she whispered.

"They're in prison, Mom."

Sam snuck a nervous look at his watch. He needed to
get to his departure gate soon, but he'd been having this
discussion for the last twenty minutes. In fact, he'd been
having it for the last three weeks, ever since Hayden had
invited him to the reunion.

"And if they escape?" she asked. "Who's going to protect you?"

He smiled. "Mom, they're supervillains. How would
you protect me? I'm going to be with the rest of the group.

It'll be perfectly safe. I'll call you as soon as I get in and before I get on the plane on Sunday. It's only two nights!"

"All right," she said reluctantly. "Are you still nervous about the flight?"

Sam's smile disappeared. "Yeah."

Even though he'd flown in both the Shadow and the League ship that had brought him home after the battle at the mansion, Sam had never been on a normal plane, and he was terrified.

"You'll do great," she said, and then enveloped him in a hug. "You better go, but make sure you call right away when you get there. Can you . . . contact me from there?"

Sam shook his head. "No, it would be too far."

Because Sam's telepathic abilities were naturally occurring, he'd been allowed to tell his mother about them. However, she couldn't tell anyone else, including his father and brother, until Sam and the others were presented to the public in two months.

That is, if they all decided to join the League of Heroes.

At first, Sam had been unsure of whether he was cut out to be a superhero. Actually, he still was. But he knew the others were going to join, and the thought of being with his friends again was enough for Sam to push his fear aside. He'd missed them terribly over the last four months.

Though he'd been a bit of a celebrity when he got home, things didn't get much better. Sam still had a hard time at home. People talked to him, but they were more curious for details about the Vindico and their powers than they were to find out about Sam's involvement. His dad and brother were nicer to him for a while, but as time went on, even that went back to normal. Except now it was worse than before because Sam could hear what they were thinking. And it hurt.

"I have to go," Sam said, giving her a hug. "Love you, Mom. Talk to you soon!"

He started for the gate, lugging his enormous suitcase behind him. It was packed with at least a week's worth of spare clothes.

"Love you too, Sammy!" she called. "I'll wait in the parking lot until the plane takes off!"

He waved and hurried on. After spending twenty anxious minutes in line, Sam finally reached the luggage check-in and plopped his suitcase on the scale. A young woman with dark eyes and a severe ponytail stood behind the desk, eyeing him.

Sam was short for a twelve-year-old and very skinny. Combined with his mop of curly black hair, which he'd at least trimmed this week, he knew he looked a little like a mocha-colored Q-tip. The woman probably thought an eight-year-old was checking himself in.

"Do you have your ticket and passport?" she asked.

Sam nodded and fumbled in his jacket. "Here you go."

She started typing. "That's strange. They must have oversold this flight."

"What? How could that happen?" Sam asked.

"It happens sometimes. All that's left are a few first-class seats."

He frowned. "How much more are those?"

"It would be an additional two hundred dollars."

Sam's eyes widened. "I don't have that much. My mom bought the ticket."

"Well, we can reschedule you for the next flight." She continued typing. "It leaves tomorrow at noon."

"That's no good," Sam mumbled. "I need to get there tonight."

"There's nothing else I can do."

Sam bit his lip, glancing behind him. He *really* wanted to get on that flight. But Thunderbolt had made it very clear they weren't to use their powers, especially for anything morally questionable.

But how would they know if he broke the rules just this one time?

"I'd like one of those first-class tickets," he said quietly.

She raised her sharply plucked eyebrows. "Now you have the money?"

Taking one last nervous glance behind him, Sam extended his thoughts toward the woman's mind. A swirl of emotions flooded through him. Strange, half-formed thoughts, spoken in the woman's cool, disdainful voice, floated around his head. He detected a dull sense of boredom first, and beneath that, an overarching desire to go home and have a glass of wine.

Give him the ticket, Sam whispered into her mind.

"I don't have the money," he said aloud, "but I kind of need to get on there. Can I go first class, please?"

A confused look came over the woman's face and she

glanced between Sam and the screen. "But . . . it costs more."

That's okay. Sam continued to reach into her mind. *It won't bother you later. You'll be enjoying a nice glass of wine with your friends, talking about how much you hate work. Just give him the ticket,* he added, a little stronger this time.

"I'll just give you the ticket," she whispered.

She began typing again and produced a new ticket, her eyes a little glazed. "Okay, you're good to go. Proceed to gate nine. Have a nice trip."

"Thank you," Sam said, feeling very guilty.

He tucked the new ticket into his pocket and then hurried toward the gate.

For the first time, it occurred to him he could pretty much do anything he wanted. It was a strange feeling.

He found the woman's mental voice again, just to make sure she was back to normal. She had already forgotten the encounter and was busy informing someone that their luggage was too heavy. Turning back toward the gate entrances, he felt an odd sensation pulling at the edge of his mind. An intense curiosity was emanating from somewhere nearby, and it was directed at him.

Sam stopped quickly to look around and heard a muffled curse as someone almost barreled into him. "Sorry," he said as a stocky man in a suit stepped around him and scowled.

Sam scanned the crowd, trying to pinpoint the source of the curiosity. It was difficult with this many people, but he finally felt it flicker off to his left. He spun around but only saw a young girl with bright green eyes and pigtails.

After a moment, Sam continued to the gate, feeling a bit apprehensive.

Someone was watching him, and he sensed that they weren't friendly.

"You may now undo your seat belts."

Sam wiped his forehead and felt the sweat seeping down his face. His knuckles were still white from clutching the armrest, and the pressure in his ears was only now returning to normal. He was pretty sure he had momentarily fainted when they hit the runway.

He hoisted his backpack over his shoulders and started for the exit. The first-class section got off first, so Sam was soon hurrying down the long white tunnel ahead of everyone else into the airport.

After retrieving his suitcase, he headed for the waiting area, dragging it behind him. He couldn't see any familiar faces in the crowd, so he decided to aim for the front entrance, figuring the others might be there. He was almost to the doors when a hand roughly grabbed his shoulder.

Sam yelped and spun around, raising his arms to defend himself.

"Well, someone's gotten a little jumpy," Hayden said.

Lana and Emily were standing behind him.

Emily sighed and shook her head. "Hayden wins."

"Guess who's playing spin the bottle tonight," Hayden

said, clasping Sam on the shoulder. "We didn't get a chance last time, but I think tonight is the—"

"Shut up," Lana interjected, pushing Hayden aside. "He's going to get right back on the plane."

Sam broke into a grin. "Trust me, that's not going to happen." Lana wrapped him in a tight hug, and his eyes widened. "Hi, Lana," he wheezed.

"Sorry," she said sheepishly, loosening her grip. "I'm so happy to see you!"

"I know! Hi, Emily!"

Emily hugged him almost as tightly. "Hey, Sammy." She took a step back and studied him. "You look older."

He brightened. "I do?"

"Yeah," she said. "I think it's the shorter hair."

"Really? I thought it might be too—"

"I agree that you look dashing, Sam," Hayden said. "And I'm prepared to talk about it all the way home. But I'm starving, and airports make me cranky. Too bad Jamesy couldn't come earlier. I can't wait to meet his sister. I've heard so many wonderful stories."

"Don't harass James," Lana said.

"When have I ever harassed James?" Hayden replied defensively.

She rolled her eyes.

"Oh yeah," he said. "Those times."

Sam smiled. "It's good to see you guys again."

"Sure is," Hayden replied. "Now let's get out of here before I get even more annoyed and start throwing people through the windows." He marched off into the crowd.

Sam glanced at Lana. "So you two are still—"

"Don't remind me," she said, and easily scooped up his suitcase under her arm. "Let's go. We might have to push the van home."

"You mean the Haydenmobile," Emily said wryly.

Sam laughed and followed them out of the airport.

6

"I'M SO TIRED," ALLY WHINED, TWISTING HER LONG, AUBURN HAIR AROUND her finger. "This has been the longest trip of—"

"We're almost there," James cut in, his patience wearing thin.

The cabdriver, an older man with a scraggly brown and white beard, smirked at James in the rearview mirror. Ally had been complaining all the way from the airport.

James scanned the street signs and glanced at the directions he'd scribbled on a small sheet of paper. It was getting late, and half the streetlights didn't seem to be working.

It was lucky they were taking a cab. He doubted he could have found it on his own.

"These houses look like crap," Ally said. "What is he, a drug dealer?"

"Probably," James muttered.

The cab turned off the main street onto an even darker

side road, where the dilapidated houses were wrapped in shadows. James peered ahead, searching for an old white house with a gravel driveway.

"What's the number?" Ally asked.

"Twenty-eight, I think. He said it fell off anyway."

"That's useful."

After a few moments, James finally spotted a house perfectly matching Hayden's description. Even in the dim light seeping out from its windows, James could see the sprouting weeds on the gravel driveway and the white paint peeling off the slats. The grass in the front yard was at least a foot high.

"That's the one," he said, and the cab pulled into the driveway.

"Lovely," Ally replied. "I think calling him a drug dealer might have been too kind."

James turned to her. "How about no more sarcastic comments for the rest of the trip?"

"Coming from you," she scoffed.

"Okay, I won't make any back to you. Deal?"

"Fine," she said. "Now let's go meet Hayden. How do I look?"

James scowled as he paid the driver. "Just try and be normal—"

"Jamesy!"

They all looked up at the loud voice and James saw Hayden scurrying across the front lawn. He reached the car, whipped open the door, and looked James up and down.

"I forgot just how big your arms are—" he stopped. "Where are my manners? Ally, it is so nice to meet you! James has been singing your praises. Wait! Let me come open your door!"

Hayden scrambled around to the other side, and James groaned as he swung open the door and extended his hand with a twirling flourish.

"Allow me," he said graciously.

"Thanks," she replied, smiling and blushing as she stepped out of the car. "I love your house, by the way."

James rubbed his forehead in exasperation.

"So what has James told you about me?" Hayden asked, putting his arm around her shoulders. "That I was handsome, witty, and intelligent?"

James started pulling Ally's numerous bags out of the trunk. "Try cocky, annoying, and vain," he said.

"He says a lot of things," Ally said dismissively. "You're taller than I thought—"

"James!"

James spun around and saw Lana bounding down the porch. Grinning, he stepped forward to wrap her in a hug. "Hey, Lana."

"We were starting to think you weren't going to make it!" she said. She pulled back but kept her hands on his arms. "It seemed like a long four months."

"You're telling me. Where are the other two?"

"They both passed out on the couch, but they're probably waking up right now with all the—"

"Hi," Ally said knowingly. "You must be Lana. I've heard

a *lot* about you." She looked at James and winked. He felt his cheeks burning.

Lana shook her hand. "I am. And you must be Ally."

Ally smiled. "I've heard a lot about all of you, obviously. The famous five. It's exciting to finally meet you."

"We are a pretty big deal," Hayden said.

Lana rolled her eyes. "Ignore him."

"My friends were pretty jealous when I told them I was coming to Hayden's house," she said.

"Don't tell him that," Lana groaned.

"I knew it," Hayden said, "I'm a national sex symbol." He took Ally's arm and led her toward the house. "We're going to get along great. Let me give you the grand tour. This is the yard. We don't have a lawn mower, so we usually just wait for the winter to kill the grass. Over here we have—"

"So he hasn't changed, huh?" James said.

"Not at all," Lana agreed, grabbing the remaining bags.

He glanced at her. "How are things with you two?"

"Good," she said. "How about you? Seeing anyone?"

James forced a smile. He'd gotten a lot of attention when he went back to school, of course. But he still had his heart set on someone else.

"Nope. I figured I'd be leaving in six months anyway. Wouldn't have been fair to start dating."

"True," she said as they started inside. "Luckily, I'm bringing my boyfriend with me."

James could hear Hayden describing a hole in the wall from inside.

43

"Yes, and we're all thrilled," he muttered. Lana laughed.

James looked at her and smiled. It was definitely good to see her again.

"I think she's my favorite Renwick," Hayden said as they sat in the living room later that night watching TV. They'd been sitting there for hours catching up.

James glared at him. Hayden and Lana were sprawled across a stained brown couch, while Emily and Sam sat on a beige one across from them. James was leaning back on a tattered recliner, sleep pulling at his eyelids. He'd hoped it would be easier to see Hayden and Lana together after a few months apart, but no such luck. Hayden had his arm casually slung around her shoulders, while Lana traced a finger along the back of his hand. They looked happy. And that just made James feel guilty for still liking her, which went along with the hurt of losing out in the first place.

Ally had already gone to bed in one of Hayden's extra rooms. The room that was supposed to be for James, conveniently enough. He would be sleeping on the couch tonight.

"Yes, she's a peach," James said.

Hayden nodded. "She appreciates me. And she thinks I'm cute. Which is obvious, but it's still nice to hear."

"Just give her another day," Lana said. "She'll be over it."

"Can we not talk about my sister anymore?" James muttered.

"James is right," Emily agreed. "We have other things to talk about. Sam, tell us about Deanna."

Sam smiled uncomfortably. "She's good. Still training."

"And how about *you* and Deanna?" Hayden asked.

"We're just friends. Not, like, dating or anything, yet."

Hayden perked up. "Yet?"

"Well, I mean, we may not," he said, stumbling over his words. "I just meant—"

"You meant you'll be asking soon," Emily finished. "Good. I like her. Maybe I'll date Lyle to complete the supergroup."

"That would be lovely," Hayden said. "We'll all be so happy."

"Except me," James grumbled.

"Who are you?" Hayden asked, looking alarmed.

James scowled at him.

"Speaking of a supergroup," Emily said thoughtfully, "Hayden and I thought it might be good to have our own name."

Sam frowned. "But we'll be in the League."

"Yeah," Hayden said, "but we're the coolest part. And Emily thought of a good one."

Emily sat up a little straighter. "I was kind of inspired by the Vindico."

"Thunderbolt will love that," James muttered.

She smiled. "I was thinking: The Feros. It means the wild, the untamed. I thought it was fitting."

"The Feros," Sam repeated slowly. "Not bad."

"Just don't tell Thunderbolt," Hayden added. "It sort of violates our sentence. So," he continued before James could object, "are you all excited for the party?"

"Just how many people are you having here?" Lana asked.

"Not many. Fifty, maybe."

Her eyes widened. "Fifty? Your house is going to be destroyed."

"Pssh," he scoffed. "I'm going to put James on the door. The world's strongest bouncer."

"No way I'm standing at the door," James said.

"Wait, that reminds me," Emily said. "I already told Hayden this, but you should all know. Someone was watching me in the woods yesterday. I tried to go after them, but they got away. And I think they know where we live."

"Someone was watching me at the airport today too!" Sam said. "They were very curious about me, and not friendly."

"Did you see them?" James asked, frowning.

Sam shook his head. "It was too crowded for me to tell where the thoughts were coming from."

"Has anyone else seen anything suspicious?" Emily asked.

"No, and I change with the curtains open," Hayden said. "So they'd clearly be watching me."

"Could it be the League?" Lana speculated. "Watching over us?"

"I don't know," Sam said. "It didn't feel like any of them. And why would they be so curious? They know who I am."

The wind picked up outside, shaking the loose window-pane. James glanced at it but saw only darkness behind the faint reflection of the living room.

"Sam, you can keep track around here, right?" he said.

Sam nodded. "Already am."

James stretched his arms over his head. "Well, we can worry about it tomorrow," he said, climbing to his feet. "I've got to get some sleep."

"Probably a good idea," Hayden agreed. He switched off the television with a wave of his finger. "I'll wake you all up when breakfast is ready."

"You're going to make us breakfast?" James asked skeptically.

Emily nodded. "He always does."

"Just don't worry your pretty little head about it," Hayden said. "Good night."

Emily, Hayden, and Lana went upstairs, while Sam shuffled to his room on the other side of the main floor. James lay down on the brown couch—the cleaner-looking of his two options—and covered himself with a spare blanket.

He might have accepted the fact that Lana and Hayden were a good couple, but James still had feelings for her, even after four months apart. He tried to think of something else. Lana and Hayden were happy together, and he couldn't get in the way of that. But as much as he tried, Lana was the last thought in his mind before he went to sleep.

CRACKLING NOISES WOKE SAM THE NEXT MORNING AND HE BLINKED SLEEPILY.

The night had been a long one. The old house was constantly creaking and groaning, and the sound of the howling wind filled the entire bedroom. Once, he even thought he'd heard soft crying filtering down from upstairs. He'd spent half the night hiding under his blanket and had managed to sleep only when the morning light finally started to creep through the window.

Even then he'd been restless. The others were counting on him to keep watch over the house, and though his dreams were often mixed with half-formed images that might have been real, he knew he was leaving everyone vulnerable while he slept.

Sliding out of bed, he pulled on his jeans and shuffled down the hallway. A delicious scent was wafting through the air. He rounded the corner and saw bacon and eggs frying on two pans, which sat unmanned on the stove top. Two spatulas were whisking the contents around, and even as he watched, one of the pans floated off the stove, dumped a load of scrambled eggs onto a plate, and settled back again.

"You like scrambled, Sammy?"

Sam whirled around and saw Hayden lying on the beige couch, his right hand waving toward the kitchen. James was still sound asleep on the brown one.

"Uh, yeah," Sam replied uneasily. "I didn't know you'd gotten so good with that."

Hayden smirked. "Practice makes perfect."

Four more eggs jumped out of the carton, cracked themselves on the side of the pan, and started sizzling.

"I can't lie, they're not the best," Hayden continued. "I always overcook them a little. Hard to tell from here. But to be fair, I'm not much of a cook, even with my hands. Do me a favor and wake up the others?"

Sam started toward the staircase.

"Just call them," Hayden said casually.

Sam hesitated and then closed his eyes. He found the sleeping minds upstairs, their thoughts muted and confused. *Wake up,* he whispered, *breakfast is on the stove.*

Immediately, Lana and Emily shot awake, and he felt a touch of alarm from Lana.

Emily didn't seem surprised.

Sorry, Sam said, *it's just me.*

"It's lucky I don't have your powers, Sam," Hayden

mused. "I would mess with people all the time. You're the only one who could have them without abusing them terribly."

Sam looked at the floor, feeling guilty again. "Actually, I kind of got upgraded to first class for free on the way here."

Hayden's jaw dropped. "You did something immoral?"

"I don't know if it was immoral," Sam murmured, wringing his hands. "Well, I guess it—"

"Congratulations!" Hayden said, cutting him off. "I'm so proud!"

"You know, we're not trying to be villains anymore," Lana commented as she came down the stairs. She walked into the kitchen and sighed. "I knew it was too good to be true."

"I never said *how* I was going to make breakfast," Hayden pointed out.

She just shook her head. "How did you sleep, Sam?"

"Okay," he replied. "It was noisier than I'm used to."

"Did you hear Lana—" Hayden started, but stopped when Lana turned to glare at him. "Oh," he said, "you don't want to—"

"No," she replied sharply.

Sam looked at the floor, feeling a little uncomfortable.

"Just a bad dream," Lana muttered, and then sat down in the living room.

A steaming plate of bacon and eggs took off after her and settled in her lap. Sam joined them and another plate flew into his hands. James woke up, looking very groggy, and soon the five protégés were all gathered in the living room, eating hungrily.

"This actually isn't bad, though it feels strangely dirty to eat things you made with your mind," James remarked, and then took another piece of bacon.

Ally came down the stairs a few minutes later, stretching. She was Sam's age, and he thought she was really pretty. She had nice green eyes that stood out from her auburn hair, a small, lightly freckled nose, and thin lips that always tugged into a smirk.

"Hey, Ally!" Hayden said cheerily. "Just in time for breakfast!"

A plate started floating off the counter, and James jumped up and ran into the kitchen to grab it. "I'll get it for you," he said, giving Hayden a dirty look.

"Oh yeah," Hayden mumbled.

Ally plopped onto the recliner, giving Hayden a grateful smile as James brought over a plate. He hadn't even sat down again before she was digging in.

"So," she said with her mouth full, "what are we going to do today?"

Sam sensed James's displeasure and held back a smile.

"Well, people will come around eight," Emily said, "so we'll have to be ready by then. We only have one shower."

"Let's do something before that," Sam suggested. "It's only eleven. We still have lots of time before we need to start getting ready."

"Speak for yourself," Ally and Lana said at the same time, and then exchanged a smile.

Hayden stroked his chin. "Maybe you're right, Sammy. A fun activity, perhaps?"

"Like what?" James asked suspiciously.

He clapped his hands together. "I know exactly what to do."

Lana turned to Hayden. "Are you serious?"

They were standing in front of a run-down, wooden shack covered on all sides by brightly colored canoes, paddleboats, and kayaks. It sat on the banks of a wide, slow-moving river, lined with gnarled trees that leaned out over the murky water.

"We're renting canoes?" Ally muttered. "Why?"

"Because it's fun," Hayden said, starting for the shack. "Hey, Jimmy! I need two canoes!"

A grizzled man with a straggly beard and bloodshot eyes poked his head out of the shack.

"Does he realize it's March?" James asked, just as a cold breeze swept by. "If the canoe tips, we're going to freeze."

"It could be fun," Sam said hesitantly.

Lana shrugged. "Well, we're already here. Might as well go out for a bit."

"Let's move, people!" Hayden called. "These canoes aren't going to paddle themselves."

Sighing, Lana led them down to the riverbank, where Hayden was already dragging a canoe to the water. James grabbed another and easily carried it over his shoulder.

Ten minutes later, Lana was casually paddling from the head of a green canoe, watching the water swirl into little funnels after every stroke. The river was calm, and a light current helped pull them along.

"Okay, maybe this was a good idea," she conceded.

"Told you," Hayden replied from the back, and then whispered something to Emily in front of him.

Emily giggled and Lana turned around. "What?"

"Nothing," she said innocently.

Lana frowned and returned to her paddling. She gazed over at the other yellow canoe, where James was sitting in the rear, doing most of the work. Ally was sitting in the middle, her paddle barely breaking the surface of the water, while Sam struggled at the front. He glanced at Lana and made a face. Sam had been less than thrilled to get stuck with those two. They had been bickering all morning.

Ally had tried to get in Hayden's canoe, but Emily had jumped in before she'd had a chance. In fact, Ally had been doing her best to get close to Hayden all morning. Lana wasn't too concerned about a twelve-year-old girl's crush, except that it was swelling Hayden's already-overlarge head. She might have let Ally have the last seat otherwise, but she'd climbed in instead and left Sam with the siblings.

Lana smiled and turned to the trees lining the bank, which grew thickly here.

"What if she jumps off?" Hayden mumbled.

"Catch her," Emily whispered.

"Right."

Lana spun around. "All right, what are you two talking about?"

"Nothing," Hayden replied, though he was barely restraining a smile.

A shriek suddenly split across the water.

"You almost put me in!" Ally shouted. "Slow down!"

Out of the corner of her eye, Lana saw the other canoe rapidly picking up speed. The front end was skipping off the water as it gained momentum, sending cold splashes up at Sam, who looked absolutely terrified. James's paddle wasn't even in the water.

Emily burst out laughing. "After them!"

"Have you lost your—" Lana said, but she was cut off as their canoe leapt forward. The freezing water sprayed up over the bow, and she started laughing despite herself. A steady stream of Ally's threats to James echoed along the river.

"Watch this!" Hayden shouted.

The other canoe lifted a foot in the air and for a moment they were completely airborne. Ally shrieked even louder, though it seemed to be mixed with laughter.

"Put them down!" Lana yelled.

Their canoe dropped back to the water, skipped once, and continued to speed along. Finally, Hayden slowed both canoes down and they coasted to a stop beside each other.

Ally looked at James, her face completely white. "What was that?"

"Sorry," Hayden said, "I forgot to tell you that these canoes have motors. They're in the back, streamlined. Really cool. That's why I like coming so much."

"I didn't see any motors," Ally replied, sounding suspicious. "And I'm pretty sure we flew into the air at one point."

Hayden grinned. "They're super strong."

Ally looked unconvinced.

"That was awesome," James said. "But it's not nice to surprise people."

He swept his paddle into the water and a massive wave erupted toward them. Lana screamed and covered her eyes as the wave enveloped the canoe, almost tipping it over. Her clothes were soaked right through.

Lana scowled. "Remember how the water's cold?"

Picking up her own paddle, she sent an equally large wave back at them, swamping their canoe. Ally and Sam screamed as they tried to cover themselves.

"That's it!" James bellowed.

Soon, both sides were exchanging vicious blasts of water. James stood up to get more force just as Hayden floated a large ball of water out of the river and sent it crashing into his back. He was knocked right out of the canoe, shouting as he went.

Lana doubled over laughing, but two strong hands suddenly pushed on the side of their canoe from below. The canoe rolled and the three of them went pitching backward into the icy water. Lana shot back to the surface, blinking water out of her eyes.

Hayden and Emily were already splashing back at James, so Lana crawled on top of their overturned canoe and gripped the far side. She pulled, righting it again as she dropped back in the water. Then, with a powerful sweep of her legs, she propelled herself back inside, grunting as her face hit the wooden floor.

Lana was just helping Emily crawl over the side when Sam shouted, "Hey! Look!"

He was pointing toward the bank. Following his gaze, Lana saw a shadow detach from one of the trees and scurry into the woods.

"That looks like the same person I saw the other day!" Emily said.

"After him!" Hayden shouted.

He threw himself out of the water with an invisible push and managed to land somewhat on his feet in the canoe. James crawled up after him.

"Start the motor!" Hayden commanded.

"I think it's a little late for—" James said.

"Thanks!"

The canoe streaked forward, sending them all toppling into one another.

"Guard Ally!" Hayden shouted back to Sam in the other canoe.

"Sam's the one person we need!" Lana yelled. "He can figure out who it is!"

"Too late!" Hayden replied.

Their canoe crossed the muddied river in an instant and slid to a halt halfway up the shore. James, Lana, Emily, and Hayden bounded out, picking their way through the low-hanging branches. Lana surveyed the trees ahead for movement but saw nothing.

"Boy, that person is fast," Emily muttered. "Did anyone get a look—"

"There!" James said, pointing as the shadow reappeared between two trees.

They all took off after it, running as fast as the dense forest would allow. The shadowy figure slipped in and out of their vision, moving with incredible speed. Soon only Lana and James were keeping up, and even he began to drop back as the thick branches became more of an obstacle. Lana kept running but finally slowed down when she could no longer see the shadow. She could hear the others calling for her, and she was just turning back when she heard a branch snap. She whirled around and saw the figure watching her from about thirty feet away. She could see now that it was a man with dark hair and eyes, and he was staring at her with a cold, detached expression.

"Who are you?" she called to him, but he made no reaction.

She took a step toward him and he vanished again. Lana stood there for a moment, disturbed. Whoever it was, they were definitely superpowered. No one else could move that fast.

James finally caught up, soon followed by Emily and Hayden.

"Did you see him?" Emily asked.

"Yeah," Lana said quietly. "I didn't recognize him, though. He vanished before I could get any closer."

"Well, whoever it is got a good look at us," James said. "Nice one, Hayden."

Hayden shrugged. "It was still fun."

"We better get back," Lana said. "Ally and Sam are probably scared."

They started for the shore and climbed into the canoe. Hayden steered them beside the others and James clambered back into the second canoe.

"What was that about?" Ally asked, shivering. "What were you chasing?"

"Nothing," James replied. "Just thought it was someone we knew."

She raised an eyebrow. "Staring at you from the trees?"

"Yeah, he's a weird guy," Hayden said.

"Sam," Lana whispered, "did you . . . you know?"

Sam glanced at Ally, who was busy questioning James, and leaned over. "Nothing. It's like they weren't even there. No thoughts, no emotions."

"Has that ever happened before?"

He shook his head. "Never. From what Sliver told me, it's impossible. Even guarded minds can still be detected. Whatever that thing was, it could sneak up right behind us, and I would have no idea."

"I'M STILL SHIVERING," ALLY SAID AS SHE STRAIGHTENED HER HAIR LATER
that night, staring into the small mirror she'd brought
with her. "I probably have pneumonia."

James adjusted his shirt and used the reflection in the
window to look himself over. With considerable effort, he
held back a sarcastic remark. James was trying very hard
not to fight with her tonight. He wanted to make sure he
could keep a close eye on Ally during the party. Muffled
voices were already carrying up the stairs as the first
guests had begun arriving almost an hour earlier. Ally had
insisted that James wait with her until she finished, and
he was getting very impatient.

"Ready?" he asked for the tenth time.

"Do I look ready?" she replied calmly.

"Yes. You looked ready two hours ago. We're missing
the party."

She glared at him. "It's, like, eight thirty."

"And they're already here," he said, gesturing at the closed door. "You're not going to prom. It's a house party."

"I don't get to go to many house parties," she said. "I need to look my best."

"Just stay close to me," James told her. He turned back to the window to fix his collar.

He was wearing a black dress shirt that clung to his pronounced chest and biceps. It was probably too tight, but no one would say anything. *Except Hayden,* he thought resignedly. James was still getting used to the drastic change in his appearance. Five months ago he looked in the mirror and saw a skinny kid with untidy brown hair and a pointy nose: his mother's "little weasel." Now his short hair was shaped into purposefully messy spikes and his body was lined with rippling muscles. He still had a pointy, freckled nose, but even that seemed to fit better now.

"I still don't know how those canoes did that. I didn't see any motors. I get the impression you're not telling me something," Ally said. She pursed her glossy lips and faced the mirror from both directions. "It has something to do with the abductions, I'm sure of it."

James turned to her. "Well, to tell you the truth, we were actually experimented on by the Vindico, who forced us to be their protégés and then tried to use us to crush the League of Heroes and take over the world."

She narrowed her eyes. "Very funny. You're such a jerk."

James shrugged and swung open the bedroom door. "After you."

· · ·

Emily stared at herself in the mirror. She wore black and purple eye shadow and her lips were colored to match. Her white skin contrasted sharply with the dark colors. Her black hair was curled in loose ringlets and it fell over a frayed white blouse in a tangle. It was unusual for her to wear anything but black, but she had decided to try something different for the long-awaited reunion.

It was great to have everyone together again; it felt like they'd never even been apart. But she couldn't help but notice that everyone seemed a little stronger, a little more confident. Their powers were growing. She'd known that Hayden was perfecting his abilities, but Sam had also told her that his telepathic range had extended, and Lana and James both seemed even faster and more muscular than when they'd left. Emily hadn't changed in the slightest. She wondered if the others would outgrow her.

She exited the bathroom and headed downstairs. The house was already filling up. The bottom of the staircase was an eclectic swirl of people and more were streaming through the front doors. Dozens of loud conversations filtered up toward her, and she sighed inwardly as she joined the crowd. She did miss the quiet sometimes.

Emily located the others and hurried toward them.

"There she is!" Hayden shouted. "Get over here."

Emily sidled up on the other side of Hayden and noticed that Lana was talking with Ally while James listened in with a sour expression on his face. Ally was telling a story about James moping around the house after the whole Sara incident.

Emily glanced at Sam and saw that he was staring intently at the wall, his brown eyes glazed over. "Are you all right, Sam?"

Sam shook his head. "Yeah, just thought I heard something."

"Was it screaming teenagers?" Hayden asked seriously. "I think I hear them too," he added in a whisper.

"It's nothing," Sam said, forcing a smile. "Just imagining things."

But Emily could tell he was disturbed. "I'm going to grab my visor and have a quick look outside to make sure our little friend isn't creeping around out there," she whispered to Hayden. Lana was close enough that she overhead.

"I'll come with you," she volunteered.

Hayden waved a hand in dismissal. "I'm sure it's—"

"You stay here and watch the party," Emily said. "Let's go, Lana."

She headed for the stairs with Lana right on her tail.

"Let's catch him this time," Lana muttered. "This is weirding me out."

"Agreed," Emily said, as she bounded up the steps to her room to retrieve her visor before meeting Lana by the front door.

When they got outside, they saw more people milling around on the driveway. Emily walked to the side of the house where a narrow alley ran to the backyard, wrapped in heavy darkness. She heard Lana's soft footsteps crunching against the gravel behind her. Emily gently placed the silver visor over her left eye and felt a tiny bit of suction as it attached itself.

"On," she whispered, and the view from that eye instantly switched to red. Spots of mottled colors appeared from inside the house, clumped together in a vibrant mix.

"Ready?" Emily asked.

"Yeah," Lana said. "Let's go hunting."

"Sam, let me introduce you to Christa," Hayden said. "You're fifteen, right?" he asked her.

The girl nodded.

"Sam's sixteen," Hayden lied, patting his shoulder, "but he's got that youthful look. Isn't he cute?"

Sam flushed.

"He is," Christa agreed. "Nice to meet you, Sam."

Sam gingerly reached out and shook her hand. Christa's friend was standing close behind her, and she met Hayden's eyes, smiling.

"Do you live around here, Sam?" Christa asked.

Hayden faded out of the ensuing conversation and looked around, analyzing the party. It seemed to be going well enough. There was a decent mix of guys and girls, and they were all laughing and talking.

He spotted an ex-girlfriend, Kayla, staring at him from the corner, and he quickly looked away. He really didn't want Lana to meet any of his exes.

Stay over there, he thought, *stay over there.*

A few moments later, he felt a tug on his arm. He sighed.

"Hello," Hayden said, turning around.

"Hi," Kayla replied, pushing his arm. "You're ignoring me tonight."

"Sort of," he agreed.

"Is that blonde your new girlfriend?" she asked, eyebrows raised.

"Yep."

"She's cute," Kayla said. "Where did she go?"

"I don't know. The bathroom, I guess."

"Why don't you introduce me when she gets back?"

Hayden frowned. "Why would I do that?"

"Because I want to meet her!"

"Yeah, sure, I'll come find you," he muttered. "I should probably go see if she's all right."

"Come find me after," Kayla said, and then went to join her friends, walking with a pronounced swing of her hips.

"Yeah, I'll get right on that," he said to himself, and then turned to Sam. "Back in a sec."

Sam glanced at him in alarm.

"Christa will keep you company," Hayden assured him, and then headed for the front door. He strode out into the cool night air, scanning over the driveway.

"Hayden!" someone shouted.

Steve and Dan appeared out of the shadows and clambered up the porch.

"Where's the wife?" Steve asked, nudging his arm.

"That word is not allowed," Hayden replied firmly.

Dan snickered. "He's a married man."

"That word isn't allowed either," Hayden said. "And she's around."

Dan looked at him seriously. "Are you in love?"

"What is with you two?"

Steve shrugged. "Fair question."

Hayden just looked at him and shook his head, smirking. He couldn't say no.

"I knew it!" Dan said loudly. "He's in love. She must be special."

"That's an understatement," Hayden agreed. "I would be very polite when you meet her if I were you."

"Must you follow me everywhere?" Ally asked, glaring at James.

"Yes," James replied simply. "There are too many Haydens here."

He'd noticed a lot of older guys checking out his sister throughout the night, and he was starting to get annoyed. He needed a sign that said she was only twelve. With her makeup and the new outfit she'd gotten for the trip, she looked a lot older than that.

Ally rolled her eyes. "Why don't you go flirt with Lana?"

"What?" James asked, feeling his cheeks flush.

"It's obvious you're in love with her," Ally said dismissively, smiling at a group of guys.

James stepped in front of her, blocking their view. "I am not."

"Whatever." Ally looked around the kitchen. "Where is Hayden? I should get a picture while I'm all done up."

"He is dating Lana, you know," James said.

Ally shrugged. "I like Hayden, you like Lana . . . it's perfect. Let's make a switch."

James sighed deeply. He did notice a few girls looking his way, but he still wasn't interested. His sister might be annoying, but she was also right. That just made it worse.

He was going to suggest they find Lana and Emily when he heard something—a quiet voice. But before he could discern the words, it was gone again. James blinked, confused. He was pretty tired; he hadn't slept very well on the couch. Maybe he'd sit down for a minute.

"Let's sit on the couch," he suggested.

"Yeah, I want to sit on the couch with my older brother at my first house party," Ally said. "That sounds awesome. Can I at least just go talk to that group of girls?"

James considered that. "Just stay close—"

She was gone before he finished his sentence. Shaking his head, he found a free spot on the couch and plopped into it. Then he heard the voice again. And this time, he couldn't help but listen.

Christa giggled. "So how do you know Hayden?"

Did I say something funny? Sam wondered. She seemed to laugh a lot, even when he gave simple answers to her questions.

"We were both kidnapped by the Villains."

She put her hand over her mouth. "You're one of *those* kids? You're famous!"

"I guess," Sam said awkwardly.

She took a small step toward him. "It must have been terrible. I recognize you now. I saw you on the news! I still can't believe Hayden was one of them too. It was *so* crazy when I saw that he was taken. Were you scared?"

"Yeah," Sam told her. "But it ended up okay."

"You're so brave. I would still be having nightmares. But I'm a baby," she said, laughing. Her hand landed on Sam's arm.

Sam thought her dimpled cheeks and dark eyes were very cute. But the more he talked to her, the more he missed Deanna. Both times she'd come to visit him, they'd only had an afternoon together before a League member picked her up again. But it was still great. They spoke with their minds as much as their mouths, and it made their conversations extremely intimate. He'd never felt so close to someone in his life.

"So, do you have a girlfriend?" Christa asked.

"No," Sam said. "Do you?"

She laughed again. "No, I prefer guys."

"Oh yeah, I meant—"

He stopped as a strange voice brushed against his mind. The words were faint and intangible, like someone calling from far away. It was the same thing he'd heard in the kitchen earlier, except now it was louder.

"Are you all right?" Christa asked, breaking into his thoughts. "You just phased out there."

"Sorry," he mumbled. "Can you excuse me for a minute?"

Without waiting for an answer, Sam headed to the bathroom. He saw Emily and Lana coming down the hallway from the back door. Emily was tucking her visor under her arm, and they were talking in low voices.

"Anything?" Sam asked.

Emily shook her head. "The heat signatures were all in the houses. Nothing sneaking around outside."

"Where's Hayden?" Lana asked.

Sam shrugged. "I don't know. Said he'd be right back."

"Well, let's just enjoy the party," Emily said. "Even if someone is watching, they're not going to try anything with this many people around."

"Yeah," Sam agreed quietly. "I'm just going to go to the bathroom."

"You okay?" Lana asked, frowning.

"Fine. See you in a minute."

He hurried to the bathroom, closing the door behind him. The roiling conversations quieted somewhat, and he leaned against the wall and closed his eyes.

Extending his thoughts, he trailed over the emotions of the partygoers: a vibrant mix of joy, jealousy, lust, and nausea. He touched against each one for just a moment and then moved on, listening for the soft voice. It wasn't long before he heard it again.

This time he concentrated on it and realized it was so quiet because it was being directed at a specific person. Sam focused until he found the person it was aimed at. Suddenly, the words became clear.

Lana and Emily looked around the crowded room.

"See Hayden anywhere?" Lana asked.

"No," Emily said. "He's probably showing off the Haydenmobile. He loves that thing."

Lana smiled and tried to ignore her nagging feeling of worry. They'd searched the shadowy backyard, and up and down the street, but hadn't found a thing. Still, something seemed wrong. *Just relax,* she told herself, *this is your last night here.*

"I'm going to get some water," she told Emily.

She'd taken one step toward the kitchen when an extremely strong hand grabbed her shoulder and whirled her around. Her muscles tensed, ready to lash out, but she stopped when she saw it was just James. His eyes were narrowed and his lips were drawn in a thin line.

"What's wrong?" she asked.

Without warning, he cupped her chin in his hands and kissed her.

Lana pushed hard on James's chest and he stumbled away.

She turned to see Hayden standing there, arms planted on his hips.

"What are you doing, James?" he asked coolly.

James wheeled on Hayden and shoved him. Hayden went toppling backward, slamming into the ground.

"James!" Lana gasped.

Sam sprinted down the hallway, waving his hand. "Hayden, wait!"

"Now you pissed me off," Hayden said.

He lifted a hand and James was blown off his feet, as if a tremendous gust of wind had swept through the room.

He smashed through a section of the wall behind him, the wood and brick splintering with an earsplitting crack. James and all the debris went careening across the alley before crashing into the neighbor's house, and he flew right through that wall as well.

The party erupted into chaos. Screaming kids scattered in all directions, tripping over each other to get to the front doors.

Ally pushed her way through the crowd. "What just happened?" she shouted.

Lana ignored her and turned to Sam.

"I was trying to warn you," he murmured.

"Of what?" Lana asked.

"The voice I heard—it was a telepath. He was telling James to kiss you."

Lana frowned. "Why would it do that?"

James emerged from the other house, completely covered in dust. He scowled as he picked his way across the alley and climbed back inside. Ally looked like she was about to faint.

James turned to Lana. "Sorry, I didn't—"

"We know," she cut in. "Sam just told us."

He shook his head. "I just snapped out of it. I didn't even realize what was happening."

"Sorry for what?" Ally asked. "What just happened?"

"My bad, James," Hayden said.

"Yeah, thanks," he muttered.

"What is going on?" Ally said sharply. "Someone had better explain this to me!"

They heard sirens wailing in the distance and shouting voices as the neighbors began to stream outside.

"How will we explain this?" Sam asked nervously.

"We'll just say we're as confused as everyone else," Hayden said. "The cops aren't going to—"

"Don't move," a loud voice commanded, and the Flame suddenly appeared on the other side of the hole, his right hand wreathed in a blaze of red and yellow fire.

Three others stepped up beside him: Sinio, Jada, and Gali.

"You're under arrest," the Flame continued, climbing into the house. "The ship is on its way. We'll discuss the matter further once we get to headquarters."

9

THE BLARING SIRENS GREW LOUDER, AND THE FLAME REACHED INTO HIS POCKET and pulled out a small silver device. "Hurry up," he said into it. "They're on the way." Then he looked up at the protégés and gestured behind him. "Out into the street. Now."

"All right, don't get testy," Hayden said, starting for the hole.

"No," Sam said. Everyone turned to him in surprise. "We're not going anywhere."

"Sam?" Lana whispered.

The Flame turned to him. "What did you say?" he snarled.

"It was Sinio," Sam said, nodding toward the thin, sallow-faced League member. "He set up James. I recognized his voice."

Sinio shifted uncomfortably.

"What?" James asked him. "Why?"

The Flame narrowed his dark brown eyes. "I don't

know what you kids are talking about. You have violated the terms of your sentence. End of story. Now, you will proceed outside to wait for pickup. As I said, we can discuss this when—"

"I don't think we'll be doing that," Hayden said, folding his arms. "How did you get here so fast anyway?"

"We were assigned to watch you," he said. "For good reason, obviously."

"So why did you tell James to kiss Lana?" Sam asked suspiciously.

The Flame scowled. "I told you, I don't know what you're talking—"

"There's the ship," Gali said. "Let's move."

James shook his head. "We're not getting on that ship. This doesn't make any sense. Where's Thunderbolt? We want to talk to him."

The fire swirling around the Flame's hand immediately grew brighter. "Get into the ship," he ordered.

"No," James said. "Not until we hear from Thunderbolt."

The Flame stepped toward him. "Then we're forced to detain—"

James reacted instantly. He put his shoulder down and bodychecked the Flame in the chest, sending him sprawling backward through the hole. He hit the ground with a thud and the other three League members scrambled through the blown-out opening.

"Get Ally!" James shouted to Emily, just as Gali charged him.

He slammed into James with the force of a truck and

they both crashed into the beige couch. James heard the wood frame splinter beneath the cushions. He strained against the enormous weight of Gali, who was trying to pin his arms.

"Stop resisting—" Gali managed.

He was interrupted as James kneed him fiercely in the stomach. He grunted and rolled off. James leapt back to his feet, sparing a quick look at the others.

Sam was locked in concentration with Sinio, but Hayden waved a hand and sent the League telepath spiraling across the kitchen. He crashed into the cupboards, shattering all the glasses. Lana was grappling with Jada nearby, while Ally was watching in horror with Emily from the stairs.

"Just stay there, Ally!" James called to her. "It's okay—"

Gali suddenly pushed James from behind, and he smacked into the wall. Spinning around, he faced the huge man, who was a foot taller and almost twice as wide. His huge, muscular arms and powerful chest looked like they might burst out of his navy-blue League uniform at any moment.

James met his eyes.

Gali charged and James dropped to the ground, hip checking him over his shoulder. The big man tripped and crashed into the floor, shaking the whole room. But just as James prepared to jump on him, a blast of fire hit his left arm, burning through his shirt. He dove behind the recliner as more flames streaked past.

James heard a muffled curse, and he peeked around the armrest just in time to see the Flame get pinned against the wall by an invisible force.

"That wasn't nice," Hayden said to him. "You ruined James's skintight shirt."

Jada and Sinio were already lying on the floor, unconscious. Gali heaved himself to his feet, but when he saw that the rest of his group was already defeated, he just stood there for a moment. Using the hesitation, James picked up the recliner and threw it at him. It sandwiched him against the wall and he dropped to the ground, dazed.

"Nice one, Jamesy," Hayden said, and then turned back to the Flame. "Now, what's going on? Why did you set up James?"

"I don't know what you're talking about," the Flame growled. Tongues of fire started to run up and down his body, but he couldn't penetrate the invisible grip holding him against the wall. "Now you've attacked League members," he snarled, looking completely enraged. "You're all going to the Perch. Thunderbolt isn't in charge anymore. I am."

"How can that be?" Lana asked skeptically. "We just saw Thunderbolt giving that news conference a few days ago."

"Things have changed. He's left headquarters. Now release me!"

"Where is Thunderbolt?" Emily asked.

"I don't know," the Flame said. "He didn't tell anybody where he was going."

"Something's wrong here," Sam murmured.

"I think we better figure this out ourselves," James said. He glanced at Emily. "Is the League ship outside?"

She turned to the front door and focused on the infrared in her visor. "Yes."

"What are you going to do?" the Flame asked.

"We need a ship," James said, "so we'll take yours. Hold him here, Hayden. Everyone else, come with me."

James ran for the front door, but Ally grabbed his arm on the way.

"How did you do—" she asked, looking confused.

"Later," he said. "Come on."

James hurried outside and saw one of the the League's gleaming white ships, the Mediator, sitting in the front yard. Its ramp was already lowered to the gravel. Farther down the street, he saw the first cop cars wheel around the corner. They had to move fast.

James charged up the ramp to find Noran in the belly of the ship holding a large black rifle. James quickly swiped the gun from Noran's hands and grabbed his shoulders, pitching him out onto the lawn, where he flopped into a tangled heap and lay still.

"Let's go!" James called to the others. Hayden was still in the house, holding the Flame.

They scurried up the ramp. James dropped into the pilot's chair and was relieved to see that the controls were very similar to the Shadow's. Outside, the cop cars screeched to a halt twenty feet from the ship and the officers stepped out uncertainly, weapons drawn.

A few seconds later, Hayden ran out the front door and into the ship.

"Everyone in?" James shouted.

"Good to go!" Emily said, sliding into the copilot's chair and running over the controls. "Ramp's closed."

James pulled back on the throttle, and the Mediator jumped into the night sky, the flashing red and blue lights disappearing below them.

Hayden slapped James on the back. "That was pretty reckless," he said. "I'm so proud."

"What just happened?" Ally breathed, leaning against the doorway. She was still completely white. "James?"

Hayden put his arm around her shoulders. "You should probably know that we're kind of supervillains."

"Well, we *were* going to be superheroes," Emily said. "We were supposed to join the League, but now we're probably villains again."

"I hope you were right, Sam," Lana muttered.

"Me too," he said weakly.

The night sky suddenly opened up as the ship passed through the clouds, the stars clear and endless. James leveled them out and felt a moment of weightlessness as they stopped their rapid ascent.

"I hate flying," Sam said, sitting down against the wall.

Ally looked at James. "All this time, you didn't tell me you had superpowers?"

"I wasn't allowed to," James said. "Even Mom and Dad don't know."

"See, your brother's cooler than you thought," Hayden

added, grinning. "Not as cool as some of the other group members . . . myself, Lana, Emily, Sam . . . but definitely cooler than the old James."

"Thanks, Hayden," James muttered.

Ally just shook her head. "I think I need a minute to process."

"I told you your house would be destroyed," Lana said to Hayden.

"True, but you didn't say that I would be the one doing it," he replied. "It's not all bad. I don't have air-conditioning, so that hole should really bring in a nice breeze."

Emily activated the communications relay and signaled League headquarters. The relay beeped, but there was no answer. "That's not good," she said.

"Now what?" James asked. "We can't go to headquarters if Thunderbolt's not there. The Flame will get another ship, and that will be his first stop."

They were all silent for a moment.

"Yep," Sam said. "We're in trouble."

10

"YOU SURE YOUR PARENTS ARE GONE?" HAYDEN ASKED.

They were standing at the bottom of James's driveway, staring up at the darkened house. The Mediator was
parked in a patch of forest a few blocks over, tucked right
in the midst of the trees so that the canopy partially obscured it from above.

"Yeah," James said. "They're away at a spelling bee.
That's why I have Ally."

"We have to leave soon anyway," Lana said. "If the Flame
doesn't find us at headquarters, he'll check our houses
next."

James nodded. "But at least we can drop off Ally and
think about what to do now. She's safer home alone than
with us."

Ally stood beside him, tightly hugging herself and
shivering. She'd asked about a hundred questions on the
flight, and James had tried to explain everything. Even

though she was scared, she looked positively delighted to be involved in League affairs. She was already speculating as to where Thunderbolt might be by the time they landed.

"You don't *have* to drop me off," she said.

James scowled. "Yes, we do."

He'd left his house key in his bag at Hayden's, but there was always a spare under one of the flowerpots. Scooping it up, he unlocked the door and stepped inside. The others were just coming through the door behind him when James's mother and father came hurrying down the stairs, wearing identical red bathrobes. His father was holding a slipper like a baseball bat.

"I thought you weren't coming home until tonight," he said, seeing James. He looked past James at the other protégés. "Are these your friends?"

"I thought you were at a spelling bee," James said.

His father frowned. "Jen lost in the first round, so we left early. She spelled *plankton* wrong. I'm pretty sure she lost on purpose so she didn't have to spend another night in the hotel with us. She can't stand our snoring."

"*Your* snoring," his mother corrected. "Now, what's going on?"

"Let's go in the kitchen," James said.

"Sorry about this," Lana apologized to James's parents.

"James?" his mother asked sternly.

"Kitchen," James repeated, and started down the short hallway.

The green walls were dotted with old family photos, and James desperately hoped Hayden wouldn't notice them.

Just as the thought crossed his mind, he heard a muted snicker from behind him. He sighed.

James flicked on the kitchen light and gestured to the table. "You should probably sit down, guys."

Emily, Sam, Lana, and Hayden all sat down at the table, while James's parents remained in the doorway, Ally beside them.

"Now, what's going on?" James's mother repeated.

"Does anyone want a drink?" his father added.

"I'd love some orange juice," Hayden said.

James rubbed his forehead in exasperation. "Mom, these are the other kids who got abducted."

"I know that," she said. "I recognize them from the news. And it's very nice to meet you all. But if you wanted to have your friends over, James, you should have given us a little more notice. I mean, it's past midnight and—"

"Anyone else?" James's father asked as he poured a tall glass of orange juice.

"Is that really necessary right now?" his mother snarled.

"Can I have some, please?" Emily asked.

James's father smiled. "See? Maybe I should make some pancakes—"

"We're here," James interrupted, "because we just had a run-in with the League. We're not sure what happened, but they set us up and then tried to arrest us."

His mother frowned. "Why would they do that?"

"We're not sure," Emily told her. "Thank you," she said as James's father set one of the glasses down in front of her. "But we fought them and—"

"You *fought* them?" James's mother put her hand over her mouth.

Hayden nodded. "Yeah. You should have seen James. He stole their ship."

She whirled on James, her eyes wide. "You did *what*?"

"We had to," James said, glaring at Hayden.

"So what now?" she asked worriedly.

James started pacing around the kitchen. "We have to leave soon. The League might come here, and we can't be here when they do." He looked at the others. "But where are we going to go?"

"We need to find Thunderbolt," Emily said.

"Where do we find him?" Lana asked. "If he's not at headquarters, he could be anywhere."

"I could log on to the League network," Emily said. "Maybe there will be some information on what's going on. And we could try and track down Deanna and Lyle too. Maybe they're with Thunderbolt."

"Who are Deanna and Lyle?" James's mother asked, sounding confused.

"The other two kids that helped them, remember?" his father said, taking a large frying pan out of the cupboard. "The ones who joined the League."

"Are you making pancakes?" she asked quietly.

"Well, they probably didn't get breakfast."

James shook his head. "Dad, we're leaving in like—"

"Pancakes would be great," Hayden cut in. "I'm starving."

"I knew it," James's father said.

He immediately took out the butter and put the pan on the stove.

"Can we please focus?" James said. "The network—how do we get in?"

Emily frowned. "You can't just log in from any computer, even with my pass code. Only certain computers are cleared for access, unless you hack your way in. My computer at Hayden's house is authorized, but obviously we can't go there now. It's probably swarming with police. We need to get to one of the bases."

"Except we don't know where their bases are," Lana pointed out.

James stopped pacing. "We know where one of them is."

"I can't believe you didn't tell me any of this." Ally shook her head.

They were standing by the front door, where James was nervously keeping watch while the others ate breakfast. He knew the Flame would probably go to headquarters first, but he wanted to make sure there were no surprises. Not with his family here.

"I told you, I couldn't. That was the rule."

She grinned. "But it doesn't matter now, right? I can tell everyone? Jen is going to faint. She's going to be so mad she slept through this. I love it. Can I tell her?"

"I guess," James said.

"Excellent." She peered through the window. "What if they show up?"

James glanced at her. "Then you run."

She mulled this over. "I knew you were different when you got back. I mean, besides the muscles. You seemed . . . confident or something. Which makes sense, I guess, since you just beat up Gali. That was awesome, by the way."

"Thanks."

"I can't believe they can give people powers," she said. "I've always wanted to fly."

"It's illegal," James told her. "We were the exception. And you can't give flight."

"Oh," she said, sounding disappointed. "That sucks. So can I come with you?"

He sighed. "For the tenth time, no. It's too dangerous."

"You're no fun," she muttered.

"You're telling me," Hayden said, coming around the corner from the dining room. "He's always ruining my fun."

"Were you eavesdropping?" James asked.

"Yes," Hayden said matter-of-factly. "We better go. I've already eaten my weight in pancakes anyway. Your dad is the best."

"I'll be sure to tell him," James said.

The other three hurried down the hallway, Emily holding some pancakes in a paper towel. James's parents followed close behind.

"You're leaving now?" his mother asked nervously.

James nodded. "Yeah, the League might be here soon."

His father handed James some wrapped pancakes. "For

the road. I already put syrup on them, so don't wait too long or they'll get soggy."

"Are you sure we shouldn't call the police?" James's mother asked.

"Definitely," Emily replied. "Don't worry, we're getting good at this."

They put on their shoes and stood by the door. James exchanged brief hugs with his parents. To his surprise, even Ally gave him a hug.

"Be careful," she said quietly.

"Call us soon," his mother added, her brown eyes watering.

His father put a hand on James's shoulder. "Want me to come along?"

James smiled. "No thanks. We'll be fine. I'll call you soon."

With a chorus of farewells, the five teens hurried back to the small forest and wound their way through the trees until they reached the ship. Several trunks had snapped under its weight, and it was perched lopsidedly on the stumps. They all clambered into the cockpit.

James gently pulled back on the throttle, and the branches scraped against the hull as they lifted out of the trees.

"Do you remember how to get there?" Sam asked.

"I have a general idea," James said.

He'd driven from the Baron's estate to Cambilsford with the Torturer, and knew the general direction. But he had slept for a decent part of the trip there and been preoccupied on the way back, worried that they'd just killed Mark Dilson. He was hoping that they would spot the huge property from above.

"I can't wait to go back," Hayden said. "So many good memories."

"And now we're fighting the League again," Sam muttered. "Just like before."

"Yes," Hayden agreed, "I think we were always meant to be villains."

The ship streaked across the night sky, and they all scanned the darkened landscape as they went.

"LOOKS A LITTLE UNLOVED," HAYDEN WHISPERED AS THEY STARED AT THE Baron's dark mansion across the estate.

They stood at the edge of the forest, mostly obscured by shadows and the thick undergrowth. After spotting the Baron's former property from above, they'd set the Mediator down into a small clearing some ways away, at Emily's suggestion. If anyone was manning the defenses, their ship would be blown out of the sky by the four massive antiaircraft cannons that ringed the estate.

The walk from the ship had felt long and eerie, with faint traces of moonlight creeping through the canopy and branches stretching across their path like grasping fingers.

By the time they'd reached the property line, the sky was beginning to lighten. Now they could see that the yellowed grass was becoming long, and the once-trimmed bushes were growing unevenly. Even the manicured gardens were sprouting weeds. The redbrick mansion itself still rose up ominously in the center of the property, and no lights shone from any of the windows. It looked abandoned.

"Anything, Sam?" James asked.

"One guarded mind," he said, his eyes closed. "Must be a League member."

"It could be a trick," Emily pointed out. She was crouching low to the ground, peering ahead with her visor and clutching a rifle she'd found in the ship. "I don't see any heat signatures at all. It seems empty."

"Well, we don't have much choice," Hayden said. "This is the only base we know of."

"What's our plan?" Lana asked.

"We should split up," James suggested. "One or two through the front and have the rest of us come in from the back. Just in case there's an ambush at the front door."

"So who gets to go through the front?" Hayden asked.

Everyone looked at him.

He sighed. "I figured."

"I'll go too," Lana said, glancing at James. "Someone has to protect this idiot."

James nodded. "See you inside."

He took off toward a line of tall hedges, and Emily and Sam scurried after him. Together, they circled toward the back of the estate, staying low to the ground and moving quickly from cover to cover.

Lana and Hayden took a straight line to the front entrance, their feet skimming over the moist grass. Hayden stopped behind a large shrub to examine the front doors.

"Kind of scary," he commented.

"You blow open the front doors," Lana said. "I'll go in first."

"You're so brave," he whispered.

"Shut up."

Lana sprinted toward the front doors and Hayden followed close behind, having a hard time keeping up with her speed.

"Now!" she said.

Hayden stuck out his hands and used all his force to mentally shove the doors inward. The lock snapped out of the heavy wooden frame and the towering doors flew open. But Hayden forgot to stop them before they swung out and hit the walls—the glass windows on either side shattered under the impact.

"Very inconspicuous," Lana said.

Hayden put up a mental shield around them to protect against any sudden attacks and they burst into the lobby.

It was completely empty. Their footsteps echoed in the silence.

"Hmm," Hayden said, stepping up beside her, "this is odd. Why would they have abandoned this place?"

"Let's get to the monitoring room," Lana suggested. "We can use the sensors to see where that guarded mind is. Emily will probably take the others right there anyway."

They hurried through the silent hallways and heard a distant smash as the others broke in through the back of the mansion. Lana slowed her pace, looking distracted.

"Sam says he still feels the mind somewhere," she said quietly. "They're going to meet us at the monitoring room."

When the two groups met up in front of the door, Emily immediately triggered the control panel, trying to open it. But nothing happened.

She frowned. "It's locked."

"What would you do without me?" Hayden asked airily.

He closed his eyes and mentally pushed against the reinforced locking mechanism. Gradually, the doors began to slide apart, screeching. When they had opened wide enough for them to almost see inside the room, a powerful stream of water shot out of the opening and struck Hayden in the face.

The ice-cold water knocked him right onto his tailbone and pain lanced up his back. Blinking, he saw another blast streak out of the room, hitting Emily in the shoulder, and she spun to the ground.

"What the . . ." Hayden managed, just as Lana dove into the room.

Scrambling back to his feet, Hayden headed after her. Inside, Lana was standing over a pale woman with vivid blue hair. It was another League member, Blue.

"That water was cold," Hayden said. "Good thing you don't shoot fire. This face is the moneymaker."

Blue frowned. "I didn't know it was you kids."

"So that's why I didn't see you on the infrared," Emily

said on her way to the control panel. "You're ice cold." She scanned over the monitors. "Everything is online; we just weren't close enough to activate the guns. The League will have to do the same thing we did and come in on foot."

"Why are you here?" Blue asked. "I thought you weren't joining us for two more months."

"We're here because your friends are chasing us," Lana said sharply. "They set us up and tried to arrest us."

Blue started to climb to her feet.

"Don't try anything," Lana warned.

"Who set you up?" she asked.

"Flame, Gali, Sinio, Jada, and Noran," James told her.

Blue sighed. "I thought so. The Flame has been the most vocal. And Gali as well. Sinio, Jada, and Noran are a bit more surprising. Obviously he's gotten to them."

"What do you mean?" Lana asked.

"I can explain what I know," Blue said, "which isn't much, I'm afraid. Something else is going on, that much I'm sure of. But I've been here alone for about a month now, and things are happening without me."

"Where are Deanna and Lyle?" Sam asked.

"They were at headquarters, but I think Thunderbolt has taken them elsewhere." She limped over to one of the chairs and sat down. "You didn't have to tackle me quite so hard," she said to Lana, scowling.

"You didn't have to shoot water at us," Lana replied coolly.

Blue held her gaze for a moment, rubbing her elbow. "I guess I'll start from when you kids got dropped off after the battle. It seemed like everything was finished. The Vindico were in prison and the war was over. But for some time before that, the League had its own troubles. There were . . . divisions in the ranks.

"Thunderbolt is our official leader, but for a few years now, some have begun to think he is too passive. They thought he could have destroyed the Vindico earlier if we'd pressed more. When Nighthawk died, the pressure really started again. And then there was Septer. At first, we didn't think he was going to make it." Her eyes darted back to Lana. "At that point, the only thing holding us together was the hatred of the Vindico.

"They gave everyone a target to go after. We attacked this mansion, and we were almost destroyed as a result. Thunderbolt had been hesitant for a reason: we were unprepared for battle. I think we had all grown complacent. We hadn't been training anymore; we hadn't been working on developing our powers. With you five on their side, we were totally overwhelmed.

"Thankfully, you turned against them and saved the League. And after that battle, everything quieted down again. We'd won, so the divisions among us could be healed. Or so we thought. As it turned out, the wounds were too deep. A power struggle began, centered around something that could change the entire structure of the League. You."

"The Feros," Hayden whispered dramatically.

Blue frowned. "What?"

"Ignore him," Lana said.

Blue gave Hayden another confused look and continued.

"You are a powerful resource. You're all very talented, more so than many League members, and you're also naturally loyal to each other. There are barely five League members who really trust each other anymore, so that makes you very influential. Was this the first time you've all seen each other since you went home?"

"Yeah," Hayden said. "The Flame ruined my reunion party."

"So this was his first real chance to make a move. But as I said, something else is happening. As you know, two League members have disappeared. That doesn't just happen. But we don't know who did it or why. The Vindico are still on the Perch, so it wasn't them. The League is nervous now and the tension is building. That's why the Flame took his risk. Thunderbolt will be furious. He'll have no choice but to arrest the traitors. The League is going to crumble."

"Sam and I were both being watched," Emily said. "Was Thunderbolt having us followed?"

"I don't think so. He's only got a few people he can trust. I'm one of them, and I've been stuck here. Maybe he knew that if something went wrong, you would come here."

"So who was following us?" Sam asked.

"I don't know. There are other players in this game now. Someone took my friends, and maybe they're on to you as well."

"That's great," Hayden said. "So now what? Did Thunderbolt leave any orders?"

"No," she replied grimly. "And I don't know how to get

in touch with him. I alerted headquarters that I was under attack and no one replied. I don't think anyone's there."

"Where is the Perch?" Emily asked.

"Why?" Blue replied suspiciously.

"Are the Vindico being guarded?"

Blue nodded. "Of course. There's always a member stationed there. And there are plenty of sentries. They're not going anywhere."

"So what do we do?" Sam asked, sounding nervous.

"Blue, you keep trying to call Thunderbolt," James said. "Emily, you can still get on the network like we planned and see what you can dig up. The rest of us can go get the ship and bring it back to—"

"Wait," Emily cut in. She looked up from the monitors. "Someone else is here."

12

THEY HURRIED TOWARD THE LOBBY, EMILY AT THE LEAD.

"They tripped a sensor outside," she explained. "Right near the perimeter."

"You're sure it's just one person?" James asked.

She glanced back at him. "No."

She led them outside, where the sun was now breaching the tips of the trees. They crossed the lawn again, and Emily scanned the forest with her infrared. There was a lot of life scurrying about and everything was muddled with red.

"Sam?" she asked.

"Nothing," he replied. "But it could be the same thing that was watching us at the water."

"Should we go into the woods to look?" Lana said.

Emily continued to survey the forest and then shook her head. "There's no point. The Wraiths could easily hide in there. Better to wait for them in the mansion."

"The Wraiths?" Hayden asked.

"That's what I'm calling them," Emily said. "They dress in black, they vanish in seconds, and Sam can't even sense them. It's like they're ghosts."

"Great," Sam murmured.

Despite Emily's suggestion, they stood there for a few minutes more, as if expecting something to burst out of the trees. Finally, the cold air drove them back inside and they settled into the monitoring room.

"You sure the Mediator is locked down?" Lana asked Emily.

She nodded. "Definitely. We'll just have to keep an eye on the sensors. I'll take first watch. I want to look around the network anyway. You can all get some sleep."

"Good idea," Hayden said. "It's been a long night. Back to our old quarters!"

"You sure you're okay, Emily?" James asked, blinking back sleep.

"Yeah. Someone else can take over in a few hours."

James nodded and they left Emily alone with Blue at the controls.

"I'll try Thunderbolt again," Blue said, sitting down in front of the communications relay.

"Sounds good," Emily replied. She turned to the computer console and accessed the League network. "Now," she whispered to herself, "let's see what we can find out."

Sam gazed around his former bedroom, his forehead soaked with sweat.

He had no idea how long he'd been trying to sleep, but it was impossible. He kept expecting voices in the dark or freezing jets of water. And that wasn't the only reason. He couldn't ignore the growing uneasiness in the back of his mind: he had a bad feeling that they were all missing something.

He got out of bed and wandered into the common room, which was still furnished as it had been during their training. It already felt like years since they'd been there. He stepped through the smashed mirror door and went to the monitoring room. Emily was leaning back in the chair, her head bobbing.

"Emily?"

She jerked into alertness, snatching her rifle off the floor and whirling to face the door.

Sam put his hands up. "Just me!"

"Oh, sorry," she muttered. "Getting a little tired."

"Well, I can take over. I can't sleep anyway."

"Is something wrong?"

"I'm not sure." Sam sat down beside her. "Where's Blue?"

"She went to bed. Couldn't keep her eyes open."

"Can you show me what I need to watch?"

Emily quickly ran over the console, explaining each alarm and how to activate the antiaircraft guns. When she finished, she looked at him.

"How was the outside world for you, Sam? Did it go back to normal?"

Sam was silent for a moment. "Not really," he said at last. "I talked to my mom about the surveillance video that

Sliver showed me. She cried when I asked her about how she moved on so quickly to do normal stuff again. She said she didn't know what else she could have done, but that on the inside, she was heartbroken. It was just like Hayden told me." He bit his lip. "So with her, it was okay. But my dad and brother, they treated me better at first, and I felt guilt in their minds. But after a few weeks, it was the same again, or worse maybe, because I could sense their dislike. I sensed that from lots of people actually. Even from some of my teachers, ones who I went out of my way to impress. Eventually, I shut it all out. But it hurt to know that so many people didn't like me."

Sam felt tears forming in the corners of his eyes. He blinked, trying to hold them back.

"I know what you mean," Emily said quietly.

"Sometimes I thought about *making* them like me," he said. "I could do that, you know. It's tempting to have this power. Sliver told me he talked rich people into giving him houses and cars and boats, and I could do the same, but I know I shouldn't."

Emily nodded. "Of course you won't. You're too good of a person. I always said you're going to be the best superhero out of all of us. You're the only one who doesn't have a dark side."

"I don't know about that," Sam murmured.

"It's true. And we're your friends, Sam. We like you. We're all going to join the League, and you won't have to worry about those people anymore." She patted his back. "But first, we have to figure out what's going on. And before that, I need some sleep. Sound the alarm if you see anything, or just wake us up your usual way."

She put her rifle on the floor but then seemed to think better of it and picked it back up. "It's nice to have it back," she said. "I feel like I can help again. Night, Sam."

She walked out of the room, and Sam turned to the console, smiling. It was good to be back with friends.

"This was a grand idea," Hayden said, gesturing at the lawn. "A little fresh air, food, a blue-haired woman—"

"I still think we should be watching the sensors," Blue cut in. "We'll be caught in the open out here."

"I have the feed linked to my visor," Emily said. "We'll be fine. Plus, we thought you could use some fresh air after being cooped up in that mansion for so long."

They were sitting around a circular wooden table that Hayden had found and floated onto the front lawn. The night had passed without incident, and so they had decided to have lunch outside. It was a clear, sunny day, but it was still cool, and they were all wrapped in thick blankets they had taken from the mansion.

Lana glanced at the forest along the outer edges of the property. Even though the perimeter sensors were on, she felt like the Flame and the others could emerge from the woods at any moment. It made for an unsettling meal.

"So, Blue," Hayden said casually. "Are you seeing anybody?"

Blue rolled her eyes. "Yes, I have a lot of free time while I guard this mansion."

"There aren't many good-looking guys in the League," Hayden mused. "Maybe Junkit, and I suppose the Flame. He's kind of a jerk, though. Gali too, if you like muscles that big—"

"I dated the Flame," Blue said, cutting him off. "But that was a long time ago."

"Really?" Emily asked. "Ironic."

"Yeah," Blue murmured, and she seemed to grow somber.

James shifted uncomfortably. "So if Thunderbolt isn't answering, and none of the League members are communicating on the network, what do we do? All we have are the base locations. Do we check them one by one?"

"That might be dangerous," Sam pointed out.

"Well, we can't sit here and wait until someone attacks," James argued.

Hayden plunked his glass on the table. "Why not? We could capture them and get answers that way."

"Wait," Sam said, turning to Blue. "What did the League do with Sliver's amplifier?"

She frowned. "I don't know. Thunderbolt wouldn't have left it here."

His face fell. "Oh. I might have been able to use it to contact Deanna."

"Well, we can try and—" James started.

Emily suddenly grabbed her rifle off the table. "Stop!"

Lana whirled around and saw someone darting toward the trees. Emily fired.

A burst of blue energy leapt across the lawn, but it sailed wide and hit a tree.

"Come on!" Emily shouted.

They scrambled out of their chairs and took off across the lawn. Lana was the fastest and she pulled ahead of the others, her legs pumping beneath her. The Wraith plunged into the woods and she crashed after it, swatting the branches aside.

"Split up!" James shouted to the others. "Cut it off!"

Lana jumped over a fallen log and heard a snap as James barreled through a tree.

She was closing in. She could tell it was a man now, with jet-black hair and a matching uniform. It really was like chasing a stray shadow. All of a sudden she saw his arm move and he cast something over his shoulder. Lana reacted instantly.

"Duck!" she screamed, and dove to her left.

An earsplitting wave of sound tore through the air, catching Lana in midair. It carried her even farther, and she landed flat on her stomach, her face smacking into the ground. Lana blinked and slowly pushed herself back to her feet. Behind her, all the trees in a twenty-foot radius had been snapped in half. She spotted James shakily standing up and she hurried over.

"What was that?" he asked, sounding dazed.

"I don't know. A concussion grenade or something."

James scowled. "Good thing it was only me and you up here. Some of the others could have been killed!"

"I know." She glanced behind him. "Where *are* the others?"

A shriek split through the air and Lana and James exchanged a quick glance before hurrying toward the sound.

"Where did it come from?" James called over his shoulder.

"I don't know! Keep going this way!"

They ran for a minute more, but all they could hear was the wind over the canopy of trees. They slowed down, looking around frantically.

Lana, a quiet voice said into Lana's mind. *It's Sam. Stay there.*

"Sam's coming," Lana said. "But who screamed?"

"It must have been Blue or Emily," James replied, scanning the trees. "It was definitely a girl."

She frowned. "I doubt Emily would scream like that."

Lana heard something crashing through the foliage, and then Hayden and Sam appeared.

"What happened?" James asked quickly.

"We don't know," Hayden said. "Emily and Blue went left, and we went right. We heard the huge boom, though, and then the scream."

"The boom was a grenade or something," Lana explained. "It went off over here. But the scream wasn't from us."

"It was Blue," Sam said. "I felt her panic."

"Where are they now?" James asked.

"I can't sense either of them," he answered quietly.

"We need to search the property," Hayden said. "Together this time."

Two hours later, they gave up their search and started back to the mansion. The sun was just beginning to set, glowing orange on the horizon. No one spoke. Their eyes were all glued to the ground, faces grim. A cold weight had settled into Lana's stomach somewhere along the way.

Emily and Blue were gone.

JAMES SAT IN THE CORNER, HIS FISTS CLENCHED HARD ENOUGH TO CRUSH IRON.
I'm the one who said split up, he thought. Now Emily was gone because of him.

"I just don't see how it could have been the Flame," Lana said. "We saw a Wraith."

"Maybe they're working with the Wraiths," Hayden countered. "And if it's these guys who abducted the other two League members, we don't even know where to start looking for them anyway."

They were gathered in the monitoring room and had already been debating for twenty minutes. No one could decide what to do next.

"So we go to headquarters?" Sam asked. He had his arms wrapped around his legs and looked like he was on the verge of tears.

"It could be a trap," Hayden said. "If Thunderbolt is gone, the Flame is in charge there."

"But if it was the League traitors, then why did Blue scream?" Lana asked.

"She did say she was on Thunderbolt's side," Sam said. "And she seemed upset when you mentioned the Flame. The only way to know is to go to headquarters."

Lana shook her head. "If it was the Flame and the others, they wouldn't bring Emily to headquarters. They'd bring her to—"

"The Perch," Hayden finished. "They'd bring her to the Perch." He walked over to the computer console. "And we know where that is now. All the bases, including the Perch, are listed on the network. Emily gave me her pass code for emergencies."

James glanced up. "And we have the Mediator."

"I don't think it will be that easy to break into the Perch," Sam said nervously.

"That might be where Thunderbolt is anyway," Hayden reasoned, logging in to the network. "It's secluded, probably defensible, and he'd want to make sure no one got to the Vindico. If they were released into all this, it would be game over for the League."

He found the coordinates for the Perch and typed them into a map. A glowing dot appeared on the screen, highlighting the prison's location.

"And if Thunderbolt isn't at the Perch?" Lana argued. "If the Flame's in charge there too?"

"Than we smash down the walls and rescue Emily," Hayden replied. "Right after we take out those traitors and throw them in a cell."

James jumped to his feet. "Let's get moving."

"Yeah, let's try and get there while it's dark," Hayden said. "We better find some jackets: this place is pretty much in the Arctic Circle."

"How are we going to break in?" Sam asked.

Hayden turned to James. "That ship's got missile launchers, right?"

Sam put his forehead on his knees. "Not again."

The rolling green landscape passed beneath them, wrapped in darkness. In the distance, a massive body of water appeared, stretching as far as James could see.

He sat beside Lana in the cockpit, while Hayden and Sam waited in the hold. They were still at least two hours from the Perch. James glanced at Lana and then turned back to the instruments. Lana's gaze was fixed on the view below.

"You know," he mumbled, "I've been thinking about getting back to this world every day for four months now. But I don't think I ever realized that we were actually in danger. That something could actually happen to us."

"I know," she said softly.

He looked at her. "What if she was killed, Lana?"

"Don't even say that."

"We just got away with it so easy last time and then right away now, *bam*, one of us is gone."

"Easy?" Lana said. "I almost killed someone, James. I've had nightmares every single night since we were sent home. I didn't think it was so easy."

James flushed. "I'm sorry. I didn't mean that."

"I know. I know what you meant." She leaned back in the seat. "Do you ever wish they left you alone—chose someone else?"

"No," James replied simply. "Even now, I want to be a superhero."

"Or villain?" she countered. "I mean, I don't regret anything. Not really. I love the powers, and I wouldn't have met any of you if they didn't take me. But if Emily, if she was . . . then I don't know. Maybe I'm not cut out for this."

"We'll find her," James said.

Lana gazed out the window. "Let's talk about something else. We can't do anything about it now." She smirked. "Whatever happened with Sara?"

James shrugged. "Nothing really. I thought I would come back and show off and get my revenge, but when I got there, I didn't see the point. Wasn't worth it, I guess." He paused. "Well, it was kind of nice when the girls started showing a little more interest. She definitely noticed."

"And what about those other girls . . ."

"I didn't date anyone, no."

She glanced at him. "Why not?"

"I don't know. Just figured I'd be leaving soon, I guess. How are things with Hayden? You guys seem good together."

"Yeah . . . we are," she agreed. She laughed and shook her head. "We're talking about relationships. I almost feel like a normal teenager."

"Yeah," he said. "Except it's a Monday night and we're about to attack the most heavily guarded prison in the world."

Lana became somber. "I hope she's there."

"Me too."

They didn't speak again until the ground below had become a patchwork of scattered, snow-covered islands. The Arctic Ocean was roiling in the darkness.

James grimaced as the ship rolled in a strong gust of wind.

"All right, I'm gonna puke back here," Hayden said, stumbling into the cockpit. "Sam's already leaning over the toilet."

"It's not far now," James said distractedly.

Another gust rocked the ship. They heard a yelp from the bathroom.

"Lovely place for a prison," Hayden commented.

"No kidding," James muttered. "It's definitely effective. Nowhere to go even if you do escape."

"I think we're coming up on it," Lana said, eyeing the sensors.

James gripped the throttle a little tighter. "Keep your eyes open."

He steered the Mediator down and felt the weightlessness return as they descended toward the dark, turbulent ocean. Many tiny islands dotted the waters now, some no more than pointed outcroppings of wind-blasted rock.

"All right, it must be bigger than . . ." James said, but

stopped when he noticed a red light on the control panel begin to flash. "What's that?"

"Press the button next to it," Hayden suggested, reaching for it.

James frowned. "Wait a second, maybe—"

Hayden pressed the button and a robotic voice filled the cockpit.

"Please transmit the proper clearance code. Failure to do so will result in your destruction. Please transmit the proper—"

Hayden pressed the button again and the voice shut off.

"Well that wasn't a very friendly greeting," he said.

"See if you can find a code, Lana," James said quickly. "Is there a way to log on to the ship's computer? Try that screen."

"I don't know what any of this means," Lana muttered. She began typing into the keypad. "We need Emily."

"Search 'prison code,'" Hayden suggested.

"Yes, I'm sure there's a search feature," James replied sarcastically.

"Someone's a bit tense. Maybe a massage would help. You've been flying for a while," Hayden said as he started to rub James's shoulders. James swatted at him with one hand and the ship veered sharply to the left. Hayden toppled over as James jerked the controls straight again and another yelp sounded from the back.

"Can you two grow—" Lana started, but she was cut off

as a red blast suddenly lanced out of one of the jagged islands and cut through the air toward them. James sent the ship diving toward the sea and there was a screech as the powerful blast skimmed over the roof. He heard Hayden fall over again.

"There!" Lana screamed, and James yanked the controls to the right just as another blast filled the space where they'd been.

Hayden slid across the floor and crashed into the far wall. "This is not fun!"

"There's the Perch!" Lana said, pointing ahead.

A larger island appeared in the gloom—rocky and barren, and the waves crashing against its sheer cliff face with terrible force. Sitting in the middle of the island was a huge, gray building with a single tower rising up on one side. They could see two massive weapons emplacements on the ground in front of it. Before the teens even had time to process what they were seeing, both cannons fired directly at them.

James sent the ship diving downward again, skimming the water. Enormous waves swirled up around them, almost crashing against the hull. Two red blasts streaked overhead and Lana screamed as James just barely steered the ship over a towering wave. The cliff was rushing toward them.

"Get ready!" James yelled tightly. "We're going in—".

"Flame?" a male voice suddenly came over the comm unit. "Did you forget the codes again? Sorry about that—

I was asleep and just heard the alarms. You're lucky you weren't blown out of the sky! I deactivated the guns. You can set her down."

James pulled back on the accelerator and glanced at Lana, relieved. "Looks like we just got an invitation."

JAMES PULLED BACK ON THE THROTTLE TO CLEAR THE JAGGED CLIFF. THE ROCK was at least a hundred feet high and plunged straight down into the frozen ocean. There was definitely no escaping this island. Even if you could fly, the fierce wind would probably send you spinning out of the air.

"This looks like a happy place," Hayden said as he climbed back to his feet.

The Perch itself looked like a bomb shelter. It was built of dark gray metal and completely devoid of windows, except for the tower, where another gun emplacement protruded from the roof. This one was aimed at the massive front door, seemingly the only entrance or exit from the ominous, boxlike structure.

James set the Mediator down on the landing pad.

"How long do you think it'll take for him to figure out we're not the Flame and the others?" Lana asked quietly.

"Probably about one second," James said. "The better question is: what will he do about it?"

A few moments later, they were all standing at the hatch. James and Sam were clutching rifles, while Lana and Hayden had decided against them. Lana still didn't want to take the risk of shooting anybody, and Hayden said he didn't need one. The ship was still shaking as the wind howled fiercely outside the closed door.

"Ready, team?" Hayden asked.

Sam's face looked green, but he managed a short nod.

"Ready," James said.

Lana clenched her fists. "Ready."

"All right," Hayden replied, his hand resting on the hatch control. "Game time."

The savage wind hit them instantly as the ramp descended, and Hayden felt his whole body go cold. He stepped out onto the landing pad, trying to shield his face with his arm, and started for the towering front entrance. Gusts of snow whipped up with the wind and stung his eyes.

"Did I mention I hate the cold?" he shouted.

The entrance to the Perch started sliding to the left, and he broke into a run, barreling through the doorway and wiping the snow from his face. The others hurried in after him.

"That was easy—" James started.

"Drop your weapons," a deep, robotic voice commanded.

Four massive robot sentries were standing in front of them, clutching very threatening-looking stun poles. They each stood at least eight feet tall, looked vaguely humanoid, and had two scarlet eyes that glowed from thick, domed heads. Hayden looked up at them, wide-eyed, and he heard two rifles clatter against the floor.

"Hello," Hayden said slowly, "robot . . . man. Can we speak with—"

"Follow us," the robot interrupted, its eyes fixated on Hayden. "Any resistance will be met with force."

With that, the four sentries pivoted in perfect synchronization and started down the long white corridor they were all standing in. Hayden glanced at the others and followed. Sneaking a peak into the shadowy room they'd emerged from, he saw ten more robots lined up and powered down. There was another line behind them. He doubted there were many uprisings in the Perch.

They continued down the seemingly endless white corridor, passing one unmarked white door after another. A few of them had glass windows, but every time Hayden looked in one of them, it was empty. Circular lights ran along the ceiling.

"So many cells," James muttered.

"And none of them have Emily," Sam said.

They all looked back at him.

"What?" Lana asked sharply.

"I can't sense her," he said. "Not even asleep."

Hayden sighed. "Well, we might as well see what we can find out."

"Keep walking," the lead sentry ordered. Their footsteps continued to rise and fall in perfect unison, pounding off the sterile white tiles. The protégés hurried to catch up.

"This place is kind of creepy," Hayden said.

"Very creepy," James agreed.

"Sliver's in there," Sam whispered, pointing to a white door. It had no window.

"You sure?" James asked uneasily.

"Definitely," Sam replied. "The others are all along here too."

Lana stared at the other doors. "Is Avaria?"

Sam nodded and pointed at another one. "She's in that cell, I think. And there's a few others too," he murmured. "I don't recognize them. But they don't seem friendly."

"If they're in here, they're definitely not friendly," James said.

Hayden shivered when he thought of how many super-powered murderers were around them, just waiting to pounce. He was suddenly glad the sentries were here.

They reached the end of the corridor and the sentries took up positions beside another seamless white door. It looked exactly like all the others. As soon as the robots were facing the protégés, their stun poles extended, the white door slid into the ceiling.

Hayden led the way through the doorway. They found themselves in the prison's central control room. The first thing Hayden saw was a display of six different screens, each containing a feed of their former mentors, all standing expectantly against their cell doors.

And there, sitting in front of the screens, was Jay Junkit.

His face, now much paler than Hayden remembered, was contorted into a scowl, and his muscular arms were folded across his chest.

"I have plenty more guards, in case you're wondering, and they can be here very quickly." He put his hand over the console. "And if that doesn't work, I'll blow this place sky high. The Vindico are not leaving this prison."

"Don't worry, Junkit," Hayden said. "We don't want to let them out."

"I didn't see why you would," he replied slowly. "But why else would you be here? And why do you have the Mediator? Where is the Flame?"

"He tried to set us up and arrest us," Lana told him. "We know that he's a traitor. And I'm guessing you are too, since you seemed happy to see him when you thought he was in the Mediator."

Junkit narrowed his eyes. "Who have you been talking to?"

"Blue," Hayden answered. "And she told us an interesting story before she got taken."

"Taken?" Junkit said quickly. "By who?"

"We thought by the traitors," James said. "That's why we came here. They took Emily too."

Junkit looked troubled. "Another one," he said softly.

"Who's taking them?" Sam asked.

"I don't know. None of us do. I can't believe they got Blue," he whispered.

"We need some answers," Lana said. "We need to find Emily."

Junkit shook his head. "I don't have any. I've been up here for weeks. I was with Ceri, but she got called away. Thunderbolt basically exiled me here."

"Why would he exile you?" Hayden asked suspiciously.

Junkit shrugged. "Because I'm friends with Flame, and I agreed with him that we should have gone after the Vindico years ago. And now we're being picked off again." He waved a hand at the screens. "But here, Thunderbolt could use me as a trustworthy guard. No one hates the Vindico as much as me."

Junkit frowned before asking, "What did you mean when you said Flame 'set you up'?"

Hayden glanced at James. "Sinio made James kiss Lana so that I would react . . . unfavorably. I threw him into a wall. Well, through a wall actually. Then they tried to arrest us for using our powers, but Sam figured it out so we took their ship."

Junkit looked thoughtful. "He wanted to get you first, I guess. But if he just took you guys like that, it would be full-blown civil war. That doesn't make any sense." He hesitated. "If Flame gets a ship, he'll come to the Perch. He knows I'm in charge here."

"Great," Hayden muttered. "Listen, we need to know where Thunderbolt is."

He laughed. "You think I know? He wouldn't tell me anything. Probably hiding away somewhere with the others. They're nervous now."

"Why?" Lana asked.

"All three abductions have been members loyal to Thunderbolt."

"What a coincidence," James snarled.

"It's not the Flame, I'm telling you," Junkit said. "He would never hurt Blue. And why would he take Emily? He wants to win you over. Taking one of you would turn you all against him. Someone else is playing this game."

"Have you asked the Vindico?" Hayden said.

"Asked them what?"

"If they know what's going on," Hayden continued. "Did you not wonder if they had something to do with these abductions, seeing as how they are fracturing your group, igniting a civil war, and undermining Thunderbolt's leadership?"

"But they're here," Junkit argued. "How could they—"

James looked at Hayden. "What if they had a backup plan in case they were captured? That makes sense."

"You see?" Hayden replied. "I'm not just all about good looks."

"We better move fast," Sam said. "Before the Flame gets here."

"Right," Hayden agreed. "Junkit, you better grab a gun." He started for the door and then paused. "And maybe those robots. This could get ugly."

EMILY OPENED HER EYES AND FELT A SHARP PAIN COURSING UP AND DOWN HER back. She was staring at roughly hewn stone, lit up with a flickering orange light, as if from a fire.

The last thing she remembered was a flash of movement in the trees and hearing Blue's shrill scream as she was tackled from behind. She must have blacked out after that.

She tried to wiggle a finger and found that she could, despite the pain. Soon all her fingers were moving, and she slowly rolled herself onto her stomach. Planting her hands beside her, Emily pushed herself to her knees, grimacing all the way. She was in a small, misshapen cavern of dark stone. A black, iron door was built into the wall, and the light was coming in from a small, barred opening that looked out on a corridor. She gingerly planted one foot onto the ground and heaved herself up. For a moment she thought she might topple back to the hard floor, but she wobbled and held her footing.

Then she saw Blue lying in the corner.

The slender woman was sprawled out on her back, her fingers curled limply upward. Her cobalt hair was splayed out around her like a puddle. Emily bent down at Blue's side and gently shook her arm.

"Blue," she whispered. "Blue. Wake up." She shook her harder. "Blue!"

"She'll be a few hours yet."

Emily turned to see a very strange-looking man step inside the room. Though it was dark, Emily could tell that his skin was purple or a very dark blue. His eyes were even more disconcerting. One was a piercing yellow and the other as dark as his black clothes and hair. But his features were almost regal: he had a broad chin and high cheekbones, and he was tall and thin. He seemed to blend into the shadows as he took another step toward her.

"She will live. But she is fragile. Unlike you, it seems." His voice was strong and melodious. "Leave her. We must discuss a few things, now that you are awake."

Emily stood up again, remaining expressionless. She didn't want to reveal that she was in pain. "Were you the one following me in the woods a few days ago?"

"No. That was one of my operatives. We have been watching you and your friends ever since you were returned home by the League of Heroes."

"So you're not part of the League?" Emily asked, straining to remain upright.

The man folded his hands behind his back. "No. We are . . . independent. Suffice to say we have our own agenda, quite apart from their little war. For some time our paths have run in different directions. But that is no longer the case."

"Who are you? What do you want with us?"

He smiled. "My name is Dolus. As for why I took you, that answer will have to wait. Now I will ask a few questions," he said, meeting her eyes. "We have uncovered as much as we can about the circumstances of your group's powers and the reasons surrounding the battle at the Baron's mansion. Most we have gathered from our other guests, but they were not completely informed. Why did the Vindico choose you five kids specifically?"

"Why should I tell you anything?"

"Because if you give me information, you will eventually get some in return. And if that isn't enough . . ." His hand fell on a sleek black plasma discharger strapped to his thigh. "Then I'll have to kill Blue to show you I'm serious. Now please, answer my question."

Emily frowned, but she didn't see how it could be damaging to the others to answer him. "Because they believed we were the best candidates, I suppose. For Sam and Hayden, they had the natural potential."

"Yes, Hayden intrigues me," Dolus replied thoughtfully. "He is extremely powerful, and after such a short time. And the others? James and Lana?"

"Why are you so curious about my friends?" Emily countered.

His fingers closed on the handle.

"I don't know," Emily said reluctantly, eyeing his gun. She wondered if she could possibly grab it from him. "James told me the Torturer was from his hometown, so I guess he just picked someone who reminded him of himself. I don't know why Avaria picked Lana. Rono found me through my online identity, Black Arrow."

"How long were you with them?"

"A month."

He began to pace. "They developed your powers that quickly? Why didn't they take protégés earlier?"

Emily studied his movements, which seemed exceptionally languid and controlled. "I don't know."

He turned back to her. "You fought for them, correct?"

"We went on a few missions."

"Including the raid to abduct Deanna and Lyle."

"Yes."

"The circumstances of the battle at the mansion trouble me. Why did you release the Vindico again after you had already imprisoned them?"

"The League was trying to arrest us," Emily explained, feeling a little defensive. He sounded almost accusatory. "We didn't have much choice."

"But it was Sam who defeated them again, was it not?"

"Yes. We realized that we were fighting on the wrong side."

Dolus stared at her for a moment. "I see. So where do your loyalties lie, then? With the League?"

"We don't know. The League betrayed us, as I'm sure you know."

"How did they betray you? My informant only saw James fly through the wall."

"Sinio coerced James into kissing Lana," Emily replied. "It was a setup so they could arrest us."

"So that the Flame could take you before Thunderbolt," he mused. "Except he underestimated you, which seems to be a common error."

Emily planted her hands on her hips. "And one you're repeating. You know the others will be looking for me right now."

He chuckled. "I wouldn't doubt it. But they won't find you here, I'm afraid. There are many things unfolding and your capture was an unplanned but useful addition. It will drive your friends to take a more active role in the upcoming action. I'm sure it already has. They are the wild cards in this."

"You have no idea," Emily snarled. "They won't give up until they find me."

"I certainly hope not," Dolus replied calmly. "That would ruin all my plans."

He walked toward the door but paused before leaving.

"Settle in: you'll be here for a while. I expect it will be a few days before things are prepared. I admire your courage, Emily, among other things. I will have a cot brought for you, and food and water. Rest; I know the effects of the stun wear heavily on the body. I assure you, this is the safest place you can be for the next few days. Your friends aren't so lucky. They're going to be right in the middle of all this, and they will be extremely fortunate to survive."

Emily leapt toward him, despite her pain, but he stepped through the door and swung it shut. His dark lips pulled back in a grin. "I see why Rono picked you, at least. Good night, Emily. I will return tomorrow."

With that, he stalked out of sight, leaving Emily a narrow view of a rough stone hallway. A torch was burning on the wall. Emily pulled on the bars with all her strength, but they didn't budge. Sighing, she went to try and wake up Blue.

They needed to get out of this cell.

16

THE CELL DOOR SLID INTO THE CEILING, AND THE BARON STEPPED OUT, SMILING. He came to an abrupt halt when he saw who was standing in front of him.

"This is not the rescue I had in mind," he said, raising his eyebrows.

Sam and James had their rifles trained on him, as did Junkit, while Hayden and Lana both had their arms raised threateningly. Behind them, eight more robotic sentries filled in the spaces, each with a stun pole at the ready.

"Why would we rescue you?" Lana asked coldly. "We're here to make a deal."

"I see. What sort of deal did you have in mind?"

As they had planned, Sam extended his mind, trying to break into the Baron's consciousness. But he encountered only an impenetrable wall. The Baron turned to him and tapped lightly on his temple.

"Many years of practice, Sam," he said. "You won't get anything that way."

"Do you know anything about the recent abductions?" Junkit asked sharply.

The Baron turned to him. "You'll have to be more specific."

Junkit narrowed his eyes. "The abductions of League members. And now one of your former protégés."

"Emily has been abducted?" the Baron said, scanning over the group. Though he wore a white prison jumpsuit, he still looked poised and arrogant. "Which League members?"

"What does that matter?" Junkit snapped, lifting his rifle. The barrel was now hovering a few inches from the Baron's forehead. "Do you know anything about it?"

The Baron didn't flinch. "No. I'm afraid my personal organization was likely disassembled in my absence. I can't speak for other members of the Vindico, though."

"That's what we were afraid of," Hayden said. "Well, thanks for your time, Baron. Back in the cell now."

The Baron glanced at him. "Just because I'm not responsible doesn't mean I can't be of some help. I know more about Leni's organization than anyone but him. And I somehow doubt he will be cooperative."

"We'll keep that in mind," Lana replied sarcastically.

"Good. I will expect your return shortly," he said, and walked back into the cell. "Always a pleasure, Junkit."

"Just give me a reason, Baron," he hissed, his finger tightening on the trigger.

"Now, now," Hayden said, "save it for Leni."

Junkit lowered the rifle and pressed something on his belt. The cell door slid shut again, locking the Baron in.

"That was helpful," James said.

"Well, I had kind of hoped Sam would be able to get something," Hayden said. "The old man's a tough nut to crack, apparently."

Sam nodded. "Leni will be the same. I really don't even want to try."

"I don't blame you," Hayden said. "Who knows what's going on in there." He gestured toward the next door down. "Well, let's get this over with."

The group shifted down one door and set up the same formation. Sam could feel everyone's nervousness permeating around him.

"How do these cells even work?" James asked, glancing at Junkit. "I get that the door is reinforced, but can't he mentally reach through and send us all flying? Or even just trigger the door controls from in there?"

Junkit shook his head. "The walls in these cells are lined with special sensors, just like the ones in the Baron's mansion. They're actually Rono's design. They detect abnormal mental activity. If Leni or Sliver tries to use their powers, they're hit with a very nasty shock. They know better. But we have to be careful. The sensors don't work when the door's open."

"Make sure you hold him in place," Lana whispered to Hayden.

"On it," he said. "You have the activator, Junkit."

"Yeah," Junkit muttered, and fished it out of his pocket. "Ready?"

"Ready," they all replied.

He punched in the code and the thick double doors slid open. Leni stood on the threshold, his hands folded behind his back. He still held an unmistakable air of authority.

His dark eyes flicked immediately to Hayden. "Ah, my former protégé," he said with a sneer. "How nice of you to visit. And you've brought the rest of your little team."

"Hey, Teach," Hayden said. "Still as pleasant as I remember. I see the rehabilitation aspect of prison life is really making an impact."

"Get to the point," James whispered.

"That would be wise," Leni replied imperiously. "It appears the Baron was wrong again. This is clearly not a rescue mission."

"You guys are really deluded," Hayden remarked, shaking his head. "Do you know anything about Emily's abduction?"

"And the three League members," Junkit added.

Leni stared at Junkit. "Falling apart, are you? Yes, I know about your little rift. If you recall, I'm the one who started it." He smiled. "The Flame is just the latest to realize Thunderbolt's weakness. And you're going along with him, aren't you?"

"What would you know about it?" Junkit hissed.

"I haven't been in here that long," Leni replied smoothly. "And I know a traitor when I see one."

Junkit growled, and Sam suddenly felt a flash of rage course through his guarded mind. Junkit's finger moved.

The gun was abruptly wrenched upward and a blast of red energy struck the ceiling, scorching the crisp white metal. Sparks rained down on the group, and Sam winced as one landed on his nose. He quickly batted it off.

"That would have been unpleasant," Hayden said, lowering his hand. "Much as he might deserve it."

Leni smirked. "I'm so touched, protégé."

"Don't be," Hayden said. "We still need information. Do you have Emily?"

Junkit glared at Hayden and slowly straightened his weapon again.

"What do I get in return for my help?" Leni asked. "I don't answer questions for free."

"If you tell us where she is, we'll come back and let you go," Lana said.

Leni chuckled, shaking his head. "Somehow I doubt that. Let me out now or no deal."

"And we're supposed to trust you?" James scoffed. "You'd try and kill us the first chance you got."

"The League is my enemy," Leni said coolly, "not you kids. We created you and were in turn betrayed. But we should have expected no less. I would agree to a truce."

"And what would you do with your freedom?" Hayden asked. "Take up knitting?"

"I would create a new, stronger League, as I have always intended." He glanced at Junkit. "Just like you wanted."

A beep sounded from Junkit's pocket, and he took out another small device.

"A ship is approaching," he said. "They've transmitted the code."

"Who is it?" Lana asked.

"Must be Flame."

Sam shifted uneasily, his eyes darting between Leni and the others. Lana and Hayden were looking at each other.

"I seem to be missing something," Leni said. "Trouble with the Flame?"

"We need to get to the ship," James muttered. "Or they might just blow it up and trap us here."

Hayden turned to Leni. "Back up. We'll come talk to you again later."

"And what if Emily doesn't have that much time?" Leni asked quietly.

"What do you know?" James snapped.

"I know who *might* have taken her," Leni replied, "and I know how to find them."

"He's not leaving," Junkit said. "The deal is off."

Leni shrugged. "It's up to you. I can find Emily and this fool can't. Who are you going to side with?"

Sam felt his hands moistening with sweat. The others all seemed unsure.

Finally, Hayden sighed deeply. "No dice," he said.

Leni jerked his hands upward, but Hayden was faster. Leni was blown off his feet, and he flew into the cell.

"Shut the door!" Hayden yelled.

Junkit punched the controls and both doors locked with a clang. Sam sagged with relief as Lana turned to Hayden.

"You actually made a good decision," she said, sounding shocked.

Hayden smiled. "I've lied enough in my day to recognize a liar when I see one."

"Flame is going to be here any second," Junkit pointed out.

"Right," Hayden said. "Let's get out of here before that jerk blows up our ship. Then we'd have to steal theirs again. Thanks, Junkit. This wasn't very helpful, but the hospitality was great."

"Where are you going now?" Junkit asked suspiciously.

"It's time to stop beating around the bush," Hayden replied. "We're going to visit headquarters."

"And find Thunderbolt," James said.

Junkit nodded. "I think that's a good idea. Get going."

They took off down the corridor. Once again, Sam felt the presence of some captives he didn't recognize. Even from that brief contact, he could sense dark, murderous thoughts. He was definitely happy to be leaving the Perch. They burst out of the still-opening front door, and Sam was hit by a blast of freezing wind and snow. They bounded up the Mediator's ramp and into the cockpit.

"There they are," James said, pointing.

Another white vessel was quickly approaching the island, barely visible in the gusting snow. As it approached the landing pad, its ramp started descending, and Sam could make out a massive silhouette standing in the opening. Gali.

"I think it's time to go," Hayden said.

"For once, I agree with you," James replied. "You might want to hold onto something."

Hayden enveloped Sam in a hug.

"You're an idiot," James said, and then he pulled back on the throttle.

The Mediator streaked toward the other vessel, and Sam and Hayden slammed into the back wall.

"Pull up!" Lana shrieked.

James yanked on the controls, and they skimmed over the other ship with a screech of protesting metal. Sam closed his eyes and hugged Hayden even tighter as they burst over the edge of the cliff. The Mediator dropped twenty feet toward the water, causing Sam to yelp in terror, and then James accelerated again, almost crashing into a wave. He pulled back on the throttle, and they shot into the sky.

The Mediator climbed rapidly, and Sam and Hayden were squeezed against the wall, unable to move. Sam whimpered as the ship began to shake violently in the heavy winds. The view out the cockpit window was completely black now.

Finally, they emerged on the other side of the turbulent cloudscape and a huge expanse of stars lit up the sky in front of them. Wisps of light covered the space between like soft brushstrokes of paint.

"This is just like I always dreamed," Hayden whispered into Sam's ear.

Sam hastily released him. "Sorry," he muttered.

"I'm not," Hayden said.

"You really are annoying, you know that?" Lana remarked, leaning back. "That was too close."

"But did you see Leni's face when I threw him back in the cell?" Hayden said. "That was hilarious."

"Classic," James agreed.

"This is so beautiful," Lana said. "I've never seen stars like this."

"Emily would love this," Sam said quietly. "This view."

They all fell silent.

"I hope she's okay," Lana murmured.

"I'm sure she is," Hayden said. "If I know Emily, whoever took her has their hands full. They're probably wishing they had any one of us but her."

EMILY'S MUSCLES SCREAMED IN PROTEST AS SHE TRIED TO TWIST THE SOPPING-wet fabric. Ice-cold water, fresh from Blue's fingertips, ran down her shivering arms. A large puddle had already formed beneath her and spilled out into the corridor. Finally, she released the jacket and it flopped against the door, held up from where it was wrapped around two of the iron window bars.

"That looked easier in the movies," she muttered, wiping her arms.

"I told you it was a waste of time," Blue said. "Even if you somehow managed to pull those bars apart, I doubt there's a door handle on the other side."

Emily turned to her. Blue was lying on the cot, curled into a ball to conserve heat. The cot itself was narrow and stiff and didn't even have a blanket. A Wraith with cold eyes had delivered it a few hours earlier, along with a tray of stale bread and a pitcher of water. He had refused to answer any of Emily's questions.

"Well, I would rather try to escape than sit here and rot," Emily said calmly. "I never had much patience for the captured princess who fiddled with her hair and stared forlornly out the window."

"Except that we have no window. Only solid, impenetrable rock and a solid, impenetrable door. And now you've used my jacket and gotten it soaking wet."

"Do you have a better suggestion?" Emily asked.

"Wait. Save your energy. Be ready if someone comes along to rescue us. Maybe we can get the jump on one of these guards." Blue hoisted herself up into a sitting position, wrapping her arms around her slender legs. "Someone is bound to slip up."

Emily frowned. "I doubt it. They seem pretty professional."

"I wish I'd met the first one. If he's the leader, like you said."

"He'll be back," Emily said. "Just wait."

"Well, either the League or your friends are bound to find us eventually. If they're not killing each other," she added. She picked up the empty pitcher. "You thirsty?"

A stream of water burst out of her fingertips, filling the pitcher.

"I still feel strange drinking water you create," Emily said, taking it from her. "But it's very good."

"It's from the air," Blue replied defensively. "It's as clean as you can get." She looked around at their dank surroundings. "Well, usually anyway."

Emily peered at Blue's fingers. "I'd be curious to study how it works."

"We've got time," Blue muttered. She stuck her hand out and Emily watched in fascination as condensation began to form on her pale skin. "Useless power for fighting, really. Your friend James beat me with a chunk of drywall."

She turned her hand over, and water began to collect in her palm.

"You seemed to do all right when you took down me and Hayden," Emily reasoned.

Blue smirked. "Through a door. And you were still just a little wet." She dumped the icy water onto the floor. "Probably why Thunderbolt stuck me at the mansion. Knows I won't be much help in an actual battle. It was the same way when I first joined the League. Every time the Vindico attacked, he'd send me off to some distant base to hide."

"I know the feeling," Emily muttered. "At least you have a superpower. Without my weapons, I'm just a liability. The others remind me of that once in a while without even meaning to. And now here we are."

"In the exact situation that they were afraid of," Blue agreed somberly. "Even if we get out of here, Thunderbolt will never let me near a battle again."

"Sounds like he cares about you."

"Maybe," she said quietly. "But he has a funny way of showing it."

"How long have you been in the League?" Emily asked.

"Six years now. Joined when I was eighteen. I'd been hiding my powers for four years before that. I didn't want to join the League at the time. Had a boyfriend and a life and a close family. I was happy. Then there was a fire. Woke up in the middle of the night to thick, black smoke and my parents screaming. The whole staircase was in flames. Well, not for long." She smiled thinly. "You should have seen their faces. I came out in my pink pajama pants, water shooting out of my hands, and put out the whole fire. After that, I decided it was just selfish to hide. I figured I was meant to do something with these powers, so I joined the League. And I haven't done a single thing but hide since then."

Emily could hear the bitterness in her voice. "I have a feeling you'll have a chance to do something soon," she said. "They're going to need your help—"

She was interrupted by a click at the door. Someone slipped inside and quickly shut it again. Emily clenched her fists, ready to charge, but stopped when the shadowy figure stepped into the light from the barred window. It was a woman.

She was beautiful, with flawless almond skin, full round lips, and captivating green eyes. Her dark hair fell almost to the belt on her black jumpsuit.

"My brother indicated that you might attempt escape," the woman said, gesturing at the door where Blue's jacket was still wrapped around the bars. "I see that his concerns were not unfounded." She met Emily's eyes. "My name is Veridus. Dolus doesn't know I'm here. And

I don't have much time. He is a bit . . . perturbed. Emily, your friends did not perform quite the way he envisioned. I think he's going to do something rash. He's going too far, but I have no power to stop him. He does not take well to objections."

"You know where my friends are?" Emily asked quickly.

"We're not exactly sure," Veridus said, glancing back at the door. "But Dolus thinks they're going to League headquarters."

"If you're his sister, why would you help us?" Blue asked suspiciously.

She slowly pulled up her sleeve. Vicious black and purple bruises covered her entire arm, punctuated by thin cuts. "These cover my entire body," she whispered, pulling her sleeve down again. "You aren't the only ones stuck here. I want to escape just as much as you."

"So release us and the others, and we'll fight," Blue said.

Veridus shook her head. "You'd be killed. There are too many of his minions here, and they are all abnormally fast and strong. Besides, the other League members aren't here."

"Where are they?" Blue asked quickly, getting to her feet.

"I don't know," she replied. "Maybe dead."

Blue sat down again, her hands shakily finding the cot. Emily considered the situation. Unless she could get her hands on some weapons, she couldn't do much in a fight. Without reinforcements, they were stuck.

"So, what then?" Emily asked.

Veridus turned to her. "We need to contact Thunderbolt.

If we can coordinate an attack, we might be able to over-run this base."

"We don't know where he is," Blue said quietly, her eyes on the floor. "We've been trying to find him."

Veridus bit her lip. "My brother can't find him either. I was hoping Thunderbolt might have said something to you."

"No," Blue said. "He took some of the others and disap-peared. He's been gone for weeks."

"My friends can get us out," Emily suggested. "If we can get ahold of them to let them know where we are. They're very powerful."

She nodded. "Yes, they are. But not enough, I'm afraid. They'll need all the forces they can muster to get into this place, trust me. We've been hidden here for years."

"Who is 'we'?" Emily asked.

"A society," she replied, "dedicated to studying super-powers and perfecting ways to transfer them. And for years, that was our simple goal. But now my brother has something else in mind. He won't tell any of us what it is. I think he means to destroy the League, the Villains, all of them. For what reason, I don't know."

"What about my friends?" Emily asked. "What does he plan for them?"

Emily didn't trust this woman, but she was eager for any information she could get. She at least seemed more talkative than her brother, if she was telling the truth.

"The same. But only after he's used them to achieve his goals."

Emily frowned. "You said they didn't perform like he envisioned. Do you know what he meant?"

"Yes. They went to the Perch a few hours ago—looking for you, maybe. They spoke to your former mentors, perhaps suspicious that they knew of your whereabouts. Leni offered them a deal, just like my brother suspected. He knows Leni well. Dolus assumed they'd take it and release the Villains, or at least Leni. But they didn't. They locked him up again. He was very surprised."

"I don't know why he would be," Emily said. "The Vindico would try and kill us the first chance they got."

"That's what I said. But he thought they might agree for the chance to rescue you. He said your friends had a history of making rash decisions."

"That's true," Emily murmured. "So he wanted them to release the Vindico?"

"Yes. That's what I mean when I say he's going too far."

"Why would he want to release them?" Blue asked.

"Because he wants them to wipe out the League and face off against my friends," Emily answered slowly. "He wants them all to destroy each other. That's why he needed the League to split and then alienate us. Otherwise we would have been one united front, and we would have beaten the Vindico again, and probably him too."

"He said you were clever," Veridus commented. "That is what I suspect too. But why my brother wants to do this, I still don't know."

"But his plan didn't work," Blue pointed out. "So it's all right."

Veridus smiled grimly. "He wanted the kids to do it, but that doesn't mean he can't. My brother knows a great deal about the League. He has all the pass codes for the Perch. Override commands. He can shut down the security systems from the outside."

"Impossible!" Blue said.

Veridus looked into Emily's eyes. "He's already sent men to release the Villains. They'll be free within the hour."

"And the first thing they'll do—" Emily started.

"—is go after your friends, yes," she finished. She put her hand on Emily's arm. "You both need to think of a way to find Thunderbolt. I'll come back the first chance I get. Don't worry, I'll do everything I can to help your friends. If they die, this war is over, and my brother wins. Then I will never be free of him, and the whole world will suffer. I've heard him whispering to himself in the darkness. He has something planned. Something bad."

She turned and hurried out the black iron door, closing it firmly behind her. Emily listened to her quiet footsteps dart back down the corridor.

"They'll kill them all," Blue whispered.

"They'll certainly try," Emily agreed softly.

Avaria stood up as the cell door slid into the ceiling. Though she had sat motionless for months now, her muscles were primed and ready. They always were.

She stalked toward the doorway, her eyes trained on the tall, handsome man who stood there, holding the activator. He took a quick step backward, allowing her to pass. She glanced to her right and saw that the others were emerging as well. The black-clad man hurried to the last two doors on her left, and the Baron and Leni strode out of their cells.

"About time," the Torturer grumbled, stretching his massive arms over his head.

"Why did you release us?" the Baron asked the man.

"Orders," he replied crisply. "There is a ship waiting for you on the landing pad."

Avaria glared at him. "Who are you?"

"That doesn't matter."

"Where's Junkit?" the Torturer asked eagerly, rubbing his hands together.

The man shook his head. "He comes with us."

"I don't think so—" the Torturer started.

"Enough chatter," Leni cut in. "I know who sent you. Tell him this means nothing to me."

"He expects nothing," the man replied.

"I doubt that," Leni snarled. "Do you know where our protégés went?"

"He says there is only one plausible destination."

Leni nodded. "As I suspected." He turned to the rest of them. "Let's move."

"Your ship is outside," the man said.

Leni led the others down the long white corridor, and Avaria stared at the strange man as she went by him. He was lean and muscular beneath his black uniform, and she could tell by the way he moved that he was dangerous.

A killer. But there was something strange about his expression. His cold eyes. Frowning, Avaria hurried after the others. They walked through the sentry room, passing a long row of massive robots standing in the darkness, powered down. Somehow they'd been turned off.

The entrance to the Perch slid open at their approach, and the freezing wind burst into the prison and swept across Avaria's face. She smiled. She'd been in this box for far too long.

Leni calmly walked toward an angular black ship sitting on the landing pad, almost invisible through the gusting snow. There was an identical vessel hovering on the other side of the pad.

"Feels good to be free," the Torturer said as they all crowded into the cockpit. "But what was that all about? Who was that?"

"His boss is an old acquaintance," Leni answered smoothly, "who clearly has an ulterior motive."

"Who is it?" Sliver asked.

"I'll explain later," Leni told them. "Let's get off this cursed rock."

Rono pulled back on the throttle, and they shot toward the clouds.

"Where did our protégés go?" Avaria hissed.

"After they couldn't find Emily at the prison," Leni said, "and after turning down my proposition, they must have gone straight to the source."

"League headquarters," the Baron mused. "Good. I've been meaning to visit."

"Now we can crush the fractured League," Leni said, "and this time, we will destroy our former protégés as well. In fact, maybe we should do that first."

There were murmurs of assent around the cockpit, and Avaria smiled again.

She was going to enjoy this.

18

THE SHIP DESCENDED ONTO A GLASS TOWER PERCHED IN THE HEART OF NEW York City. There was an empty landing pad on the roof.

"I can't believe we're finally going to League headquarters," Sam said excitedly.

James grinned as he slowly eased the ship onto the roof. There was a gentle thud, and then he powered down the Mediator. He sat back, exhausted. They'd had little chance for sleep in the last few days, and it was starting to catch up to them.

Lana glanced over at him. "Do we have a plan?"

"Break down the door and see what's inside," James said. "Same as usual."

She sighed. "That's what I figured."

The sun had risen a couple hours earlier, but it was still cold, especially on the roof of the enormous tower. They hurried toward the doorway on the other side of the landing pad and James tried to access the door control. It beeped, but the door didn't open.

"We need a password!" he called over the wind.

"Stand back!" Hayden said, raising his hand. "Open sesame!"

With a titanic crash, the metal door flew inward, pulling some of its concrete frame with it. James heard the door clatter down a staircase.

"In we go!" Hayden shouted.

James went in first, stepping over the chunks of concrete. The staircase was brightly illuminated and the walls were painted navy blue and inlaid with various gold insignias. Tightly gripping his rifle, James reached the bottom of the steps, planted his back against the wall, and then spun around onto one knee. He scanned the empty room.

The stairs opened onto a large, beautifully furnished lounge area. Two walls were entirely taken up by floor-to-ceiling windows, and sunlight streamed across a variety of couches, pool and Ping-Pong tables, flat-screen televisions, and even a bar.

Hayden strode past James, patting his shoulder on the way. "Look at you, you're like a commando. Let's rip those sleeves off and tie your hair back with them."

James clambered back to his feet. "I didn't expect to find a clubhouse."

"These guys live it up, that's for sure," Hayden agreed, wandering into the lounge. He dropped onto one of the couches, sighed, and planted his feet on a glass coffee table. "Jamesy, make me a martini, will you?"

"Shut up," James snarled. He spotted a pair of white doors on the far side. "Let's keep moving."

"Anyone in here?" Hayden asked Sam.

"It's hard to tell," Sam murmured, "because there are so many people in the lower parts of the building. I don't think so, though."

James hurried toward the far doors, the others close behind. The doors slid open as soon as he reached them. His finger tightened on the trigger, and he stepped inside.

The room was smaller than the lounge and mostly filled by an enormous, circular white table that sat in the middle. It was surrounded by fourteen matching chairs, and the far wall contained a giant screen.

"Their meeting room is nice too," Hayden said. "Very bright. I don't like the circular table, though. It's too inclusive."

There was another door on the opposite side of the room, and James headed toward it, his footsteps thumping off the hardwood. The empty silence of the building was beginning to give him the creeps. Again, the door slid open as soon as he reached it, revealing a wide passageway. The navy-blue walls were dotted with numerous pictures and framed newspaper articles, and four statues lined the hall, situated at regular intervals. James recognized the Four Founders and spotted Thunderbolt, staring proudly with his arms crossed.

"Found him!" Hayden exclaimed. "Just like I remember."

James rubbed his temple and scanned the rest of the

hallway. There were doors on either end and a few more lining the walls. He turned back to the others.

"I don't want to say it, but—"

"We should split up," Lana finished. "I agree. Hayden and I will check everything to the right. You and Sam go left. Sam, keep track of anyone landing on the roof."

The two groups set off in opposite directions.

James found an empty, stainless steel kitchen area behind the first door. He hurried on to the next one and noticed a small panel beside it with a glowing green light. When he stepped closer, the door slid open to reveal a white marble bathroom.

"Find anything yet?" Hayden called from the opposite end of the hallway.

"No," James replied. "You?"

"Not really."

"Found an elevator!" Lana shouted. "We're going to go down a level!"

Sam soon found another elevator on their side of the hallway as well. There were only four floors to choose from, so James pressed the next one down and the doors slid shut. After an almost imperceptible drop, they opened again. James's eyes widened.

They were in a giant room that was completely filled with control panels, sensor arrays, monitor screens, and a whole variety of other machines that James couldn't even guess at. In the center was a large, circular device rising out of the floor.

He spotted Lana and Hayden on the far side, and Hayden

waved vigorously as soon as James and Sam stepped out of the elevator.

"Fancy meeting you here!" he called.

James ignored him. "This is incredible," he said, staring in amazement at the massive control room. "Emily would faint if she saw this."

"We could definitely use her right now," Sam agreed. "I don't even know where to start."

They slowly picked their way toward the middle of the room and came to the circular device.

"Let's all go to a computer and see if we can find anything," Lana suggested.

"Let's press something on this thing first," Hayden said. "It looks important."

James frowned. "I don't think just pressing things—"

Hayden touched a panel on the side of the device and suddenly the entire base of the platform was ringed with flashing red lights.

"Do you ever—" James snarled.

"Please provide voice identification," a deep voice said, cutting him off.

Hayden smiled. "See, it worked."

"Confirmed," the voice said.

A glowing white light emerged from the top of the circular machine, and then a holographic representation of Thunderbolt appeared, as if he was standing in front of them. James immediately noticed the dark rings under his eyes. His mouth was pulled in a grim line.

"Greetings," the holographic Thunderbolt said. "I wasn't

sure if you would find your way here, but I suspected you might. I transmitted this message after I learned of the Flame's attempt to arrest you and your subsequent escape. It was wise to run. I do not fully understand his motives. His actions seem unnecessary. He is not a fool, though his recent actions make him appear one."

Thunderbolt folded his arms.

"We have had to leave all the known bases. None of them are safe. Two of our members have been kidnapped, both right out of secondary bases. Until I learn more, we must remain hidden. I cannot tell you exactly where I am. Even though this message is voice activated, I fear that our enemy might be able to access it. I'm sorry we couldn't wait at headquarters for you, but as you may have noticed, it isn't very defensible. The Flame may follow you here, so I suggest leaving quickly. Don't engage them again. They will be more prepared this time, and they know this place far better than you. They may have decided they will never win your loyalty and try and stop you from reaching me at any cost. I don't know how far they're willing to go.

"Once you leave headquarters, proceed to the coordinates at the end of this message. We aren't there, but it's close enough that Deanna can use the amplifier to contact Sam. She'll guide you the rest of the way. I'm collecting the remaining loyal members, and then we are going to arrest the traitors and find our captured companions. I have contacted the Perch, and it remains secure, but I fear these unknown assailants might make a move against it. We have to act swiftly to find them before that can happen.

"Now, get moving. Transfer the following coordinates to the ship's computer and fly there with all speed. We'll wait for you here."

He recited a brief string of numbers, and then the image disappeared.

"Probably should have come here first," Hayden said.

Lana shook her head. "I really wish he sent this to the Baron's mansion."

"I guess he figured this was the logical choice for us," James muttered.

"Well, we better get going," Sam said. "The Flame is probably right behind us."

Lana nodded. "Remember the numbers?"

"Yeah," James said.

They hurried back to the elevator. After it shot upward, James hastily led them through the meeting room and into the lounge.

"Wait!" Sam shouted.

James spun around. "We don't have—"

"It's too late," Sam said quietly. "They're already here."

"They'll blow us to pieces if we come out that door," Lana cautioned.

James glanced upward, where he knew the other ship was resting right over their heads.

"If I was them, I might just blow a hole in this roof," Hayden said, and everyone looked at him in alarm. "Let's go back to the control room and wait for them. We'll do Thunderbolt a favor and arrest these traitors right now. It's their fault Emily got kidnapped, so let's make them pay."

"Agreed," James said. "Once they're out of the way, we can find Thunderbolt."

"But Thunderbolt said—" Sam started.

Hayden waved a hand. "Don't worry, Sammy. These guys are chumps. This battle will be five minutes at most."

"We better move before they send a missile at our heads," James said, looking up again. "Remember, they might actually be trying to kill us this time."

Everyone ran back to the meeting room, with James at the rear. He had just made it to the white doors when a massive fireball careened across the lounge and exploded two feet from his head. The impact sent him hurtling into the meeting room, and he hit the far wall with a crunch. Flames billowed out of the doorway behind him.

"Yep," James said, climbing to his feet. "They're definitely trying to kill us."

19

LANA SLAPPED THE BUTTON ON THE ELEVATOR'S PANEL, CLOSING THE DOORS just as they heard another blast of fire hit the metal.

"Sam," Lana said, "come with me to the far side of the control room. We need a gun on both elevators."

The doors slid open again, and Lana and Sam sprinted across the room. She glanced back and saw Hayden standing between the elevator doors, not allowing them to close.

"Got this one!" he called.

Lana and Sam reached the far elevator and slid to a halt. James arrived soon after and they trained their rifles on the door. Sam closed his eyes.

"Where are they?" James asked nervously.

"I think they're still up there," Sam murmured. "They seem very agitated. They're not in the elevator yet."

Lana quickly pressed the button. As soon as the doors opened, she planted herself between them. "Now what?" she asked.

James shrugged. "I guess we wait."

Then the ceiling exploded.

Shrapnel and dust fell from above, followed by flickering tongues of fire. They dove to the floor as the debris and flames rolled over their heads. Lana looked up just in time to see a huge shadow drop through the blown-out hole, barely visible through the smoke. The shadow opened fire. Fizzling blue blasts peppered the wall above their heads.

"Fire back!" Lana screamed.

James propped himself on one knee and returned fire, and the huge shadow hastily ducked behind a console. Lana saw two smaller shadows drop in through the hole. The Flame lifted his hands and fire sprayed toward them.

Lana sprinted to her right, circling back to Hayden. Gali opened fire, trying to take her down, and she was forced to dive behind a sensor array. She somersaulted into a crouch on the far side. *Where is Hayden?* she thought desperately.

On cue, she heard a roar and saw Gali go spinning through the air. He smashed into a console and it exploded in a shower of sparks. Suddenly the thick smoke and dust began swirling in unnatural patterns, and Hayden stepped into view. But just as he was about to reach Jada and the Flame, Gali stood up again and fired. Hayden was forced to deflect the shots and leap out of the way.

The Flame was still shooting fire at Sam and James, keeping them pinned, but the scarlet flames were passing uselessly over their heads. Lana was thinking it seemed like a terrible waste of energy when she realized that the Flame was only making sure he had their attention.

Lana took off toward Sam and James, and she was about ten feet away when the elevator door opened behind them. Sinio stepped out, his plasma rifle aimed at Sam's back. Lana leapt through the air and collided with the thin man. They landed in a heap, and Sinio slammed against the metal floor. She thought she heard something break.

"I wasn't going to shoot," he managed.

"Wasn't about to take that chance," Lana replied coldly.

The Flame had obviously accepted that the ambush had failed, and he was now huddled behind the circular projector as Sam and James returned fire. Lana spotted Jada slinking behind a large console on the other side of the room, trying to circle back in their direction. But the console was suddenly ripped from the floor, and it slammed into her, sending her flying. She hit the ground twenty feet away, and the machine landed on top of her.

Hayden appeared again, crouching low to the ground. The Flame knew he was being outflanked and sent a huge fireball in Hayden's direction before running toward Gali, who was still shooting at them from the far side of the room.

"We'll discuss the terms of your surrender now!" Hayden called after him, and then hurried to Lana's side. "This is going well."

"They almost killed Sam," Lana said, gesturing at Sinio.

Hayden shook his head. "Once you mess with Sam, you've gone too far. James, Sam!" he shouted. "Cover us!" Then he glanced at Lana. "Shall we charge?"

"We shall," she said. "Go!"

. . .

Sam popped back under cover as a flurry of bolts streaked over his head. He bit his lip and prepared to return fire. But just as he was lifting his rifle, he felt a familiar voice touch his mind. He frowned, straining to listen over the noisy battle.

James glanced at him. "What is it?"

"I'm not sure! It feels like . . ." He stopped. "How could that be?" he whispered.

James fired another volley of shots and then ducked down again. "What?"

Sam didn't answer. He didn't need to.

An angular black ship descended outside the wall of windows. It hovered for a moment, facing the battle. Then it fired.

Two missiles exploded into the glass, shattering the entire glass wall that ran along that side of the floor. Sam hit the ground as the earsplitting explosion filled the room, and the barrel of his gun jammed painfully into his stomach. Spots swam in his vision as he tried to get up again.

"They're coming in!" James screamed.

Sam planted his hands beside him and stood up. The black ship was floating right through the shattered window.

"It's them!" Sam said, grabbing James's arm. "Run!"

Sam quickly found Lana across the room and mentally told her to grab Hayden and escape. Feeling a sense of understanding, he spared a look at the ship. Just as it reached the edge of the floor, the Torturer bounded out, his boots hitting with a loud thump. Avaria and Leni jumped out behind him, and then the ship floated upward out of sight.

"Get to the elevator!" James snapped. He fired a quick volley at the three Villains, but they were redirected in midair. Leni turned toward them, smiling.

James and Sam bolted into the elevator. Sam punched the lowest button and the doors began to slide shut. Just as it was closing, one of the consoles ripped free from the ground and flew toward them. The doors closed right before it hit, denting the heavy metal inward. The elevator plunged down two more floors.

James glanced at him. "Why are we going down?"

"They're covering the roof," Sam replied. "Their ship went up."

He quickly reached out to find Lana's mind. *Go down,* he said, *they're on the roof.* This time, he sensed only fear.

The doors opened into a wide, richly decorated hallway. Paintings hung on the wood-paneled walls and the spotless white carpet looked thick and soft.

"Living quarters," James said. "There must be a way to get to the rest of the building. We need to get to the street. Where are Lana and Hayden?"

"I don't know," Sam said nervously. "They're still okay, I think. I just can't—"

The far elevator opened and Lana and Hayden emerged, both looking the worse for wear. They were covered in soot and dust, and Hayden was clutching his right arm. Placing his gun between the elevator doors, James hurried across the hallway with Sam close behind.

"You okay?" James asked.

"No problem," Hayden wheezed. "Just a scratch."

"He got hit by a blast of fire," Lana explained, looking at his arm with concern.

Sam saw that Hayden's shirt was blackened beneath his fingers. The exposed skin was just as charred.

"You can all fuss over me later," Hayden said weakly. "We need to get out of here."

"Leni almost killed us," Lana added. "Collapsed some of the ceiling on us."

James shook his head. "This is as far as the elevators go. We can't get to the ship either. They've got it covered."

"We need to get into the city and get lost in the crowd," Lana said. "Sam, can you block your mind and make sure Sliver can't find you?"

He nodded. "Yeah. But how are we going to get down?"

A massive boom sounded from above them, and they all jerked their heads back to look up.

"Leni's coming through the floor," Hayden said. "Stand back."

"What are you gonna do?" Lana asked.

"Same thing. Sam, is there anyone directly below me?"

Sam extended his thoughts and found numerous people all over the floor beneath them. None seemed directly below, however.

"It's hard to tell exactly, but I don't think—"

"Good," Hayden cut in. Taking his right hand off his charred arm, Hayden extended it toward the floor and closed his eyes.

The other three backed against the wall behind him.

"Shouldn't you aim a little farther—" James said.

The carpeted floor suddenly crashed inward, as if an enormous weight had landed on it. The sounds of splintering wood, screeching metal, and cracking concrete filled the air as a twisted hole appeared. They heard screaming from below.

"Go!" Hayden said.

James immediately stepped forward and jumped down into the hole. Lana glanced at the other two. "We'll catch you," she said, and leapt down after James.

"After you," Hayden said politely.

Sam frowned, peered over the opening, and saw Lana and James waiting ten feet down in the rubble, arms outstretched. Sam closed his eyes and jumped.

James caught him easily.

"I'm coming, Jamesy!" Hayden called from above.

He stepped over the edge, holding his injured arm close to his chest. James caught him and then scowled as Hayden stroked his cheek.

"My hero," Hayden whispered.

They were surrounded by gray cubicles dotting the entire floor. Sam saw some people staring curiously over the tops of them, while everyone else was already scrambling for the exits, tripping over each other to get out first.

He turned to the others. "Let's get to the—"

There was an enormous crash as the floor two stories up collapsed. They all scattered out of the way as debris rained through the hole, sending up more plumes of dust.

"Run!" Lana screamed.

An emergency exit sign was visible on the far wall, and they took off toward it, jostling their way through the narrow aisles. They scurried down the concrete steps of the emergency stairwell. Urgent voices echoed all around them as they ran.

The descent seemed endless. Sam just kept moving, sandwiched between Hayden and James, as they marched down staircase after staircase, each looking the same as the last. Finally, after Sam had lost count of the floors, they ran out into the main lobby.

A rapidly growing crowd had formed, and Lana pushed through it and led them toward the front entrance. Sam noticed that the people in front of them were hastily backing out of their way.

"Let's find somewhere to hide out for a while," James said quietly. "Then we'll go to the hospital."

"No hospital," Hayden replied. "I just need some aloe."

"You got hit with a fireball!" James said.

"Uh-oh," Sam muttered.

A police car was driving right up the sidewalk toward the building, its sirens blaring. Pedestrians scattered out of the way.

"Lose the rifle, Sam," James muttered, and only then did Sam remember that he was still holding his large gun.

He quickly dropped it and kept walking. The police car pulled up to the main entrance and two officers jumped out, hands on their guns. They surveyed the scene for a moment, and Lana quickly led the group toward another set of doors on the side of the lobby.

They had just reached them when a shout cut through the noise. "Hey! Stop!"

Sam saw the officers hurrying toward them, their guns out of their holsters now. He prepared to extend his thoughts, wondering if he could convince both of them to drop their guns at once. But Hayden was faster.

"Sorry!" he called. "We really can't!"

He waved his hand and the two cops went flying backward. They hit the tiled floor and slid into the crowd some thirty feet back.

"Move!" Lana snapped, and they ran out into the cool morning air.

They took a sharp right, rounding the building. Sam heard sirens wailing from every direction now. The streets were busy with traffic and businesspeople hurrying past, seemingly unfazed by the sirens. Sam tried to politely apologize to everyone as they pushed their way through the crowds to the road. Lana stopped at the curb, looking uncertain.

"We need a car," James said, and he and Hayden marched right past Lana to a red sedan that was waiting for the light to change.

James went around the front of the car and swung open the driver's door. A large, clean-shaven man wearing a suit looked up in shock.

"Can we borrow this?" Hayden asked sweetly from the passenger side window.

"What?" he said, looking confused. He scowled. "Get your hands off my door."

"Sorry," James said. "We're gonna have to take it anyway."

James reached into the car and lifted the man out like a small child. He planted him on his feet and then climbed into the driver's seat.

"What are you doing?" the man shrieked, flushing a deep red.

"We'll give it back," James assured him. "Everyone in!"

Cars were honking all around them now, and people were pointing toward them from the sidewalks. Lana climbed into the passenger's seat, while Hayden and Sam clambered into the backseat just before James hit the gas.

He turned left, almost losing control of the car immediately and skidding across the road, and then he made a few more quick turns before settling into the slow-moving traffic. Sam leaned back in the seat, overwhelmed.

"Well, that was exciting," Hayden muttered, clutching his arm.

"Too exciting," James said.

Lana shook her head. "Every cop in the city will be looking for us now."

"How did the Vindico get out?" Sam asked. "That's what I don't understand. Junkit would have never let them out."

"Not a chance," James said. "Maybe the Flame made a deal with them?"

"I don't think so," Lana replied. "They seemed just as surprised to see them. Gali and the Flame were trapped under the ceiling too. I didn't see them get out."

"The Vindico aren't going to stop until they find us," Sam murmured.

"Nope," Hayden agreed quietly. "We'll just have to be ready when they do."

20

"LOOK WHAT WE HAVE HERE," LENI SAID MOCKINGLY.

The Flame stared up at Leni from under a heap of debris. Gali was unconscious beside him.

"Two more over here," the Torturer called. "Both of them knocked out."

"Looks like the children got the best of you," Leni said. He gestured sharply with one hand and the Flame was yanked out of the pile and left to dangle limply in midair. His blue outfit was torn and streaks of blood glistened on his exposed skin. Sparks played along his fingertips, but he seemed unable to muster any fire.

"Kill him and let's go," Avaria hissed. She glanced at Rono, who was busy uploading all the data he could retrieve off the heavily damaged equipment. "Rono's almost done."

Leni smiled. "Not so fast. I want some answers from these fools."

The Flame's arms squeezed against his body and his face flushed red.

"Why were you attacking our former protégés?" Leni asked.

The Flame managed to shake his head, his lips pressed in a firm line. "I don't need to tell you anything," he wheezed. "You'll kill me either way."

"The manner of your death is always a factor," Leni reasoned. "But in fact, your fate has not yet been decided. It strikes me that your little band might be of some use to us."

Avaria glared at him. "How so?"

"They are irreparably against Thunderbolt and our protégés now," Leni replied. "They may give the old man one more thing to consider."

"And us," Avaria said coolly.

"True," Leni conceded. "But at this stage, the most dangerous thing for us would be the reunion of our protégés with Thunderbolt and the other loyal members. Combined, they would be powerful enough to defeat us."

"So what do you suggest?"

"First things first," Leni said, turning back to the Flame. "Answer my question. And remember now, the lives of your three companions rest on my satisfaction with your answers."

The Flame frowned, looking uncertain. "We were trying to stop them from finding Thunderbolt too. For our own reasons."

"I know of your treachery," Leni told him, "and I

support it. You are correct to think that Thunderbolt is weak. He should have killed us when he had the chance. So, you were trying to kill them?"

"No. We were just trying to detain them."

"What's the holdup?" the Torturer shouted from the other side of demolished control room. "Rono's done here. Sliver says he's picking up approaching fighter jets on the radar."

"We'll only be a moment," Leni replied. "What is your goal?" he continued, turning back to the Flame. "To supplant Thunderbolt? You must know you were doomed to failure. You were outnumbered."

The Flame scowled. "To create a new League. And we weren't alone."

"That's what I thought," Leni said. "You would never be ambitious enough to do this alone. Do you have any idea where Thunderbolt is?"

The Flame shook his head and then grimaced as the invisible grip tightened. "I don't," he said, almost in a whimper. "He didn't tell any of us where he was going."

"Very well," Leni said. "Here's what's going to happen. We will leave you your ship. For now, we have the same goals. Find the kids before they reach Thunderbolt. If you succeed, we will allow you to live after we've wiped out the rest of the loyal members. If you attempt to rejoin Thunderbolt and fight against us, I assure you I will personally find you and kill you myself. You've been warned."

Leni released the Flame, and he crashed into the pile of debris.

"I hope you know what you're doing," Avaria muttered.

"Those kids need to be dealt with," Leni replied, starting for the staircase. "They are becoming too powerful. If they rejoin Thunderbolt, they may best us again. I refuse to let that happen."

They climbed the stairs and emerged onto the windy landing pad. Their black ship was hovering next to the entrance, piloted by Sliver, while the Mediator was powered up as well, with the Baron at the helm. The second League ship remained on the pad.

"Where to now?" Rono shouted over the wind.

"You go with the Baron and see what you can get out of those discs," Leni said. "We're going to find the children."

"About time," Sliver muttered as Leni, Avaria and the Torturer climbed aboard the black ship. "Those jets are getting close."

Leni leaned forward and hit the comm unit. "Rono, find the codes for—"

"Already done," Rono said. "The air force thinks this is official League business and that everything is now under control. The jets have been recalled."

"Can you sense Sam?" Leni asked Sliver.

Sliver shook his head as he steered them into the forest of towers. "He must be blocking himself off. He hasn't perfected it yet, though. He'll slip up eventually."

"They can't have gone too far," the Torturer reasoned. He stared down at the bustling cityscape. "But it will still be hard to track them down."

"We'll find them," Leni said. "And when they're gone, we'll crush Thunderbolt and the others with ease."

"And who is this other shadowy figure?" Avaria asked. "Who you seem so reluctant to name? What's his goal in all this?"

"His name is Dolus," Leni said. "I've known him for many years. He has a whole organization of superpowered men like the one who released us from the Perch."

Avaria frowned. "Why didn't you mention him before?"

"He's been hiding away somewhere for years, and until now he's shown no interest in our affairs. I'd hoped he was dead. As far as his end goal, I have no idea. We'll have to wait until he plays his hand. But we're doing exactly what he wants, that I'm sure of."

"Maybe he doesn't mean us any harm," the Torturer suggested.

Leni turned to him. "I wouldn't count on that."

"Hello, Emily."

Emily jerked awake on the cot. Blue was asleep beside her, curled in a tiny ball. Dolus stepped inside their cell, his yellow eye blazing through the shadows. Emily looked for similarities with his beautiful sister. She saw the same proud chin and high cheekbones, but other than that, he was too discolored to look much like her. A high-powered plasma handgun was slung on his belt.

"Are you comfortable?"

"Just great," Emily replied sarcastically. "You could bring a blanket for Blue, you know. She's freezing in here."

"I'll see what I can do. I'm sorry your stay continues to be extended. Events on the outside are being delayed. Your friends are resourceful."

"Are they all right?" Emily asked.

"Yes, for now. They've already visited the Perch."

Emily feigned surprise. Obviously he hadn't found out that his sister had already paid them a visit.

"They acted . . . differently than I had expected," he continued thoughtfully. "They left your mentors there. Wise, of course, but I had assumed they cared enough for you to take their chances. I know at least one of your mentors offered them a deal."

"They're smarter than you think," Emily said, folding her arms.

"Maybe so," he conceded. "But alas, not smart enough. They should have killed them when they had the chance. Because I released the Vindico and gave them a ship."

Emily scowled. "Why are you doing this? My friends didn't do anything to you. They didn't have a choice to get involved."

He nodded, and for a moment, he actually looked remorseful. "I know. It's unfortunate, but necessary. We don't always get a choice of what we're involved in. But they are playing an intrinsic role in these events, one that you were supposed to be involved in, by all rights."

"So let me out," Emily countered.

"I can't. For a number of reasons. One is that you are much safer here, and if I can save at least your life, that would be of some relief to me."

"I'm so pleased," she muttered, getting to her feet. Her body was stiff and sore from lying on the uncomfortable cot. "I want to fight with my friends."

"I know. But they are off the radar, so to speak, so it doesn't matter. You wouldn't be able to find them. They've managed to lose themselves in the middle of New York City. But the Vindico are hunting them now, and so are the Flame and his little rogue group. I hope they do not overwhelm them too easily."

"Obviously my friends are doing just fine," Emily said.

"They are. They are even stronger than I imagined. They will be trying to find Thunderbolt as quickly as possible now. It's their only chance. I of course can't allow that to happen. I must put my own men into the fray. With this many people after them, even New York will not hide them for long."

"Why are you involved in this?" Emily asked. "What do you want?"

Dolus smiled. "I've been involved since well before you were born. I am a man of many faces, Emily, and many pasts. Unlike you and your friends, I *chose* to become a part of this a long time ago. I wasn't always like this, you know. I used to be a good man, or as close as we can be. But that man died, and I woke up in the darkness."

Emily thought briefly about attacking him, but there was something about his stance that warned her against it. She suspected that his gun would be aimed squarely at her forehead before she even finished her first step.

"I didn't come here just to worry you," he said. "I will

attempt to capture your friends, not kill them. The others won't be so kind. Do you have any idea where they might go?"

"To find Thunderbolt," Emily answered. "And no, I still don't know where that is."

"I see. Think about it very carefully, and I will return again soon." He turned to the door, but paused. "One more thing. When this is done, what would you have me do with you? The League will be gone, and your friends may not survive."

Emily narrowed her eyes. "If you hurt them, I'll come after you."

He smiled and swung open the door. "You are a rare specimen, Emily. The safe answer would have been to go home. But you're not one for the safe answer." He sighed. "I suppose I'll have something to think about too."

He shut the door, and it clanged loudly into place. Emily bent over and shook Blue. She groggily opened her eyes.

"What is it?" she murmured.

"We need to figure out where Thunderbolt might be," Emily said, "before that woman gets back. We need to help her find him soon, or her brother is going to kill everyone." She glanced at the door. "Including us."

21

"I MUST SAY, I EXPECT A BIT MORE FROM A HOTEL BATHROOM," HAYDEN said as Lana rubbed the antibacterial cream into his scorch marks.

The skin was blackened all along his forearm, and it had begun to blister. The wound was horrendously painful, but Hayden had never been one to complain, so he continued to occupy himself with a thorough inspection of the bathroom.

They were holed up in a very cheap, dingy hotel in one of the less pristine parts of the city. Lana had found the car owner's wallet in his briefcase, which had contained a decent amount of cash. They'd used it to buy the cream and some painkillers at a pharmacy, and then they'd passed the hotel and decided it might be a good idea to get off the street.

"For one," Hayden continued, biting back a surge of pain, "that red color on the bottom of the curtains, that's mold. I have the same thing at my house. And look at all those water stains. Clearly they aren't wiping the tiles. Who knows what James and Sam are getting from those beds—" He jerked back as she touched his arm again. "Okay, ow!"

"Sorry," Lana mumbled as she tightened the tensor bandage. "You're good to go. Let's get your shirt back on."

"What's the rush?" he said. "Actually, we should probably take a shower. We are pretty dirty. Let me help you get your shirt off."

"Shut up. You might be right, though. I'll take one. You go lie down. I just put the bandage on, so you can't go getting it wet."

"I can't stay in here?"

"Get out."

Sighing, Hayden traipsed out of the bathroom and slowly eased himself onto the bed beside James.

"You should try not wearing a shirt," Hayden whispered to him. "It's liberating."

"Just stay on your side," James replied sharply.

"I've been waiting so long for this," Hayden said, shuffling a bit closer. "Do you want to be the little spoon or me?"

James abruptly climbed off the bed and lay down beside Sam on the other one.

"So what are we going to do now?" Sam asked.

"We have the coordinates to Thunderbolt's location," James reasoned. "We just have to figure out where it is and then drive there."

"What if it's in Hawaii?" Hayden asked.

James hesitated. "Then we're screwed."

"Sweet," Hayden said. "When's that pizza getting here? I'm starving."

James glanced at the clock. "They said forty minutes."

"How long has it been?" Hayden asked.

"Five."

"Crap." Hayden shifted and pain lanced up his arm. Biting his lip, he readjusted himself again and closed his eyes.

They lay around for a while longer and then quickly devoured three pizzas. Once the discarded boxes were lying on the stained beige carpet, they decided to have a quick nap. They all knew they could have a long drive ahead.

As Lana settled in beside Hayden, he ran his fingers through her freshly washed hair. James and Sam were already asleep on the other bed.

"That hotel conditioner worked wonders," he said. "Very soft."

"Thanks." She looked at him. "How's your arm?"

"Better. Maybe a kiss would help."

"Don't push your luck," she said.

He smiled. "I love you." It was the first time he'd said it, but it wasn't scary. It just felt right.

"I love you too," she said, sounding surprised.

He leaned down and kissed her. Then he wrapped her in his arms, and they fell asleep.

James frowned and shuffled closer to his end of the bed. Sam was rolling back and forth, muttering under his breath. He'd been doing it for at least twenty minutes now.

James considered waking him but decided that bad dream or not, Sam could use the rest. James closed his eyes and tried to fall asleep.

Sam abruptly rolled again, coming right up to James's back.

"No," Sam whispered fiercely. "Stay away!" Then he rolled back to the other side.

James sighed, and after a moment of quiet, he began to doze. Just as he was fading out of consciousness, a disturbing thought struck him. He turned to Sam.

Sam was lying flat on his back now. His eyes were still closed, but his forehead, already glistening with a sheen of sweat, was creased with intense concentration. His mouth continued to move slightly, but no words were coming out.

"Sam," James said, gently shaking his arm. "Sam?"

Sam didn't stir. James shook him harder.

Sam's eyes suddenly shot open, staring at the ceiling. "They're coming."

James leapt off the bed. "Wake up!" he shouted.

"What?" Lana mumbled.

"They're coming," James said sharply. "We need to leave."

Hayden and Lana scrambled off the bed, and Sam groggily stood up as well, looking dazed. He teetered and leaned against the nightstand.

"How far are they?" James asked him.

Sam closed his eyes for a moment. "They're getting closer. I don't think they know exactly where we are. I tried to fight him."

James nodded. "Let's get the car."

They cautiously opened the door, peering down the pale yellow hallway. The paint was peeling off the ceiling, and the carpet was matted with dirt. Several of the lights were flickering. It was empty, though, so they crept toward the staircase and hurried down the concrete steps.

When they reached the lobby, James peeked in through the small glass window on the door. The same pudgy man who had checked them in was sitting at the desk, watching television.

"I wish we had our guns," Sam whispered.

"That might have alarmed the fat guy on the way in," Hayden said quietly.

They descended the next set of stairs toward the underground parking lot. Only four cars sat in the garage, including theirs. James glanced nervously at the garage door.

"Didn't he say he'd open it when we checked out?" he asked.

"Yep," Lana said. "That's why we have Hayden."

"Glad to be of service," Hayden said.

James climbed into the driver's seat and started the car. As soon as the others were in, he drove toward the steep ramp, half expecting the garage doors to explode at any moment.

He glanced in the rearview mirror. "Hayden?"

"Right." Hayden closed his eyes and extended his left hand. With a labored grinding noise, the large door began to rise. Sunlight poured in the opening, causing them all to squint.

As soon as the door was about five feet up, James hit the gas. The car leapt up the steep ramp and burst out of the garage. Sam shouted as they left the ground for an instant, sailing up over the lip of the ramp, and then they hit the pavement again with a screech. James veered right just as a booming horn sounded, and they all turned to see a bus heading straight toward them. Everyone yelled at once as James hit the gas again and their car barely accelerated ahead of the bus, shooting down the street into traffic.

They slowed at a red light. James checked the rearview mirror and saw a black ship hovering right in front of the dingy hotel. Traffic had come to a stop and large crowds were already forming on the sidewalk, pointing up at the vessel.

"That was close," James said, turning to Lana.

She nodded tightly. "Too close."

"No more rest breaks, I guess," Sam muttered.

Hayden stretched in the back. "But I'm so very sleepy."

"We need to figure out what those coordinates mean," Lana said. "Let's get to an Internet café and look it up."

Twenty minutes later, they were all gathered around one computer tucked in the corner of a seedy Internet café. James really wished he'd written the coordinates down. A fair amount had happened since they'd received Thunderbolt's message.

"I think this is it," he said uncertainly, "if I got that last number right."

"What's with them and Canada?" Hayden asked. "How long of a drive is that?"

James punched in the information. "Ten hours," he grumbled.

"You know it could be on the other side of the world if you have that number wrong," Lana pointed out.

"I think this makes sense," James said. "The League's original base was in Canada."

He leaned back and stretched his hands over his head. There was only one other person in the café, and he was intently bent over his own computer, seemingly unaware of his surroundings.

"Maybe we should e-mail our families," Lana said. "Tell them we're okay."

Sam brightened at that and wheeled his chair a little closer. Lana went first, and then Sam followed. He was halfway through his e-mail when James noticed the man at the other computer was staring at them curiously. He quickly looked away when James made eye contact with him.

Lana noticed too, and she and James exchanged a quick look.

"How long was he staring?" James whispered.

"Too long," Lana said.

Sam finished, and James rolled his chair up. He hadn't even started typing when the man stood up quickly and exited the café, pulling out a cell phone as he went.

"He was very anxious," Sam said.

"Maybe we should check a news site?" Hayden suggested.

James pulled up a news website. A picture of League

headquarters dominated the front page, with black smoke roiling out of the windows. Below that were smaller pictures of the twisted holes blown through the floors.

The headline read: League Headquarters Attacked by Teenagers. And at the bottom of the page was a video link with the subtitle: "Surveillance video of the four teenagers who were abducted by the Vindico four months ago, assaulting two police officers before stealing a vehicle and fleeing the scene."

"Click on it," Lana said softly.

They sat in silence as they watched themselves hurry across the lobby and then as Hayden waved his hand and sent the two cops flying across the room.

"That looks even funnier from this angle," Hayden said.

"My mom's probably watching this right now," Sam whispered.

"This is bad," James agreed. He glanced at the door. "And that guy—"

"Was probably watching it too," Lana finished. "And is now calling the cops as we speak."

They had taken about five steps toward the door when they heard the first siren.

22

"WE NEED TO GET TO THE CAR," LANA SAID. THEY HURRIED DOWN THE NARROW staircase to the entrance of the small building and then stepped back again. "Too late."

Outside, four police cruisers were already coming around the corner. They pulled up in front of the café, forming a loose perimeter.

"Should we give ourselves up?" Sam asked nervously. "At least then we'd be protected."

"You think those cops would be able to stop the Vindico from getting to us?" James said. "We need to get to Thunderbolt."

The police officers stepped out of their cars, weapons drawn. More cop cars pulled up and James spotted two large black vans as well. Armored SWAT police poured out of them.

"We're screwed," James said.

Hayden sighed. "This is going to be messy. Sam, can you keep some of them occupied?"

"I think so," he said uncertainly. "Why?"

"James, you run to the car and get it started," Hayden said, then turned to Lana. "Feel like flipping some cop cars?"

"No," she replied. "But we don't have much of a choice do we?"

Hayden lifted his hands. "Ready?"

"Ready," they all said quietly.

One of the police cars slowly floated upward, and the terrified officer behind it scrambled on his hands and knees toward another vehicle. The car stopped its ascent and hovered in midair. Then it abruptly flew across the street and smashed into one of the black vans.

"Charge!" Hayden shouted.

James kicked open the door, snapping it right off its hinges, and saw the black van toppling over in the corner of his vision, its windows shattering. Hayden ran out behind him, and with a vicious wave of his hand, another cruiser went skidding into a pole.

James sprinted toward their red sedan and realized a cop car was parked directly in the way. The officer behind it fired, hitting James in the arm. Sharp pain lanced up his arm as the bullet bounced off his hardened skin, and he knew it was going to leave a nasty bruise.

James lowered his shoulder and plowed into the vehicle,

sending the officer flying and the gun spilling from his hands. He risked a glance backward at the scene of chaos. Cruisers were overturned everywhere, and he watched as Lana tossed one officer onto the hood of a parked car. He bounced off it, shattering the window.

Several other officers were standing by with weapons lowered, obviously under Sam's control. Hayden sent them clattering to the ground with a wave of his hand.

James jumped into the car. A few seconds later, Sam barreled into the front seat.

"Tell them to hurry up," James said.

He watched in the rearview mirror as Lana ripped a gun out of one armored cop's hands and then dispatched him with a swift kick to the stomach. Then she shouted something at Hayden and sprinted toward the car. Hayden took an unnatural leap, throwing himself across the street. He stumbled on the landing, but Lana caught his arm, and they fell through the open door into the backseat.

"Canada, please," Hayden said.

James hit the gas. The car jumped forward, leaving the tangle of destroyed cop cars behind them. The remaining officers opened fire at their retreating vehicle.

James whipped the car into a turn. But before they'd rounded the corner, he saw two cruisers streak out of the pile after them. He veered right into opposing traffic, and a chorus of horns sounded from all directions. Another cop car suddenly flew out of the intersection in front of them, skidding in a tight turn. They were going to crash.

"Hayden!" James screamed.

The cruiser rose off the ground, and James drove right underneath.

As soon as they were past, the car dropped back to the street, shattering its windows on impact.

"In the future, drive *around* things," Hayden said, sounding exhausted.

Ahead, the traffic thickened at a red light.

"Hold on!" James yelled, and veered to the right onto the sidewalk.

People jumped out of the way as they sped past. They burst into the intersection, narrowly missing another car, and then James wrenched them into a sharp turn. Two of their tires lifted off the street, and there was a collective scream as they dropped back to solid ground and accelerated again.

"Play a lot of video games?" Hayden asked.

"A few," James said tightly.

"What are we gonna do?" Sam shouted. "I've seen reality shows like this. No one ever escapes in these chases!"

"Most of them can't throw cop cars across the street," Hayden pointed out.

"Watch out!" Lana shrieked.

James turned sharply left as an elderly woman walked right into their path. James watched her shake her fist in the rearview mirror.

"Almost killed her," he muttered.

"We need to get out of Manhattan," Lana said. "Get to a bridge."

All James could see around them were endless buildings. The flashing lights were still behind them, and he gripped the steering wheel, feeling the sweat forming beneath his fingers. They sped down the road for another two minutes, during which Hayden had to push two separate unsuspecting cars aside, as well as a man on a bike, before they finally emerged onto a wide-lane highway bordering the murky river. James sped down the highway toward the Brooklyn Bridge.

"And here come the choppers," Hayden said, staring out the window.

James weaved in and around the other vehicles as they crossed the bridge. They'd made it about a quarter of the way across when they saw more red and blue lights speeding toward them from the other direction. James looked in the rearview mirror and saw a stream of cop cars coming onto the bridge after them.

"This was a bad idea," he said grimly. "We're going to have to go right through."

"I'm getting a little tired," Hayden said, leaning over James's shoulder to see in front of the car. "That's a lot of cops."

All the other vehicles on the bridge were hastily pulling to the sides, revealing a straight line between their car and the rapidly approaching cruisers. James tightened his grip on the wheel again and prepared to charge.

Just then, a white ship dropped out of the air between them and the police, stopping its swift descent only a few feet from the road. Its nose was pointed right at them, the missile launcher visible beneath the cockpit.

"Hayden—" James started, feeling the panic rise.

But the ship turned and its ramp swung downward. The Flame rushed out, waving his hands over his head. James slammed on the brakes and their heads all snapped forward as the car skidded across the pavement, heading right for the ramp. They screeched to a stop a few feet from the Flame.

He hurried to James's door and flung it open. "Get in the ship!"

James frowned, but they didn't have much choice.

"Hurry up!" the Flame shouted. "The Vindico will be here any second!"

They all scrambled out of the car and followed him up the ramp. Hayden had just made it through the door when the ship leapt into the air. The ramp swung shut, blocking out the roaring wind.

"I thought you were trying to kill us," James snarled.

The Flame shook his head. "We have the same enemy. And we need all the help we can get. Do you know where Thunderbolt is?"

James hesitated. But once again, they didn't have much choice.

23

"IS IT TRANSMITTING?" LENI ASKED CALMLY.

Rono's voice came back over the comm. "Yep. They're heading north."

"You knew they were going to betray us," Avaria said.

Leni nodded. "Of course. They hate us enough to risk death, and they guessed correctly that I would have killed them even if they helped us. I had Rono plant the homing device on the Liberator as a backup in case they got to the children first. I would have preferred to just catch the brats ourselves and be done with it, but this might be even better. Now we can destroy the whole lot at once."

"But that defeats the purpose," Avaria argued. "If they are all reunited, they may be strong enough to defeat us."

"We will have some support as well," Leni said. "I will make these coordinates known to our rescuers. They clearly also have an interest in destroying the League."

Sliver glanced at Leni. "So why aren't we following them?"

"We'll let them settle in first," Leni replied. "Perhaps they will succumb to their own infighting. Thunderbolt might even arrest the traitors. Plus, if our rescuers decide to attack first, it saves us the trouble."

"Those kids are really getting powerful," the Torturer muttered, peering out the cockpit window.

They were flying over the path of their protégés' escape. Outside the Internet café, ten cop cars had been severely damaged, most of them overturned, and the street was littered with glass and debris, as well as massive crowds of onlookers and news vans.

"I know," Sliver agreed, turning the ship north. They could see fast-approaching air force jets coming to the scene—obviously having figured out that the League did not have the situation under control. But even military jets couldn't catch the highly advanced vessel they were in, and they wouldn't want to if they could. "If we had just managed to keep those kids on our side, we'd be unstoppable."

"Do you think we have to kill them?" the Torturer asked.

They all glanced at him in surprise.

"What?" Leni said.

The Torturer shrugged. "Well, they're pretty powerful. They could be useful. I think I can get James on our side if I had another crack at him."

"They put us in prison," Leni reminded him icily. "They betrayed us. Twice."

"I know, but to be fair, they were kind of in a tough spot—"

Sliver snickered. "You're going soft, old man."

"If you don't want to kill James, fine," Leni said. "I'll do it."

The Torturer frowned. Who were they to tell him what he should do with his own protégé? His eyes darted back and forth to Sliver and Leni, and not for the first time, he wondered what it would be like to be rid of them.

Emily could see him searching in the long grass.

She didn't say anything. She just stood on a small bluff as the stalks billowed in the wind. He continued to walk among them, calling her name. And though she felt a powerful affection for the old man, she remained where she was and still said nothing.

So he walked in the wrong direction, eventually passing out of view in the distance. She called out for him. But she had waited too long and there was no answer. Only the wind howling away. She sat down on the bluff and began to cry.

"Emily?"

Emily's eyes blinked open, and she immediately felt the wetness on her cheeks. She was staring up at the stone ceiling once again. She glanced over to see Blue sitting beside her, a concerned look on her face. One of her slender hands was resting on Emily's arm. Emily sniffled again and wiped her eyes with her free hand.

"I was crying," she said matter-of-factly.

"Yeah," Blue replied softly. "Bad dream?"

"Yeah."

"Do you want to talk about it?"

Emily hesitated. "Just something I regret. It's not the first time I've had this same dream."

"You'll fit right in with the League," Blue told her. "If we survive. We all have nightmares. Things we've seen. Members we've lost. I missed most of the darker times, but the older members, they barely sleep. Thunderbolt suffers the most. He sits in the lounge for hours, staring out at the city. I always used to find him there. He takes things very hard. He's seen so many die, yet he just keeps on going." She brushed the cobalt hair from her eyes.

"I had no idea," Emily said.

"No one does. Why would you? He puts on a brave face for the world because he has to. But he breaks a little more with each member that disappears."

"What do you have nightmares about?" Emily asked.

Blue smiled wanly. "Things I regret."

She seemed sad about something, so Emily changed the subject. "Did anyone come in while I was asleep?"

"No. I thought I saw someone look in at one point, but it was probably my imagination."

Emily pushed herself up into a sitting position, trying to shake off the sick feeling in her stomach. It had been a few weeks since she'd last had that dream. Every time, she woke up crying. She stared at the iron door, willing it to snap off its hinges. As she did, a shadow passed in front of the light. Straining, Emily thought she heard faint footsteps moving down the tunnel, and then there was silence again.

"Maybe I didn't imagine it," Blue whispered.

They sat there for a while longer, and soon Emily heard soft footsteps again. The door swung open and Dolus stepped inside.

"Emily, come with me."

"I'm coming too," Blue snarled, getting to her feet.

In a blur of motion, his gun was pointed at her forehead. "I asked for Emily."

He took a step back to clear the doorway, and as soon as Emily was through, he swung it shut again. Then he gestured down the hallway with the gun.

They started down the tunnel, neither speaking. Emily saw four more cell doors carved into the rock. They looked empty now, but she wondered if they had been used for the other League members at one point.

The stone floor rose steadily upward until they came to another black iron door. Dolus knocked once and it swung open, revealing a wide cavern illuminated by torches. Emily saw a Wraith step aside from where he was guarding the door from inside the room. She saw two more guards within the chamber, each standing by a respective door. Their faces were expressionless, and all three men were meticulously clean shaven.

They walked across the tavern to one of the far doors. The guard swung the door open at their approach, and Emily's eyes widened when she walked inside. Ten large cylinders lined the far wall of this smaller room. Each was connected by tubes and wiring to a number of consoles, and several men and women were hunched over the controls, staring intently at the data coming across the panels.

"Do you know what these are, Emily?" Dolus asked her.

She turned to him. "I can guess. Avaria used a cylinder like this to give Lana her superpowers. This is where you transform your subjects."

"Correct. We've only mastered strength and agility, though we have begun to understand the principles of flight. So far I've given powers to twenty-five individuals. I am very selective about my subjects. They must be intelligent, loyal, and stable."

"What are you using them for?"

"Our goal remains a secret, for now. I have given some thought to you, Emily. You have many of the qualities that I highly value. I brought you here to make you an offer."

He smiled, revealing flawless white teeth.

"I can give you powers equal to or even greater than those of your friends. You would no longer need to rely solely on your weapons. I want you to join us. I know your immediate response, and I can hardly blame you, seeing as you're being held here against your will. But when you know my goal, I am sure you'll see its wisdom. You're too clever not to. If you join me, you may be able to convince your friends to do the same. In one stroke, you could save them and end this coming battle before too many lives are claimed. It's too late for the League, and certainly for the Vindico, but you and your friends are young and relatively innocent in this. There is no need for you to be killed."

Emily met his mismatched eyes with her own. His yellow eye glowed with a fiery intelligence, while the darker one was almost indiscernible against his skin.

She didn't doubt that he had the ability to give her powers. The men who had captured her and Blue had been incredibly fast and strong. No one could argue that she didn't belong in the League if she had superstrength. And she also knew that powers would give her a greater opportunity to escape.

But she'd been betrayed by Rono before, and this time she wouldn't be so quick to trust a supervillain.

"And when will I know what your goal is?" she asked suspiciously.

"Very soon. Will you consider the offer?"

She nodded. "I'll consider it. But I'll make no decisions until I know more."

"I wouldn't expect it."

One of the cylinders suddenly swung open, and Emily turned to see a nude, muscular man emerge and wrap himself in a robe. He looked young, maybe in his twenties, and handsome, with deeply tanned skin and high cheekbones. His movements were unnaturally graceful.

"Let's return to your cell," Dolus said. "Think about my offer. And don't concern yourself with Thunderbolt's destination anymore. Unfortunately for him, that won't be secret for long."

He led her back the way they had come and pulled the cell door open.

"I'll be back soon" he promised right before the door clanged shut behind her.

"What was that about?" Blue asked.

Emily frowned. "He wants to give me superpowers."

"Why would he do that?"

"I don't know," Emily said. "But I obviously don't trust him."

Blue seemed to think about this as she stared at the closed door. She shook her head. "So someone else has figured it out. This is worse than I thought. This is the League's worst nightmare."

Emily glanced at her. "He said there are already twenty-five of these superpowered Wraiths."

"We need to warn Thunderbolt."

Emily could hear the longing in Blue's voice. A chance to finally help the League. But Emily had seen the black iron doors and the silent, stone-faced men. She knew they weren't getting out of here. Not like this.

She sat down on the cot, curling her arms around her legs, and though she tried not to, she began to consider Dolus's offer.

24

"SO, LET'S TALK," HAYDEN SAID, TAPPING HIS FINGERS AGAINST THE TABLE.

The Flame, Gali, and Jada sat on one side of the Liberator's gleaming white conference room, facing the protégés. Sinio was in the cockpit, piloting them toward the coordinates James had provided.

"Very well," the Flame said. "To begin, you should know that we never meant to harm you."

"How nice," Lana said sarcastically. "You just tried to arrest us, got Emily kidnapped, and then blew up half of League headquarters coming after us again."

The Flame folded his arms imperiously. "We can hardly be blamed for Emily's disappearance. You should have been more careful."

"More careful?" James snarled. "Maybe you should have warned us we were being stalked instead of trying to arrest us."

The Flame started rising from his chair. "Maybe you should have opened your eyes and—"

"Easy," Gali cut in, laying a massive hand on the Flame's shoulder.

"We've lost people too," Jada said. "You aren't alone there."

The Flame sat back down, looking venomous.

"Do you have any idea who would have taken them?" James asked.

The League members looked at each other darkly.

"We have a guess," the Flame muttered.

Lana studied him for a moment. His black hair was unkempt and greasy, and thick stubble was creeping down his neck. His eyes were ringed by dark circles, giving them a haunted look.

"Go on . . ." Hayden said.

The Flame sighed. "As you know, right before you were first abducted, the Torturer managed to capture one of our members. His name was Nighthawk, and he was a close friend of mine. He and I were out on a routine patrol mission, having heard a report that someone matching the Torturer's description was prowling around the area. We get a lot of reports like that, so we didn't think much of it."

He looked away. "Well, this time it was a trap. Just as we were walking by an abandoned mill, the brick wall burst, catching us both by surprise. Clouds of dust and debris enveloped us; I couldn't see anything. I stumbled around, calling Nighthawk's name. But when the dust cleared, he was already gone." The Flame clenched his fists and tendrils of fire curled off his knuckles. "We never saw him again."

"What does that have to do with you betraying the League?" James asked.

"We didn't betray the League," Jada replied. "We just wanted a new leader."

"Oh, you're right," Hayden said. "Totally different."

The Flame narrowed his eyes. "After Nighthawk disappeared, I pressed for a full search for the Vindico's new base. We knew the Baron must have built one. We even guessed the area. But Thunderbolt was always reluctant to attack. It was almost as if he felt guilty."

Lana glanced at James.

"What?" Gali asked, looking between them.

"The Baron told us that he started the League," Lana said. "That he was the one who got the original four together. But they kicked him out after he tried to give himself superpowers."

"Impossible," the Flame scoffed.

"Thunderbolt didn't deny it," Hayden said. "I told him everything after the battle at the mansion."

"It would explain a lot," Gali muttered.

"Maybe," the Flame said, sounding unconvinced, "but it just reaffirms my point. If we'd struck earlier, we might have wiped them out. Instead you were abducted and we were almost destroyed. But ultimately, through no small amount of luck, we ended up capturing them, and Thunderbolt seemed to have been right. The war was over."

"Well, technically *we* captured them," Hayden noted.

"Because they were busy fighting us," the Flame replied coldly. "I disagreed with Thunderbolt that we should wait even six months to train you. I wanted you to become full members immediately. But he sent you home, and we all went back to our regular rotations. Three-and-a-half months later, Renda was gone without a trace. Then Peregrine disappeared a week later from the mansion in Ontario.

"For a few days, none of us knew what to do. Then we received an anonymous lead. This man told us he was defecting from some sort of secret organization that was planning to slowly pick off League members, one by one. He gave us a location where the two captives were being taken as a stopover, but he warned us they wouldn't remain there for long. I immediately called for a full-scale attack, and I was supported by many of our members, including these three. But Thunderbolt hesitated. He told us something 'didn't feel right' and that we had to proceed with caution. So he sent us in for a reconnaissance mission first.

"I went with Gali and Ceri, and we were almost shot out of the sky. Some ground-based weapons opened fire, and we narrowly escaped after two black ships appeared and chased us away. When we got back to headquarters, Thunderbolt finally decided to send the full team. But when we returned to the site, we found the compound already deserted. There were signs of a hurried escape, and that was all. We'd lost our chance.

"I was furious. I had an argument with Thunderbolt, but in the end I decided not to leave. I didn't think I had the support, and I didn't want to fracture the League because I knew we'd get picked apart.

"After we had no news for a few days, Thunderbolt split us up again. I was sent with these three to watch over Hayden and Emily since Thunderbolt knew about your reunion weekend. The rest of the group stayed with him at headquarters. Everyone except Blue, who he sent to stay at the mansion. Thunderbolt thought it was the safest place for her since no one but you kids, the League, and the Vindico knew of its existence. It was two days after we moved Hayden's neighbors to another location and moved in ourselves that a note was left on the doorstep addressed to me."

The Flame stared at the far wall.

"It was the deserter. He said he wanted to meet me. The next night I went to meet him, and he appeared out of nowhere, dressed all in black. He told me that the organization, which he was hesitant to name, was preparing to attack the League. He said their leader was going mad, talking about wiping out everyone. He needed to get out and he wasn't alone either. He told me he had at least ten more men like him, all superpowered, who would join the League to rebel against their leader. He said that their support was behind *me*, not Thunderbolt. In fact, he told me they'd only join if I was in charge."

"I see where this is going," Hayden said. "Did you at

least find out where these superpowered guys came from?"

"No," the Flame said. "He only said he'd been recruited."

The Liberator dipped a little as they flew through some turbulence, and Lana saw Sam nervously clutch the edge of his chair. "And so this is why you decided to rebel?" she guessed.

The Flame sighed deeply.

"I thought I had to make a move to save the League. I convinced the others, and we decided that in order to secure enough influence, we needed to recruit you. But we also knew your loyalties were with Thunderbolt since he had Deanna and Lyle on his side. So we came up with the plan to have you arrested. We were going to act as if Thunderbolt was being unreasonable, demanding that you go to the Perch, and try to win your loyalty by refusing to take you. It was ill thought, in hindsight, and things have gone downhill since.

"Talia picked us up from Hayden's house after your escape and let us borrow the Liberator. She was sympathetic, though not enough to join us. Noran decided to go back to Thunderbolt as well; he said we had gone too far. He was right. We knew we had betrayed the League; we knew Thunderbolt would arrest us if you got to him with the story. So we chased you. We were too late to get you at the Perch, and after hearing from Junkit that Blue and Emily had gone missing, we were frantic. At this point, I believed the deserter fully. I thought that if we were arrested, then the rest of the League would be killed when this organization attacked. That's why we followed you to New York."

"What were you going to do?" Lana asked coldly. "Kill us?"

The Flame shook his head. "We thought you would be frightened into surrendering. We were never going to kill you."

"Didn't seem that way when you were throwing fireballs at our heads," Hayden mused.

"Then the Vindico showed up," Gali cut in. "We still don't know how." He looked at the others, and their faces were grim. "We fear that Junkit may be dead."

"Leni left us alive," the Flame continued, "and told us to hunt you. I don't know how he would be so foolish, to tell you the truth. We would never join them. When we got back to the ship, we knew we had to try and save you, return you to Thunderbolt, and face the consequences." He sighed again. "And that was the first right move we've made in weeks. I don't know how we were so stupid."

"And what about this deserter?" James asked. "Have you heard from him since?"

"No," the Flame said, almost sheepishly. "And now I begin to wonder if he was a deserter at all."

"What do you mean?" Lana said.

"It strikes me that all he really accomplished was to split the League," the Flame said. "And where has he gone now? Why didn't he just tell us where to find the organization in the first place?" He scowled. "He may have been with them all along."

"It bothers me that Leni did something so dumb," Hayden said. "He's a jerk, but he's not stupid."

"I know," James agreed, looking concerned. "There's not much we can do, though, other than meet up with Thunderbolt. Do you think he'll arrest you guys?"

The Flame shrugged. "I don't know. Probably. But maybe he'll wait. We need to recapture the Vindico, or kill them as I'd prefer, and then deal with this organization. The deserter warned me they were very powerful, and for some reason I don't think he was lying about that, at least."

"Well," Lana said, "despite everything, I have to say I agree. We need all the help we—"

"We've arrived at the coordinates," Sinio said from the cockpit, cutting Lana off. "Now what?"

Hayden turned to Sam. "Time to find your girlfriend."

Sam closed his eyes. A minute passed, and then he suddenly broke into a smile.

"Found her," he said.

"Tell her how pretty her mind is," Hayden suggested.

"I see where they are," Sam said, opening his eyes. "It's a few miles west of here. I'll show Sinio where to go." He hurried into the cockpit.

"I guess we'll find out what's happening soon," Hayden said.

"I just want to know one thing," Lana whispered. "Where is Emily?"

25

THE RAMP TOUCHED DOWN IN A MEADOW, AND LONG GRASS CURLED UP OVER the edge. James gazed out at the sprawling property, miles away from the nearest town.

The two-story house was ancient: its faded gray bricks and peeling white windowsills looked like they'd seen too many hard winters. A huge red barn stood forty feet behind it. Forest ringed the property, past fields that had once been tilled but were now a patchwork of sun-soaked cornstalks, purple and yellow flowers, and clumps of grass.

James walked down the ramp slowly, eyeing the screen door of the farmhouse. *Sam must have this wrong,* he thought. A loud bark cut through the air, and he saw a big white dog come bounding out of the house.

"Someone's going to be *really* confused if we're at the wrong house," Hayden said.

"This is the right place," the Flame murmured from behind them.

The white dog slowed to a halt ten feet in front of them. Its coat was made of thick tufts of speckled white and gray hair and when it bared its sharp teeth James realized it wasn't a dog at all. It was a wolf.

"Nice boy," Hayden said, and the wolf growled. "Or not."

"Here!" a stern voice called, and the wolf immediately bolted back to the house.

Thunderbolt walked out of the screen door with Deanna and Lyle behind him. Four other League members followed them and spread out across the porch.

The wolf ran past Thunderbolt and perched itself on the porch.

"Why are you here?" Thunderbolt asked sharply.

The Flame stepped up to meet him as he came across the front lawn. "To bring them to you," he said. "They were about to be captured . . . or worse. We would like to rejoin you or give ourselves up, whichever you choose."

Thunderbolt didn't reply for a moment. He looked much as he did in his message: tired and old. But there was still danger resonating in his eyes. "Why?" he asked.

Deanna and Lyle were expressionless behind him, though Deanna smiled briefly at Sam before looking away again.

The Flame hesitated. "We've realized our mistakes," he explained, "and that this is the only way to save the League. If it's not already too late."

Thunderbolt scanned over the four protégés. "What's happened?"

"The Vindico are free," Hayden said.

"And Emily and Blue were taken," James added.

Thunderbolt stiffened. "I feared Blue was gone when she didn't respond to our latest attempt to contact the base. But I never thought Emily would be captured as well. How did this happen? How were the Vindico released?"

"We don't know," the Flame said. "We visited the Perch, but when we left, they were still in their cells. We can only guess that whoever is abducting League members might also have let them out. We fear . . ." He looked away. "We fear this can only mean that Junkit is dead."

The lines on Thunderbolt's face seemed to visibly deepen as he took in this information. "Things are much worse than I believed," he said quietly. "Everyone come inside. There's still room in the barn; store the Liberator in there. We will discuss our next steps together."

He started back for the house. Lyle and Deanna quickly followed him.

"I expected more hugging," Hayden said. "Or at least a firm handshake."

"Did he hurt your feelings?" Lana asked.

"Yes," Hayden replied seriously. "He did."

James nudged Sam. "Well, someone is happy to see us, at least."

"We should probably get inside," Sam said, sounding uncomfortable.

"Wouldn't want to keep Deanna waiting," Hayden agreed, and put his arm around Sam's shoulders. "Walk with me, Sam. Let's talk about courtship. The first step is to shotgun her so that there is no competition from your friends . . ."

"Did he shotgun me?" Lana asked incredulously, turning to James.

James bit back a smile and started after them.

"He shotgunned me?" she said. "Hayden!"

James looked around the crowded living room, studying the tense faces. Pale light was filtering through the closed white curtains, and he saw dust swirling through the air. He and the other protégés were sitting on an old green couch, while the rest of the remaining League members stood in two groups. Besides Thunderbolt, Deanna, and Lyle, there were five other loyal members, and across from them stood the four traitors. The Flame was leaning against the wall, staring warily at the loyal members.

"So," Thunderbolt began, standing at the entrance to the kitchen, "at last we are all gathered, though it is far later than I'd hoped. The delay has been costly. For those of you who don't know, the Vindico have escaped the Perch."

There were some curses from the other League members.

Thunderbolt glanced at them. "And Blue has been abducted, as has Emily."

James saw a few dark looks and glances stray toward the four traitors. The Flame met their eyes stonily.

"How could the Vindico have escaped?" Meirna asked.

Her voice was calm, but James could see that she was visibly shaken. "It's supposed to be impossible."

"We have to assume they were released by these unknown attackers," Thunderbolt said. "But how *they* got in, I have no idea. There's no way to get past the air defenses and sentries, and you can't blow your way through that door."

Lana frowned. "Is there any way to override the systems?"

"Not that I know of," Thunderbolt said. "The only one who would know is the man who built them, and Nimian has been dead for almost twenty years."

"Did any of the other prisoners get out?" Talia asked.

Thunderbolt shook his head. "I don't know. If they did, we're all in trouble. But if this mysterious group's goal is to help the Vindico, they wouldn't have let anyone else out. You know as well as I do that they would go after the Vindico first.

James was just about to ask who else was in the Perch when Thunderbolt turned to the protégés. "We need some answers before we can begin. Why were Emily and Blue together? Where have you been?"

Hayden recounted their actions since the failed arrest at his party, ending with the battle at League headquarters and their dramatic escape from New York.

When Hayden finished, Thunderbolt nodded and turned back to the group with a grave expression.

"So we must continue to assume all of our known bases are in danger. It was stupid of me to leave Blue at the mansion for so long by herself and to leave Junkit alone at the Perch. But I was not the only one who acted foolishly."

He turned to the Flame and narrowed his eyes.

"Perhaps it's time you give some account of yourselves," he said, the warning evident in his voice.

The Flame repeated the same story he'd told the teens on the way there. All of the loyal League members listened grimly. Thunderbolt again made little reaction, though his scowl only continued to deepen. When he was finished explaining their rescue in New York City, the Flame stepped back against the wall again, lowering his eyes.

"I wondered why your decision to return to us came so suddenly," Thunderbolt said. "What more do you know about this organization? Aside from the fact that they have been capturing our members and have now released the Vindico?"

The Flame shook his head. "Only what I've just told you. It is becoming more obvious that it was all a setup."

"As I feared in the first place," Thunderbolt snarled. "Your stupidity has almost destroyed us all."

"I only wanted what was best for the League," the Flame replied sharply.

"By betraying us?" Ceri said, her lip curling in disgust. "Blue might still be here if you hadn't acted like an idiot."

"Don't blame that on me," the Flame hissed.

Ceri clenched her fists. "Who should we blame, then? The kids? Who had to hide at the mansion after being attacked by the ones who were supposed to be protecting them?"

"We weren't attacking them!" Gali protested. "We were just going to take them in."

"Without permission," Thunderbolt said. "The entire reason I wanted the kids left at home was to keep them from becoming targets of this group. No one outside of us knew they would be future League members."

"Well, you were wrong," the Flame snapped. "They were being followed by that organization already: Emily and Sam had both seen them. It was only a matter of time before they were snatched out of their beds. They needed to be brought in so we could keep a close eye on them."

"It wasn't your decision to make," Meirna said. "And even so, after you failed, you should have reported back to Thunderbolt. Instead you chased them across the country and ultimately attacked our own headquarters! What were you thinking?"

"How was I supposed to contact him?" the Flame asked. "He was hiding here! In a place he's never seen fit to share with us. We made mistakes, we've admitted that. That's why we're here. But while you lot were hiding up here with your tails between your legs, we saved these kids!"

"We were following orders," Ceri snapped.

"Everyone calm down," Thunderbolt said. "We don't need to fight among ourselves any longer. We're already in enough trouble. We know everybody's stories now, and it's time to make some decisions. As for our next step, we need to wait for the Vindico to surface somewhere. Before anything else, we must capture them again. We'll have to think of where they would go and why. But for now, we have an immediate issue."

He folded his arms.

"What to do with the traitors. The sentence is always life imprisonment, but the conditions here are unusual. We no longer have a secure prison, nor any facilities to keep them contained, unless it's on the Defender. More importantly, we are undermanned and facing two potentially deadly enemies. My first instinct is to lock you up, but we can't let our anger override our reason."

"And what if they betray us again?" Septer asked, staring at the Flame.

"Their actions were stupid," Thunderbolt said, "but I do believe they thought they were acting in the best interests of the League. The way to save the League now is clear: capture the Vindico and destroy this shadow organization. Due punishment may follow, but it can be based on their conduct as we move forward in the coming battles. But we all must accept them, or this group cannot function. We'll put it to a vote. For myself, I vote to postpone punishment and re-admit them until the war is over."

He turned to Deanna and Lyle.

"We vote the same," Deanna said firmly.

"I vote they be arrested now," Ceri snarled.

Septer and Meirna agreed with her, while Noran and Talia sided with Thunderbolt.

"And how about you?" Thunderbolt asked, turning to the protégés. "Due to the situation, I think it makes sense to formally induct you into the League of Heroes, if you agree. I apologize for the lack of ceremony, but we will have a proper induction once this is over. Stand up, please."

James, Hayden, Lana, and Sam climbed to their feet.

Thunderbolt stepped in front of them. "On this day, I, Thunderbolt, invite you to join the League of Heroes, and in doing so, request that you pledge yourselves to preserving the justice and freedom of all peoples, and to honor and swear by our code of morality. Do you accept?"

"Yes," James said immediately. He'd been waiting for this moment his whole life. He hadn't expected it to happen in an old, dusty living room, but it didn't matter. He was a member of the League of Heroes. From this day forth, he was a superhero.

"I do," Hayden said, extending his hand, as if for a ring.

Thunderbolt scowled and moved on to Lana.

Lana hesitated but finally said, "Yes. For Emily."

Sam glanced at them and then nodded. "I accept."

"Good," Thunderbolt replied. "Your first duty is to vote."

James looked at the Flame. "I vote for them to stay."

"Me too," Lana said.

"We need their help," Sam agreed.

Hayden stroked his chin thoughtfully. "A difficult decision," he said. "On the one hand—"

"Vote's over," Thunderbolt cut in. He turned to the Flame and the other traitors. "You are re-admitted to the League and are to be treated as normal members until the conclusion of the war. At that time, we will return to this discussion. If you handle yourselves honorably and help us defeat our enemies, I will consider a pardon."

Ceri sat back down, looking sullen.

"For the moment, there's not much to be done. I suspect everyone is tired. We'll break for a few hours and then meet for a strategy session. Until then, shower, lie down, whatever you wish. You will all be rotated into guard positions. Dismissed."

"Welcome to the League," Deanna said, turning to them. She gave Sam a firm hug.

"Thanks," Hayden replied. "It looks like a happy place."

"Is there a bed I can lie down on for a bit?" James asked Deanna. "I'm exhausted."

"You guys can use our room," she said. "You must all be tired."

She and Lyle led them upstairs, the old floorboards groaning under their weight. James studied the walls, which were covered with yellowed photos of a large family. At the top of the stairs they turned into a small room with two narrow beds pressed against either wall.

"We're on guard duty soon anyway," Lyle said. "So you lie down. We'll come get you for lunch."

"Thanks," James said, dropping onto one of the small beds.

"Shotgun!" Hayden shouted, and jumped on beside him.

James immediately pushed him onto the floor.

"We'll fit right in with the League," Lana said, lying down on the other bed.

Hayden climbed to his feet and lay down beside her. "Yeah, but James and I are besties. We'd never split up."

"We'll see," James muttered as Sam awkwardly climbed onto the bed beside him, facing the other direction.

"I can't believe we're in the League of Heroes," Sam said.

James smiled. "I know."

Sam was silent for a moment. "My mom is going to kill me."

26

AVARIA GAZED INTO THE SWIFT-MOVING CREEK. SHE COULD SEE SMALL FISH near the banks, moving in and out of the tangled weeds. She closed her eyes, enjoying the soothing noise, and felt some of her tension ease. The long weeks in prison had grated on her. She despised confined areas. She needed to move. She needed to fight.

Once, things had been different. When she was a girl, she'd lived in a rural town, and her house was bordered by a forest much like this one. She had spent her days under the leaves or tending the horses out in the fields. Her parents would read to her and her brother at night, and she would sleep under a thick quilt to keep out the cold.

Avaria opened her eyes and stared at the richly colored leaves dotting the forest floor. It reminded her of those times, which seemed so faint that they could well have been a dream. Maybe it was an imaginary life she had built just to believe she was once normal. To remember that there had been something before the hate.

The only evidence she'd had was her crumpled photo. She wondered if it was still at the mansion, tucked into a drawer. Of Derias, the man she had loved, and a smiling, happy, young version of herself who had died the same night as her husband.

As it always did, the mere thought of Derias flooded her with memories that she couldn't get rid of. The feeling of his fingers running through her hair. The way the corner of his lips tugged into a smile whenever she entered the room. The way he would change his appearance as they lay together in bed, just to hear her say she liked him the way he was. The way he looked at her like she was the only thing he would ever need. Happy memories that were destroyed in an instant. Because of her.

Avaria closed her eyes again. She didn't want to think about that night. The guilt hadn't faded in fifteen years, and she knew it never would. The only thing to do was replace it with the same burning anger that had sustained her since. She would not rest until she found Captain Courage and killed him. The others could have their power and influence. She wanted none of that. When her one goal was done, she would disappear and become someone new. Someone whose hands weren't stained with blood.

"I miss you, Derias," she whispered softly.

"Avaria!" someone called, and she spun around. Rono emerged from the woods, pushing aside the low-hanging branches. "The Baron wants to talk about our next move."

Avaria took one last glance at the creek and then followed him back toward the ships.

"We haven't had much chance to talk since we were released," Rono said.

Avaria glanced at him. "About what?"

He looked around and stopped. "Are you going to kill Lana?"

"Of course," she said coldly, and then saw the look on his face. "Not you too."

He shrugged. "I just think we put a lot of work in and maybe we can still—"

"Emily betrayed you."

"I know," he murmured, "but like the Torturer said, we did teach them to be evil. I mean, they just did what we told them."

"She's not your daughter, Rono. She's gone."

Rono looked away. "I know that."

"Do you? Because it doesn't sound like it. They betrayed us. End of story."

"Yeah. I know," he said quietly.

Avaria nodded. "Good. Now let's go figure out how to make them pay."

Both vessels were parked in a grassy clearing a few hours from where the protégés had set down. The other four Vindico members were gathered between them, standing in a loose circle. Avaria and Rono joined the group.

"Now," the Baron said, "we know where the protégés are on the map, but not the conditions of their location.

They could be at a secret base, though I have no knowledge of any League structures in that area. Rono has been doing some work with satellite observations, but there aren't enough conclusive pictures of that remote area. So far, he's found nothing."

He gestured at Leni.

"At Leni's urging, we've sent a broadcast of the coordinates to the Perch, under the assumption that Dolus and his organization are still holding the facility. We're hoping they will assist in assaulting this new location. However, we have no way of knowing if they will actually receive it."

"They will," Leni said.

"Even so," the Baron replied, "it will be difficult to combine our efforts. We must consider how we are going to attack."

"Straight in," the Torturer said. "We'll catch them by surprise."

"They might have antiaircraft defenses," Rono reasoned, "in which case we need to go in on foot. Judging by the area, I'd say there's probably forest nearby."

"But think how many of them might be collected there," Sliver argued. "With the traitors and our protégés, we're outnumbered."

The Baron nodded. "Exactly."

"Maybe we should lay low for a while and wait for them to split?" Rono suggested. "They might just fall apart eventually anyway."

"Unlikely," Leni replied. "Now that we're free, they're

united. But drawing them out might not be such a bad idea."

The Baron frowned. "What do you mean?"

"Perhaps we don't need to attack their hiding spot," Leni reasoned. "Why not let our friends work on that? I just had a thought."

He looked at the others, a cruel smile forming on his lips. Avaria frowned at the smug look of satisfaction on his face.

"These kids are indeed powerful," Leni said. "With them, the League can probably defeat us. But just as they used our protégés against us, we can use them against the League. You see, they have a weakness the rest of the League doesn't."

"They do?" the Torturer asked, looking confused.

Leni met his eyes. "They haven't had a chance to learn a lesson the League figured out a long time ago. Hide your family."

"Of course," the Baron whispered.

"Let the League stay hidden in the wilderness for a while longer," Leni said. "We'll leave one ship here to keep an eye on them, and the rest of us can go collect the families. Rono, you should stay with the Baron. Contact us if there's movement. We'll be back in a day or two."

Leni smiled. "Then we send them a message and see what our protégés do when we bring the war home."

27

SAM SLIPPED OUT OF THE BEDROOM, EASING THE DOOR SHUT BEHIND HIM. THE others were still fast asleep, but he couldn't rest. His mind was on Deanna.

As he tiptoed down the stairs, he heard muted conversations coming from various parts of the old, creaky house. Sam brushed against the minds of the other League members, sensing distrust, anxiety, and from most, fatigue. He located Deanna and immediately felt a warm glow of recognition from her.

Sam smiled and hurried out the front door.

The sun was beginning to lower on the western skyline, glowing orange and bright. A cool breeze was blowing across the meadow, and it cut right through his thin T-shirt. He hugged himself and turned to find Lyle sitting on a bench.

"I'm guessing you're not looking for me?" he asked.

Sam hesitated.

"That's okay," Lyle said, smirking. "She's around back, watching the forest. Then again, you already know that, don't you? I forget you two are probably talking as we speak."

"Thanks," Sam said sheepishly.

He wandered around the house and spotted Deanna casually leaning against the back wall, staring out at the field. The shaggy wolf sat beside her, following her gaze.

"Can't sleep?" Deanna asked, glancing at him.

"No," he replied. "Anything going on back here?"

"Not a thing. Wolf's keeping me company though."

Sam frowned. "His name is Wolf?"

"Yeah," she said. "Not very creative, I know. Wolf is Thunderbolt's pet, but he's taken a liking to me."

Sam tentatively petted Wolf's back. "He's beautiful."

"He is."

Sam leaned against the coarse brick wall and followed her gaze across the field.

Not a thing out there, Deanna said into his mind. *Though I think I might have seen a deer once.*

It's been a while since I've talked like this, Sam said. He could feel a little nagging voice of concern in her mind. *Is everything all right?*

She looked away. *No,* she replied, *but you knew that. Things are bad. You heard Thunderbolt. And I can't shake this feeling that it's only going to get worse.*

"I know what you mean," Sam said softly.

Thunderbolt is worried. Deanna continued. *He tries to act like he's not, but you can see it in his face. He looks like he doesn't sleep, and he's been acting strange lately, more somber than I've ever seen him. I think he doesn't know what to do, and he's not used to that. It's keeping him awake at night.*

"How long have you been here?" Sam asked.

Too long, she thought, and then bit her lip. "A few weeks," she said out loud. "It's tough to tell here. It's always the same. We left headquarters after the second abduction and came right here."

"Where *is* here?" Sam asked, staring up at the ancient house.

"This is Captain Courage's childhood home," Deanna said. "He kept its location secret for years. This is where his family lived, or at least some of them, and he wanted to keep them safe. But when his parents died, his remaining brothers and sisters moved away with their children. Apparently he told Thunderbolt about the house, and they decided to keep it as a secret meeting place in case things ever got really bad. So here we are."

"This is *Courage's* house?" Sam whispered.

"Yeah," she said, smiling.

Sam nodded, running his hands along the gray brick. "I have to go look at those photos when we go back inside." He shook his head. "So what have you been doing here?"

"Waiting. First for the other members and then for you guys. Thunderbolt wanted to keep me and Lyle safe and didn't trust any of the other bases. We've been redirecting everyone here using the amplifier." She reached down and patted Wolf's head. "Wolf is a lot happier here, but I think he's the only one. I feel like we're just giving the bad guys time to get their plans together."

Sam glanced at her. Her curly, raven hair was blowing over her cheeks, and she was still biting her lip, as if deep in thought. He felt a little flutter in his stomach.

She smiled. "I'm glad you're here too," she said, meeting his eyes.

"Felt that one, I guess," Sam murmured.

"Yep. You're not very discreet."

"To be fair, you read my mind," he pointed out.

"You should know to be careful with your thoughts around me." She took his hand.

After a minute of content silence, she turned to him.

Thunderbolt is about to collect everyone, she said. *We better go wake the others.*

All right, he replied, trying to hide his regret. She smirked again.

"Got that too?" he asked, sighing.

"Yep."

"I need to put some walls up."

"I'd just break them down again," Deanna replied confidently. "Waste of time." She leaned over and gave him a quick kiss on the cheek. "Let's go."

They rounded the house together, and Sam didn't even bother to hold back his smile.

"We need to press the attack," the Flame said vehemently. "Before they get a chance to settle in somewhere."

"And where do you want to attack?" Ceri replied,

derision evident in her voice. "We don't know where they are!"

"They may be at headquarters still," Gali said. "Why would they leave?"

"Because you blew it to pieces," Meirna snarled.

Both sides started yelling at each other, and Hayden leaned back on the couch. He'd been having such a nice sleep, and now they had to sit in on this continual arguing. It had been fifteen minutes already, and they were no closer to a decision than when they'd started.

He glanced at Lana, and she rolled her eyes. James sat beside her, looking like he was barely awake, while Sam was with Deanna on the other side of the room. Hayden gave him a thumbs-up, and Sam quickly looked away, embarrassed.

"Stop!" Thunderbolt said loudly, rising to his feet. "This is not helping. If we're going to get out of this, we have to work together." He began to pace in the center of the living room. "I would like to strike out, but it seems unwise to commit ourselves to an offensive attack without any information. The Vindico could be anywhere, though I think they would likely have gone to the Baron's mansion. We know Leni has a base somewhere, but again, we have no idea where." He scowled. "They in turn have no idea where we are. We're both fighting shadows."

"So one of us has to turn a light on," Hayden said, and everyone in the room looked at him. "Yes, we're still here," he continued. "We're just a bit sleepy. But I'm getting bored, so I feel like I should participate."

Thunderbolt glared at him. "Do you actually have a suggestion, or do you just feel like talking?"

"Both," Hayden replied. "If you recall, I already made my suggestion. We have to turn a light on."

Thunderbolt narrowed his eyes. "Meaning . . ."

"We need to show ourselves and bring them to us. Now, I think you all have it wrong when it comes to their current location. They aren't settling in somewhere. They're not ready to let this become a drawn-out war again because they want to kill us, and soon. I saw the look on Leni's face. He wants blood."

Hayden shrugged. "When does he not, really? The point is, they're after us and you guys. Here's what's been troubling me. Leni sent the Flame to capture us, even though he knows very well that the Flame hates him and would never help him. Then, despite the fact that we destroyed *several* New York City blocks, Leni and the others were nowhere to be found, and the Flame and crew provided a timely rescue. Curious, no?"

"What are you getting at?" Thunderbolt snapped.

"Maybe I was wrong," Hayden said thoughtfully. "We may not need to turn on a light after all."

"We don't have time for this," the Flame said, turning to the others.

"Let him finish," Thunderbolt said slowly.

"Thank you. I found it strange the whole ride, but I let it go. It's just too much of a coincidence. What if the Vindico wanted the Flame and the others to get there first because they *knew* they would never turn us over? In fact, the

Vindico might have guessed that the shock of seeing them free would send you running right back to Thunderbolt."

"But why would they let us go then?" the Flame asked sharply.

"Simple," Hayden replied. "They wanted you to lead them here."

"But they didn't follow us," Gali argued. "We would have seen them on our scanners if they were anywhere close."

Thunderbolt had his arms folded across his chest, and he looked deeply troubled.

"Agreed," Hayden said. "But a homing beacon would have done the trick."

"Go check the ship," Thunderbolt said, turning to the Flame.

The Flame hurried out the door, and Gali rushed out after him.

"I bet they'll find a beacon somewhere on the Liberator's hull," Hayden said.

"Why didn't you say anything before now?" Thunderbolt snapped.

"It just came to me," Hayden replied. "I'm brilliant, but at a measured pace."

"They could be outside right now," Lana whispered.

"No," Deanna said, "they aren't in range. But Sam and I will go check with the amplifier."

Thunderbolt watched as they hurried upstairs. "If Hayden's right, we could have visitors as early as tonight."

"We need to leave," Jada said urgently.

"And go where?" Thunderbolt asked. "Maybe we should fight them here."

"This isn't the most defensible location," Lana pointed out. "Leni could knock this place over in a second."

"True," Thunderbolt agreed, "but some of our more defensible bases have already been breached. Here, at least the other group can't find us."

"So what do we do?" Ceri asked.

"First, we have to confirm that there even is a tracking device," Thunderbolt replied. "Then we wait to hear from Sam and Deanna before we decide whether to stay here or relocate."

"I'm tired of running," James muttered.

Thunderbolt glanced at him. "So am I," he agreed.

They waited a minute or two longer, and then the front door swung open. The Flame marched in, holding a circular black device.

"Didn't take long," he said bitterly. "It was on the bottom." He tossed the homing beacon on the floor and stamped on it. "They know we're here."

Everyone in the room stood up, except Hayden, who just sighed. "I hate being right all the time," he said.

Deanna and Sam came back into the living room.

"Didn't sense anyone in range," Deanna said.

"So what now?" the Flame asked, turning to Thunderbolt. "They'll come soon."

Thunderbolt was silent for a moment. "Let them come."

The other members all began talking among themselves.

"We'll keep five on guard at all times," Thunderbolt said over the noise. "Sam, Deanna, Sinio, Talia—one of you needs to be on the amplifier constantly. You may be able to overwhelm them when they get close. The first shift can eat now. I'm on guard. Flame, Gali, Hayden, and Sam, you're with me. Let's move!"

Hayden watched as everyone hurried in different directions. Lana and James looked down at him.

"Shouldn't you be doing something?" Lana asked.

Hayden sighed again and tiredly climbed to his feet. "I wish they'd let us sleep a little longer. I have a feeling this is going to be a long night."

28

JAMES ADJUSTED THE COLLAR OF HIS BORROWED FLEECE JACKET, PULLING IT UP to his chin. The night air was bitterly cold, and the breeze had become a fierce wind, piercing through to his bones. The moon was obscured by clouds, the darkness broken only by the light washing out from the windows of the house.

He had been called to relieve the first watch twenty minutes earlier, just as he'd been lying down to try to get a little more sleep. Ceri was head of this shift, and she'd sent him to the back of the house.

Figures, he thought sourly, *send the new guy on the worst job.*

Lana was pacing around out front, while Ceri and Jada were on either side. Sinio was currently manning the amplifier.

James huddled against the cold brick, scanning the field uselessly. He knew he was very exposed at the back, where there was the least amount of light. If Sinio didn't warn him, someone could sneak within ten feet of him and he wouldn't have a clue. James straightened up a little, unnerved. He supposed that's why they'd given him the position: with his dense skin, he could best survive a surprise attack.

Finally, James decided to take a walk, both to wake himself up and to warm his freezing limbs. He walked a short ways out into the field and then paced back and forth, spotting Ceri and Jada. After a few minutes, he turned back to the wall. At least there was some shelter from the wind next to the house.

He was halfway there when he saw a shadow on the house move. He froze, and the shadow stopped. It was tucked against the base of the back wall, half-concealed in the long grass that ringed the house. James took another few steps, crouching low to the ground, and then stopped, waiting for movement. A moment later, the shadow moved again.

It crept below the edge of the illuminated kitchen window and then slowly eased upward, peering through the glass. James slunk forward, his muscles tensed and alert. As he neared the shadow, he began to pick up speed. He was about fifteen feet away when the shadow abruptly whirled around.

"They're here!" James screamed, now that the surprise was gone.

Shouts filled the air and the Wraith exploded into action. He sprinted toward James with blinding speed and roundhouse-kicked him in the ribs. The blow was incredibly powerful, and James toppled sideways, landing face-first in the grass.

He hastily rolled to the side just as a foot stamped where his head had been. He looked up to see a man in a black uniform standing over him. Just then, an explosion lit up the night sky, and James felt intense heat press against his face. The Wraith tried to kick him in the face again, but James reached out and caught the boot. Then he wrenched the foot to the side and sent the man crashing to the ground.

James scrambled to his feet and saw that the back of the house had been blown apart. Flames sprouted out of the rubble. Ceri was grappling with another Wraith nearby. With a sudden twist, he threw her into the wall.

Just as James started running to help her, a sharp kick struck the back of his knee and his leg buckled. He landed in a crouch, then turned and plowed into the man's stomach. They both landed in a heap, with James on top. The Wraith tried to throw him off, but James was faster. He punched him across the chin and the man's head snapped back into the grass. When he tried to get up again, James punched him one last time, and he finally went limp.

James sprinted around the house, staying clear of the billowing flames, and saw that Lana and Jada were locked in combat with one of the attackers. There was a blinding flash as lightning leapt through the air. Thunderbolt was shouting orders from the porch.

James raced toward Lana, but something crimson sped

past him and exploded into the side of the house, blowing him off his feet.

He hit the ground hard and rolled into the field. James saw another Wraith emerging from the darkness, a huge rocket launcher propped against his shoulder. The man lifted the weapon to fire again, but it was suddenly ripped from his hands.

The man hurtled toward James, as if pulled by an invisible string. James jumped to his feet and swung a vicious uppercut directly into the helpless man's chin, sending him flying into a backflip. He landed flat on his stomach, unconscious.

James rubbed his knuckles and turned to Hayden. "Thanks."

"Anytime!" Hayden yelled as he ran toward Lana.

James hurried after him.

Lana swung at the strange man's head, but he ducked out of the way with unnerving speed and kicked her in the stomach. As she flew backward, she saw Jada launch herself at the attacker, her red hair streaming behind her.

Lana hit the ground and rolled onto her feet again. She took a moment to analyze her surroundings. Most of the League members were outside now, including Thunderbolt and his wolf, and there were shadowy figures scattered across the property. She had seen at least two of them make it inside the house after the first explosion.

She heard a gasp of pain and spun around to see Jada collapse to her knees. Lana balled her hands into fists and charged. The tall, muscular man's clean-shaven face registered no emotion; even his dark eyes were vacant. The man stepped out of her way and tried to smash her in the back with his elbow. Lana narrowly avoided the blow and then countered with a sweeping kick at his legs, which he jumped over with ease. He was still in midair when an invisible force sent him spinning into the field.

Lana glanced back and saw James and Hayden running toward her. She nodded at them and turned back to the Wraith, who was barely visible in the darkness about thirty feet away. She saw his arm move and realized too late that he was grabbing something.

A red blast lanced out toward Hayden. James shoved him to the grass just in time and took the shot in the chest himself. He gasped in pain and fell to the ground, motionless.

Lana turned and sprinted at the man. He fired again, and she ducked as the red blast sizzled past her head. He shifted his aim, but his weapon was knocked aside at the last moment and the shot went careening into the darkness. Lana jumped, sailing ten feet through the air, and kicked him in the side of the head. He spun under the force of the impact and then lay there.

Lana hurried back. Thunderbolt was still shouting commands and threats, and Lana saw one of his blue bursts of lightning connect with an attacker. Wolf chased down another Wraith nearby and let loose a piercing yelp as he was kicked in the ribs.

Lana reached Hayden, who was pulling a grimacing James to his feet.

"That was the bravest thing I've ever seen," Hayden said.

"Are you all right?" Lana asked James, staring at the scorch wound on his chest.

The shot had burned a sizable hole in his shirt, but the skin underneath just looked very red and swollen, like a bad sunburn.

"No problem," James said, though he sounded a little strained. "Where's Sam?"

Lana's eyes went immediately to the burning house. "Oh no," she whispered.

Sam crawled along the floor, staying below the thick smoke in the hallway. His hands were covered in soot, and he guessed that the rest of him was as well. He'd been lying in bed when the explosion tore through the back of the house, and he'd fallen onto the floor and smacked his head on the hardwood.

Worse still, he could sense that Deanna was hurt.

Sam had just reached the stairs when he felt a stab of pain emanating nearby. He glanced back and saw a closed door near the end of the hallway. Someone was hurt on the other side. Biting his lip, he scrambled toward it on all fours and pushed open the door.

The wall on the far side of the room was completely gone and exposed to the night air. Squinting through the blast of cold wind that blew past him as he opened the door, Sam spotted a trail of blood leading across the room.

Talia was being dragged toward the destroyed wall by an expressionless man in black. She was matted in blood and looked only partly conscious.

The man looked up and met Sam's eyes.

Sam instinctively launched a mental attack. But to his horror, it passed right around the Wraith, as if he wasn't even there. Sam tried again, but there was nothing.

The man released Talia's arm and let her drop to the floor. Sam clambered to his feet, holding his breath against the thick smoke that was collecting around his face. He was only two steps into the hallway when his feet were kicked out from under him.

Sam pitched forward and slammed into the floor. Pain raced up his body. He rolled onto his back and saw the Wraith step toward him, wrapped in smoke. The Wraith pulled a weapon out of his belt.

This is it, Sam thought. He knew that he was about to die.

But then a massive blast of fire hit the man's stomach, sending him flying down the hallway. The tremendous heat forced Sam to close his eyes, and when he opened them again, the Flame was standing over him, holding his side. Blood seeped through his fingers.

"We need to get out," he wheezed.

"Talia's in there," Sam managed, pointing at the open door.

The Flame nodded, and together they collected Talia from the burning room, hoisting her up between them. With an extremely labored effort, they carried her to the stairs. Sam felt her weight pressing down on him, his head swimming in the smoke. The Flame looked like he was about to collapse at any moment.

Somehow, they reached the bottom of the stairs and dragged her toward the front door. They had almost made it when Lana, Hayden, and James sprinted inside.

"You all right?" Lana asked.

"Yeah," Sam replied weakly. "Help the others. Deanna and Lyle are in there."

Lana and Hayden raced toward the kitchen, while James scooped up Talia easily and carried her out. Sam and the Flame shuffled after him, barely staying on their feet.

"I'm going to get the others," James said to them, and raced back inside. "Stay with her."

Sam fell to his knees, and the Flame collapsed beside him.

"Thanks for saving me," Sam said. "We need to bandage your side."

"Yeah," he replied faintly.

Sam moved the Flame's hand and saw that a piece of shattered brick had wedged itself into his skin. Blood was flowing freely from the wound. Sam pressed both his hands against it, trying to staunch the flow, but it had little effect. He looked around frantically.

There was a flash as Thunderbolt sent another burst of lightning at a departing Wraith.

"Help me!" Sam shouted.

Thunderbolt hurried over, his eyes still darting to the shadows around them. He bent over to take a closer look at the Flame's wound.

"Press your shirt against it as tightly as you can," he ordered. "I'll get the first aid supplies in the Defender."

He raced off toward the barn. Sam took off his shirt and pressed it against the wound, but that was quickly sopping with blood as well. Slowly, the others began streaming out of the house, Lana holding up a limping, soot-covered Deanna and James helping Lyle, who looked dazed. Hayden was close behind, floating two others with him, including one of the unconscious attackers.

They all gathered around Sam, lying the injured on the grass, and watched in silence as the black smoke disappeared into the night.

29

THE IRON DOOR SWUNG OPEN, FLOODING THE SHADOWY CELL WITH LIGHT.
Emily instinctively covered her face. She'd just been sitting there, staring at the wall while Blue slept restlessly
beside her. Blue slept more and more as the days wore
on in the darkness, and she was constantly shivering and
weak. Emily was worried about her. If they didn't get out
of the cell soon, Blue might not get out at all.

Veridus stepped inside and shut the door. She wore the
same black uniform she had the first time they'd met her
and her hair was tied back in a ponytail.

"I don't have much time," Veridus said, glancing at the
still-sleeping Blue. "I'm sorry I haven't been able to get to
you for a few days. My brother was keeping a watchful eye
on me. I believe he suspects something. But he's away for
the moment, so this is the first chance I've gotten to come
see you."

Emily raised her eyebrows. "Won't the guards tell him?"

She shook her head. "I have full rights to come here. Technically, I'm second-in-command. But they wouldn't support me in a rebellion. They owe him too much."

"Because of their powers?"

"Yes. They were all specially chosen and taken from unsatisfactory lives. I regret not allowing him to grant me the same. Perhaps then I would have had the strength to challenge him."

"He won't let you have powers?" Emily asked.

"No, not anymore. As I said, I believe he distrusts me. But I know he's offered them to you."

Emily remained silent for a moment, studying this strange girl in front of her. She was again struck by her flawless beauty. She seemed almost too perfect. Her almond skin didn't have a single blemish, her lips were perfectly sculpted, and her body was both curvaceous and toned. But it was her piercing, forest green eyes that Emily found so bizarre: they were extremely vivid and seemed to just be a monotone ring of color around her pupils.

"He did," Emily said slowly. "Can I ask you something?"

"Of course."

"What happened to your brother?" Emily asked. "Did he used to look like you?"

She sighed. "He was attacked a long time ago. He was severely wounded, to the point of death, but he was saved by a friend. He could heal his wounds, but he chooses not to. He wears them to remember how he was wronged, I think. I've asked him to reconsider, but he will not. He looked like me once, when we were younger." Her voice became soft. "Those days are long past."

"I wondered," Emily said, still watching her closely, "though his wounds don't look like any scars I've ever seen. What about his eyes?"

"His eyes were once green like mine," Veridus said, "but after the attack, they changed. I can't say that I understand completely what happened to him."

"Who attacked him?"

"I don't know," she said. "I wish I had more answers for you. But we need to get—"

"Was it the Vindico?" Emily interjected.

"No, I don't think so. His motives aren't vengeance. I know that. There is something else he wants."

"I wish I knew what," Emily said. There was something nagging at the back of her mind, but she couldn't place it. "He said he might tell me if I went through with the transformation." Then she realized who Veridus looked like. "You know who you remind me of?"

Veridus seemed taken aback. "Who?"

"Avaria. Do you know what she looks like?"

"Yes," she replied. "I haven't seen her in a very long time, though."

"You know her?" Emily asked, surprised.

"Yes. To my own misfortune," she said. "I'm sorry, but we must speak quickly. My brother will be back soon. Are you considering the transformation?"

Emily hesitated. "Considering, yes. But I haven't made a decision."

"Why?"

"I think he has ulterior motives. Don't you?"

Veridus was silent for a moment. "I don't know," she conceded. "He does speak highly of you, which is a rarity. It is possible he has truly become fond of you and wants you to join his organization. I can't see what else it would accomplish."

"But he must assume I would remain loyal to my friends," Emily said. "He would just be making me more powerful and more liable to escape. It doesn't make sense."

"Perhaps he's relying on your gratitude. But you're right, it isn't wise. He's making a mistake, and I'm not sure why. But we must take advantage. He might be giving us the weapon to beat him."

"What about Thunderbolt? Has he been found?"

She nodded. "There was an attack last night. Your friends and the rest of the League managed to fight off my brother's men, though they took injuries."

"Were my friends hurt?" Emily asked urgently.

"No, he thinks they're fine. But several League members may have been killed."

"Who?"

"I don't know. Not Thunderbolt, I know that much."

"Is he going to attack again? Where are the Vindico?"

"He may, if the League doesn't move somewhere else. I'm guessing they will. As for the Vindico, they haven't attacked for some reason. He said he had a guess where they've gone, and I think he went to see if he was right."

"We need to contact Thunderbolt," Emily whispered.

"How?" she asked, shaking her head. "He's probably on the run again with the others. And even if I knew where he was, there's no chance I could get a message there without my brother knowing. I think we're on our own."

Emily stared at her. "You think I should do the transformation."

"I can't tell you what to do. But if we can kill him, then I would be in charge. I could disband this organization and release the prisoners. The League could choose what to do with my brother's soldiers."

"They'll follow you even if you kill him?" Emily asked skeptically.

"No," she said. "But they will if you do."

Emily looked away, feeling the weight of that statement settle in. Despite everything Dolus was doing, Emily wondered if she could actually kill him.

"I need to think about it," Emily said. "When will he come back?"

"Later today." She reached out and put her hand on Emily's arm. "I know it won't be easy. It's not fair to ask this of you. But it might be the only way to stop him and the only way to save your friends." She glanced at the door. "I'd better go. I'll try and get back as soon as I can. Just remember, we may not have much time."

She hurried out of the cell and shut the door behind her.

"You're thinking about it, aren't you?" a quiet voice asked.

Emily turned around. "You were awake."

Blue nodded, though her eyes were still closed. "I thought it might be better just to listen. Since they only seem to want to speak to you anyway."

Emily caught the slightest hint of bitterness in the League member's voice. But she knew it wasn't directed at her. It was just bitterness that she was never quite involved.

"What do you think I should do?" Emily asked.

Blue was silent for a moment. "I don't know. If they offered me the chance, I would take it. But it just seems too convenient. I don't trust either of them."

"Neither do I," Emily agreed. "But we don't have a lot of options."

Emily thought about stepping out of the chamber, her skin tingling. Strength coursing through her body.

Then she could defeat the Wraiths, capture Dolus, and save the League.

It all made perfect sense.

"You'll make the right decision," Blue murmured, and then curled up tighter.

Emily stood for a long time, watching the light flickering through the small window in the door. Something was wrong here, she knew that. But time was running out for her friends, and Emily had to do something. There really was no choice. She had to accept Dolus's offer, and then she had to kill him.

30

HAYDEN STUDIED THE GRIM, BLACKENED FACES SITTING AROUND THE TABLE. They were all gathered in the meeting room of the Defender, which was parked in the field beside the ruined farmhouse. Thunderbolt sat at the far end, staring at the gleaming table.

The Flame, Ceri, and Talia were all in critical condition and lying unconscious in the ship's small medical facility. A few others had broken limbs, cracked ribs, or deep gashes. Most were stained with ash and soot, and everyone looked exhausted.

Hayden glanced at his friends. They had gotten out relatively easy, though James had a nasty scorch mark, Lana was severely bruised, and Sam had a mild concussion. Hayden felt like he might have sprained his wrist, but he knew it could have been much worse.

"We've been bested again," Thunderbolt said. "We captured four of the attackers, but we've temporarily lost three of our own, and many of us are now injured. It's obvious that someone else has figured out how to grant superpowers. Who knows how many more of these men are out there."

He paused. "It seems this new enemy is just as dangerous as the Vindico, if not more so. And we must guess that they are working together. It is possible that the Vindico gave them our location, though we cannot know for sure."

"We shouldn't have been caught off guard," Gali said gruffly, turning to Sinio. "Why didn't you detect them?"

"They can't be detected." Sam spoke up before Sinio had the chance. "They're immune to us."

Thunderbolt frowned. "How is that possible?"

"I don't know, but it's true," Deanna said. Her arm was wrapped in a sling and she had a bloodstained bandage tied around her forehead. "I tried to get at them too, but nothing."

"It wasn't even like a blocked mind," Sinio added. "It was as if they weren't there at all."

"Great," Thunderbolt muttered, staring at the wall. "I take responsibility for this. We underestimated our foes. We should have gotten in the ships and left."

"So what do we do now?" James asked.

"We need to get to better medical facilities," Thunderbolt said, getting to his feet. "Those three need attention, and soon. The facilities at headquarters are the best we can do right now."

"The headquarters is in shambles," Gali argued.

"And so are we," Thunderbolt said. "It's time we fix both."

He marched toward the cockpit as quiet conversations filled the room.

Hayden turned to Lana. "I told you this was going to be a long night."

She nodded. "We're in trouble."

"I know," he agreed. "Something's still bothering me about all this."

"What?"

"Why didn't the Vindico attack too?" Hayden said. "And why didn't they just fire ten missiles at the house and blow us to pieces? It seemed like a halfhearted attack."

"You call that halfhearted?" Lana said incredulously. "We were almost killed."

"I don't know, it just seems like they could have done more. James told me he saw one peek in the kitchen. But it was empty. So why fire there? The living room was full." He shook his head. "We need Emily. She'd have this figured out by now."

"And after everything, we're no closer to finding her either," Lana said. "My mom must be frantic. She would have seen us on the news. I had to beg her to let me go to your house, you know that. I told her it would be perfectly safe."

"She's not going to like me, is she?" Hayden asked.

"Nope."

"Well, when this is done, we'll go for a visit, and I'll bring some flowers."

"That should do it," Lana replied sarcastically.

"Well, that, and my irresistible charm—"

He was cut off as Thunderbolt walked back into the room. "There was a message left at headquarters," he said. His eyes fell on the four of them, and then he activated a control panel on the wall. Leni's mocking voice filled the room. "You had the right idea: you should be hiding. But our former protégés forgot something very important. If you're going to hide, you have to make sure everyone you love is hidden as well."

"No," Lana whispered.

Thunderbolt looked at her. "I'm afraid they've gone after your families."

Lana's eyes blurred with tears as she walked down the front hallway of her house, listening to the heavy silence. The table by the front door had been cast aside, and flowers lay strewn across the carpet, their petals just now beginning to wilt.

She knelt down and picked up the phone. She imagined her mother snatching if off the base before the phone went careening from her hands. Her father and brother yanked off their feet by some invisible force, clutching at the table as it tipped, the flowers spilling over their hands. All of them exhausted and confused, wearing their pajamas, rudely awoken in the middle of the night.

The tears poured down her cheeks, and she saw little droplets fall onto the phone. A hand landed on her back.

"We have to get to the others," Hayden said, sounding hesitant. "We might be able to catch up with them."

Lana nodded and gingerly placed the phone back on

the base. Composing herself, she turned around and saw James and Sam watching her. Thunderbolt stood behind them with Deanna and Lyle—they all wore sympathetic expressions.

"He's right," Thunderbolt said. "I'm sorry, Lana."

Lana roughly wiped her eyes. "How long do you think they've been gone?"

"Not long. I imagine it's only been a few hours. The carpet is still damp from the flowers."

"They would have had time to get to my house," Sam whispered. "I'm the closest to Lana. My family is probably already gone."

"Which means they're heading for mine," James said.

"Likely," Thunderbolt agreed. "We'll go straight there."

He hurried outside, and Deanna and Lyle followed.

Lana held back for a moment, staring at the open door. *I did this to them,* she thought. *I brought this on my family.*

Hayden wrapped her in a hug. "It's going to be okay."

"Yeah," Lana said quietly. "We better go."

The Defender sat in the middle of Lana's street, its white hull gleaming in the early morning sun. She spotted lights in several windows as curious neighbors watched the proceedings. Mrs. Frosia was watching out of her bedroom directly across the street, but as soon as Lana met her gaze, she quickly swung the curtains shut.

Thunderbolt stood at the base of the ramp, watching her as she hurried onto the ship and sat down on one of the stiff benches with the others.

"We'll get them back," Thunderbolt told her, closing the ramp. "Set course for Cambilsford!" he called, his voice echoing down the corridor.

"I don't want to do this anymore," Lana whispered.

They sat in silence for the entire flight.

James thumped the kitchen wall and little flakes of paint and dust dropped to the floor. His family was gone too.

A half-finished bowl of cereal sat on the counter, and there was bread in the toaster. They'd obviously been taken right in the middle of breakfast.

"How could we have been so stupid?" he said.

Lana put her hand on his arm. "I don't know."

Thunderbolt walked into the kitchen, holding a small piece of white paper. "I found this on the front table." He crumpled the note. "'Lesson learned. Come and find us.'"

"That's Leni," Hayden muttered. "I can hear him gloating."

"That means my family is definitely gone too," Sam said, and he slowly sat down at the table.

"We can check," Thunderbolt replied. "But I'm sure they are."

"Where would they go?" Lyle asked.

"I'm not sure. But we have to be careful," Thunderbolt said. "We can't just go blindly searching. Obviously they've laid a trap."

"We can't just leave our families with them either," James argued.

"No, we can't," he sighed, pacing around the kitchen. "At least they're easy to understand. They want to kill us, plain and simple. They've taken your families as bait to make sure you come to them. But then why make us guess?"

"I agree. They must have gone somewhere we would expect then," James said. "Like the Baron's mansion."

"Like the mansion," Thunderbolt agreed. "That would be my best guess too."

"I'm sick of that place," Hayden muttered.

"We'll have to go in on foot," Thunderbolt said, ignoring him. "They'll have the air defenses up and ready. But they know we have to do that, so they might be waiting in the woods."

"And Leni likes to beat people with trees," Hayden warned.

"We'll just have to be ready," Lyle said. "There are still more of us than them."

Thunderbolt scowled. "If only we hadn't lost the others, we would have easily overwhelmed them. We're missing seven members now."

"And yet it was the other group that kept picking them off," Hayden said.

"Leveling the playing field," Lyle said. "Like when they attacked us earlier. Five of them retreated, even though they might have collapsed the house and finished some more of us off."

Lana glanced at Hayden. "Just like you said earlier."

"So these other guys just wanted us to face the Vindico on even terms?" James asked. "Why?"

"To make sure we finish each other off," Hayden replied. "Or at least weaken both groups to the brink of destruction."

"Well, there's only one thing we can do," Thunderbolt said. "Attack the mansion and defeat the Vindico as quickly as possible. Sam, Deanna, we have the amplifier, so you might be able to knock them out again. If we can take out the antiaircraft guns on the perimeter, we can get the Defender in, and we'll have a heavy arsenal at our disposal."

He scanned over the kids.

"We'll go in as one group. Hayden and Lyle, you're going to have to contain Leni. You've done it before, you can do it again. Sam and Deanna, you need to knock Sliver out of the battle quickly. If you four can win your battles fast enough, the fight will be over. We all know Avaria and the Torturer can do real damage, and the rest of us need to deal with them. We'll leave someone on the Defender, and I'll assign Septer and Jada to take out Rono and the Baron."

Thunderbolt paused.

"We have to win this battle as efficiently as we can. If we're correct, we'll be attacked again soon after. We've taken enough hits. We've had family and friends stolen from us, and it's time to get them back. You are the new League of Heroes, and it's up to you now."

James felt the weight of his words sink in and looked around at the young faces in his kitchen. They were covered in soot and ash, their clothes were filthy, and dark rings circled their eyes from days with little to no sleep. They really looked like the Feros now.

We're just a bunch of kids, he thought.

But he saw the anger and resilience burning in their eyes, and he knew he looked the same. They were ready, and they weren't going to go down without a fight.

31

SAM STEPPED OVER A FALLEN LOG AND SPARED A QUICK GLANCE AT DEANNA. She had the amplifier slung on her back and held a rifle a bit awkwardly with her right hand. Her left arm was still in a sling. She looked at him, and they exchanged a brief nod.

They had set the Defender down a few kilometers from the mansion, out of range of the antiaircraft guns. Sam and Deanna could immediately sense the terrified minds of the captured families, but nothing else. Either the Vindico weren't there, or they'd found a way to block themselves from the amplifier.

Thunderbolt was visible up ahead, picking his way through the dense trees that surrounded the property. Shafts of sunlight spilled in from the sparse winter canopy, but shadows still lay among them, giving the woods an ominous feel. James, Hayden, Lyle, and Lana were all hurrying along behind Thunderbolt, while Meirna, Jada, and

Septer were taking the rear. Gali and Noran were guarding the injured members back at headquarters, while Sinio was still in the Defender, awaiting the signal that the guns had been knocked out.

A branch snapped, and everyone came to a sudden halt.

"Sorry," James mumbled.

The procession continued, and Sam kept his range extended as far as he could, trying to locate the guarded minds of the Vindico. He felt Deanna doing the same. His eyes darted back and forth with every step, looking for any signs of movement.

Quiet conversation filtered back from the front of the group, and Sam spotted the first antiaircraft gun ahead in the trees. A small clearing was carved out of the forest, and the cannon rose out of the grass. It had a circular, steel-plated base, and the enormous barrel jutted out of the top, sitting on what looked like a swivel mount.

The group stepped into the clearing and spread out around the weapon.

"Hayden and Lyle," Thunderbolt said quietly.

They both stepped forward and extended their hands. The massive, reinforced barrel wrenched to the side, and the sound of shrieking metal echoed off into the distance. Sam nervously hoisted his rifle and stared into the trees, expecting the Vindico to burst out at any moment.

"One down," Thunderbolt said. "One more on this side and the Defender can get in safely."

They plunged back into the forest and picked up their pace. Sam broke into a light jog to keep up and almost stumbled into a divot. *Careful now,* Deanna said. Sam smiled and continued on. After a few more minutes of weaving through the trees, they emerged into another grassy clearing, where a second massive cannon was pointed at the sky.

Hayden and Lyle again twisted the barrel, and Thunderbolt took a small device off his belt. "Thunderbolt to the Defender. All clear." He waited for a moment, but there was no response. Frowning, he put it to his mouth again. "Come in, Defender."

Thunderbolt slowly lowered the device.

"There's only static."

"They're jamming us," Septer said.

"Or they already got to the ship," Thunderbolt said grimly. "Deanna?"

"I can't sense him," she replied.

Sam glanced back the way they had come. That meant the Vindico could be behind them. He gripped his rifle tighter. It felt as if the trees were watching them. He wanted nothing more than to be done with this assault, but his family was in that mansion. He narrowed his eyes and trudged along.

"Stop," Lana said, and the march came to a halt in a fairly open patch of tall oak trees. "I just saw something move."

Thunderbolt hurried beside her. "What was it?"

"I don't know," she replied, shaking her head. "It was moving too fast."

Sam stepped closer to Deanna.

Thunderbolt turned to the group. "If we get attacked, split into the groups we talked about and find your target. We can get to the families after—"

He was cut off by a series of earsplitting cracks. Four enormous trees tipped over toward the group. Sam yelped and dove to the ground as one fell directly toward him. Hayden, Lyle, and Meirna managed to deflect three of them, while James caught the last before it could crush Sam. Then someone opened fire.

Crisscrossing red bursts exploded into the area, and frantic shouts sounded from all directions.

"Split up!" Thunderbolt ordered, his deep voice carrying over the noise.

One blast hit a trunk and erupted into a flurry of sparks, showering Sam as he stood up. He grabbed Deanna's arm, and they started running. Sam kept his head as low as possible, ducking beneath the laser fire, and saw the others take off into the forest.

"Get to the mansion!" Deanna said. "We'll be killed out here!"

They broke into a full sprint, and the sounds of battle faded behind them.

"It must be coming up!" Sam said, trying to ignore the cramp in his side.

They ran for a minute or two longer until they reached the edge of the property. They bounded out of the forest onto the long, unkempt grass surrounding the mansion and froze.

An angular black ship was hovering in front of them,

its two missile launchers fixated in their direction. A calm voice sounded over its loudspeaker.

"Drop your weapons, please," the Baron said, "and proceed to the house with your hands up. I assure you, there would be little more than a crater left if I were forced to use these missiles."

Sam looked at Deanna, and then they both dropped their rifles and raised their hands. *It's going to be okay,* Sam said to Deanna. *The others will be here soon.*

"Watch out!" Lyle screamed, and Hayden dropped onto his stomach as another tree trunk skimmed over his head.

Hayden felt the air whoosh out of him on impact, and then he mentally yanked himself back to his feet. A shadowy figure stepped between two trees in the distance, and Hayden recognized the flowing black cape.

"There!" he called to Lyle, and he raced toward his former mentor.

"Keep your head down!" Lyle said, sprinting after him.

I have a better idea, Hayden thought. He reached out with his mind and gripped one of the huge oak trees, snapping it like a twig. He broke it twice more until he had three manageable pieces and then glanced at Lyle. "Want one?"

Lyle nodded and one of the pieced floated toward him. Hayden took the other two, and they stalked forward together, the three jagged pieces floating in front of them like a shield. Blasts, shouts, and explosions were echoing in the distance. Hayden hoped that Lana was okay. He'd last seen her disappear into the woods with James and Thunderbolt.

"See anything?" Lyle whispered, peering through the trees.

"No," Hayden replied softly.

"So," a cold voice said behind them, "the protégé returns."

They both spun around but saw no one.

"You've grown stronger," Leni said. "You could have been powerful indeed."

Hayden looked around. "I'm pretty strong already. Come out and I'll show you."

"I think not," Leni said. "With your little friend, you are a match for me in a contest of brute strength. Alas, there's more to our powers, as you have yet to learn. It's a question of cunning, and in that regard, you are both hopelessly overmatched."

There was another loud crack, and Lyle yelped as the ground under their feet gave way. Hayden reacted instantly and sent himself hurtling sideways. But Lyle wasn't as fast, and he disappeared into a pit, his scream echoing up after him.

Hayden rolled head over feet into the brush. Scratching branches dug into his exposed skin, and he shut his eyes. He finally flopped onto his back and pushed himself up again.

"Lyle!" he shouted, but there was no response.

"He's probably just unconscious," Leni said, his voice carrying through the trees. "Don't worry, I haven't killed him yet. We came to the decision that we might as well enjoy your deaths. Nothing swift and easy for you." He chuckled. "So what now, protégé? I laid traps throughout this forest years ago. Where will you go now?"

"Do you need traps?" Hayden asked. "I would have thought such things beneath you."

"Ah, the baiting routine," Leni said. "Predictable. But now that it's just the two of us, I must agree. They were beneath me."

He stepped out from behind a tree. He wore the same black outfit he had during training, including his long cape. A silver device ran around his forehead.

"I like the headband," Hayden commented. "It holds your hair back nicely."

Leni tapped it with one finger. "This keeps your little friends out. Rono and Sliver have been perfecting the technology. You won't be getting out so easily this time."

"Very clever. I guess we'll be beating you the old-fashioned way then."

Leni smiled. "Indeed."

At once, both trees beside Hayden exploded off their stumps. Hayden lunged out of their way and swept his hand at Leni, sending a wave of invisible force streaking toward him. Several trees were uprooted by the energy, and leaves, splintered wood, and other debris swelled along with the wave, giving it a tangible shape.

Leni stuck out his hands and the two tremendous forces clashed against each other. Both of their feet slid backward, grinding into the soil.

Then the clouds of splintered wood and dust abruptly clumped together to form a spear. The spear launched itself at Hayden, who just managed to deflect it with a quick hand motion. The spear dissolved into a cloud again, which blew toward him.

Squinting against the debris, Hayden charged Leni, preparing another surprise blast. He emerged from the cloud and saw that Leni had already moved.

Hayden crouched, gathering his energy around him. "Hiding again?"

"Not quite," Leni said. His voice was right in Hayden's ear.

A violent blast struck Hayden from behind and sent him flying through the air. He hit a tree and went spinning to the ground. Hayden rolled onto his back.

Leni stepped over him. "Too easy," he said. "Perhaps I overestimated you."

"We should talk about this," Hayden wheezed.

"Oh, we will," Leni assured him. He drew a cylindrical weapon out of his belt and pulled the trigger. Blue sparks fizzled from the nozzle. "See you soon."

This did not go according to plan, Hayden thought.

Leni jabbed the weapon into his stomach and everything went black.

"Move!" Thunderbolt shouted, just as he unleashed another volley of lightning.

Lana leapt out of the way, but Avaria did the same,

disappearing behind a clump of trees as the bolt of energy sizzled by. There was a titanic roar to her right, and she saw the Torturer bat another tree aside as James hurriedly backed away.

"Go left!" Thunderbolt ordered.

Lana nodded and ducked to the left, trying to circle around her former mentor.

"Anything?" Thunderbolt asked.

"No," Lana called back as she rounded the clump of trees.

She crouched low to the ground, listening for movement. She heard the sounds of James and the Torturer's violent struggle and beyond that, some distant gunfire. And then another set of footsteps, so soft that they could barely be heard over the breeze.

She turned back to Thunderbolt and saw Avaria step out from behind a tree. Before Lana could even open her mouth in warning, Thunderbolt sensed that she was behind him. He tried to turn, his hands already glowing with another deadly blast, but Avaria was faster. She kicked him across the head and he collapsed, his arms flopping limply beside him.

"No!" Lana screamed.

Avaria met her eyes, wearing a taunting smile.

"Hello, Lana," she hissed. "Now we can fight fair."

"Where is my family?" Lana snarled.

"Alive," Avaria replied. "We left them in the front lobby, just in case you managed to get the ship in and fire on the mansion. Sliver has them under guard." The smile vanished from her face. "But their use is coming to an end. As is yours."

Lana stepped toward her. "You did this to us, in case you forgot."

"A failed experiment," Avaria said. "I thought you had promise. But as strong as I made you, you were still so weak. One near kill and you crumbled."

Lana clenched her fists. "That's because I'm not like you."

"No?" Avaria said. "If I recall, you pulled the trigger on Septer. I didn't do that."

Lana exploded into action. She swept a powerful kick at Avaria's head, who ducked and spun to the side. Lana reversed direction, swiping with the back of her fist, but again, it sailed wide. Avaria jabbed Lana in the side and then tried to knee her in the stomach. Lana narrowly avoided the blow and lashed out again. This time her fist connected with Avaria's chin, jerking her head to the side.

Avaria stepped back, rubbing her chin.

"Such a shame," she said, and then sent a kick hurtling at Lana's chest.

Lana managed to block the blow, but the force of the impact sent her flying. She landed flat on her back and rolled onto her feet, but Avaria had already closed the distance. Her right foot connected solidly with Lana's cheek, and Lana sprawled to the ground, reeling. She tasted blood and felt it drip from her mouth.

Two strong hands gripped her shoulders and slammed

her into a tree. Avaria held her there with one hand, staring into her eyes.

"You weren't quite ready, though," she said, and then pulled a stun gun out of a holster on her leg. She placed it against Lana's neck. "Good night."

"I think you're taking this a little too personally," James said, dodging yet another powerful blow.

"How did you want me to take it?" the Torturer asked, batting aside another tree. The huge man scowled. "You betrayed me."

"It was actually Hayden's idea."

"Oh, so it's his fault," the Torturer scoffed. "Well, I had to sit in the Perch because of you!"

The thought seemed to renew his anger, and he lowered his head and charged. James tried to get out of the way, but the Torturer's massive shoulder struck James in the chest and knocked him backward. He grimaced as the Torturer landed on him. James kneed the big man in the stomach, causing him to groan, and then tried to weasel out of his grip. He crawled out of the Torturer's arms and started pulling himself away.

The Torturer grabbed his legs. James strained to keep moving, his fingers digging into the dirt, but his mentor was much stronger.

"Now you've forced me . . . to have to kill you," the Torturer said.

"You . . . don't . . . have to," James replied, trying to find something to grab.

"I really . . . do," he said.

James felt something hard beneath the soil, and he yanked a large rock from the ground. Then he twisted himself and swung the rock at the Torturer's head. It impacted with a loud smack, and the Torturer cursed and released him.

James scrambled back to his feet, still clutching the rock. "Stop this."

The Torturer stood up. "I can't. You've forced my hand."

"Why?" James asked. "Is it really going to solve anything? What are you going to do once we're dead?"

He shrugged. "Kill the rest of the League."

"And then?"

"Subject the world to our rule." The Torturer frowned. "Or just live easy. I could enjoy myself and not have to worry about getting arrested by the League."

"So do that anyway. We'll get you a pardon."

"Unlikely," he said. "Besides, the others won't agree to that."

"So help us beat them."

"It's too late. For one, your friends are probably all captured. And besides, I can't trust you. You've already betrayed me twice!"

"Not this time," James said earnestly. "Help me, and I'll make sure you're pardoned."

The Torturer stared at him for a moment. "It just won't work," he said, sounding hesitant. "How would we—"

"There you are!" a voice called, and they both turned to see Rono emerge from the woods, holding a rifle. "We're waiting on you. I've already captured the Defender, taken out the other three members, and parked it. You had one kid to get. What's taking so long?"

"He's tough to get ahold of," the Torturer grumbled, glancing at James.

"I'll take care of that," Rono said, and lifted his gun.

"Wait, let's—" James started.

Rono pulled the trigger, and a blue blast erupted from the nozzle and struck him in the stomach. A strange tingling sensation raced up and down his body, and he felt his limbs weaken. Rono fired again, and he dropped to his knees, his body completely numb now. He thought of the others, already captured, and his family.

They'd failed, and they were all going to die. He wanted to feel sad, but it seemed beyond him.

Rono stepped forward, with the Torturer beside him, and he thought he saw concern in the big man's eyes, or doubt. Then Rono lifted the rifle again, and James saw one more flash of blue.

32

"COME WITH ME, EMILY," DOLUS SAID CALMLY.

Emily glanced at Blue and walked through the door. Dolus closed it behind her, and Blue was instantly at the window, her slender hands wrapped around the bars.

"Don't hurt her," she snarled.

He looked at her. "I intend to do quite the opposite, actually. I would be more concerned about yourself."

Blue gingerly released the bars and stepped back. Then, without warning, her hands shot up and a powerful stream of water erupted from her fingertips, crossing the distance between them almost instantaneously. But Dolus was ready.

He pivoted on one heel and the blast of water slammed into the stone wall behind him. In the same motion, he drew his gun from the holster and shot her in the chest.

Emily heard Blue hit the stone, and she prepared to

launch herself at him. But before she could take a step, the gun was pointed at her forehead.

"Don't try it," he warned. "A stun blast to the head from here would likely be fatal."

Emily stared down the barrel for a moment and then let her hands fall to her sides, defeated.

He nodded. "I knew you would make the wise decision. I hope you have made another. Walk with me."

Emily met his eyes and compared them to his sister's. *There's one similarity,* she thought. The yellow of Dolus's eye was as flawlessly colored as his sister's green ones. It was like a coat of paint, broken only by a small black pupil.

"All right," she said quietly, following him down the corridor. She glanced back at the iron door. "Is Blue going to be okay?"

"Most likely, though she is weak. I won't lie to you, Emily, her time here is almost at an end. I thought she and the others might be of some use, but there was no need. Events are moving very quickly, and the battle I've waited for has already arrived. Renda, Peregrine, and Blue will be disposed of."

Emily turned to him. "Why?"

"You'll find out soon. The conclusion of this game is upon us. It did not go exactly as I hoped, but things rarely do. Now, I must know: what is your decision?"

Emily felt her stomach roiling. "Are my friends alive?"

"Yes. But not for long, if you don't help them. A decision, Emily."

Emily thought of Veridus's words, warning her that this might be the only chance to beat him. The only chance to save the others.

"I'll do it."

He smiled. "Good. You will be a valued member here. We have time for only one session, and then we must proceed to the battle. You will come with me to end this, and with your help, we might be able to save your friends."

"What will one session do?" she asked as they approached the first door.

"It will be a small step of the transformation. A mild increase in strength and speed."

"And why do that now?"

"It may help convince your friends that the procedure is safe."

Emily came to a halt. "Why would my friends need this procedure?"

"Only to improve on their powers," he replied. "I want them to join us as well. The League is finished. We will be the new force of justice in this world. A new organization, untarnished by the blood and mistakes of these past conflicts. We can focus on truly righting this planet."

Emily said nothing. Despite his confident tone, she knew he was lying. *What is going on?* she thought desperately. Her plan had been to undergo the transformation so she could kill him and allow his sister to seize power. But if she was only getting a small boost in strength before they left, she would never be able to beat him. *Didn't his sister know it would be a slow process?* she wondered.

Emily kept walking, her mind racing with questions. She glanced at the guard as she passed by, at his dark eyes. They seemed emotionless. His black hair was slicked back like the rest, and though their faces were different, she got the feeling that all of these men were the same somehow. They were all empty.

And then it hit her.

I was right the first time, Emily realized. This procedure might give her strength, but it was going to strip her consciousness. It would make her follow his orders blindly, just like these men. And that's why he wanted her to go in before they left. Emily narrowed her eyes. His sister had been helping him all along.

Emily came to a stop in the middle of the room.

"Who was it that attacked you?" she asked.

Dolus was silent for a moment. "So my sister did visit you."

"Yes," Emily replied. "Twice. And she mentioned you were attacked many years ago. Who was it?"

"We do not have much—"

"Just answer the question," she said.

He turned to her with his piercing yellow eye. "Two friends of mine. They were punishing me, and rightly so. Now, we must hurry and—"

The pieces suddenly fell into place. It was his sister's story that had first triggered a memory, something she'd heard four months ago. The second clue had been the strange eyes, which, despite the difference in color, seemed equally perfect and unnatural. Combined with the fact that supposedly no one in the world apart from the Vindico and the League knew how to grant powers, it had begun to add up. And now he had just confirmed it.

"Where is your sister?" Emily asked.

He frowned. "She's away on a mission."

"I see. I don't suppose she'll be back before we leave?"

"Unlikely," he said.

"It's strange, really."

"What?"

"That you look like that. There must be a good reason, of course." Emily met his eyes. "I don't agree with you about your friends. I don't think they were right to attack you for protecting someone you loved."

He stood there for a moment, and then his lips curled in a smile. "Very good."

Dolus's eyes suddenly became green, and Emily watched in fascination as the hard angles of his face changed and his black and purple skin became a soft almond. His body shortened and curved, while his hair grew long, until it fell over his shoulders.

When he was done, Veridus was standing in front of Emily.

"What gave her away?" he asked.

"A few things," Emily said. "But in terms of appearance—the eyes. Too perfect."

He nodded and then swiftly changed back to his discolored form.

"There is a lot of detail in the eyes," he agreed. "It was always the problem in my transformations. And yet it was the manner of my accident that convinced you. So someone has told you the story."

"The Baron. It was Avaria's story he told, of course, but you figured in quite importantly. She doesn't know you're alive, does she?"

"No," he said, "she does not. And she *will* not, until the very last moment. Now, I ask you again. Will you undergo the transformation?"

"I think you know the answer."

"Such a shame," Dolus mused. "I've told you many lies, Emily, but one thing is true: I've taken a liking to you, and I would have had you spared. Alas, it was your own brilliance that killed you, a recurring theme I know all too well."

With a flicker of motion, his gun was pointing right between her eyes.

"Not yet," he whispered. "You deserve the same explanation, and you deserve to be with your friends. It's time to go. We must end this, once and for all."

33

JAMES BLEARILY OPENED HIS EYES, AND THE FIRST THING HE SAW WAS HIS parents. He frowned, feeling the throbbing pain running along his entire body, and watched as their mouths began to move. *How strange,* James thought. He could have sworn he'd been captured by the Vindico. Maybe it was all a dream, and they were waking him for school.

Then he saw the world materialize beyond them and a high, ornate ceiling took form, dotted with blackened scorch marks.

"James," his father said, the words starting to make sense. "Are you okay?"

"I'm fine," he murmured.

Beside him, his mother was crying. James planted his hands beside him and pushed himself up, feeling his head swim. He was back in the mansion.

The others were beginning to sit up as well, all looking the worse for wear. Lana and Sam were both surrounded by their anxious families. Lana began to cry as soon as she saw them and hugged her mother. Hayden was sitting beside a crying woman who must have been his mother, and near him lay Deanna, Lyle, Thunderbolt, and the four other captured League members.

And standing in a large circle around them were the Vindico. All but Leni held rifles. The amplifier was lying on the ground behind them, and they had removed their blocking devices. James looked up to see the Torturer, who met his eyes before quickly looking away again.

"What's going on, James?" his mother whispered. "Why did they bring us here?"

His younger sisters were crouching behind her, their faces white, lips quivering. He'd never seen them so scared. Ally looked at him, and he saw that her green eyes were glassy. James suddenly felt sick.

"I tried to fight them off," his father added quietly, "but before I knew it, we were in the ship, and then we were here. They dumped you in here five minutes ago."

"We tried to rescue you," James murmured, watching as Hayden climbed to his feet, eyeing the Vindico. "They were waiting."

His father nodded. "I heard them talking about a trap. What do they want?"

James hesitated. "Nothing good."

"What does that mean?" his mother whispered urgently.

"We'll get out of this," James said. "Just stay down and—"

"Now that you're all awake," Leni said loudly, "the rest of you can stop the crying. It will accomplish nothing, except to annoy me. Before anyone gets the bright idea of trying to attack us, be aware that we will kill families first."

James tentatively got to his feet.

"So what now?" Thunderbolt asked sharply. "You've kept us alive. Why?"

"Don't become accustomed to it," the Baron replied from the other side of the ring. "I assure you, it isn't an act of mercy."

"Forgiveness, then?" Hayden said.

"Not quite," Leni told them. "More like vengeance. We knew you would fall into the trap easily, so we decided we all owed ourselves some closure. You four were *our* mistakes, and it's only right that we fix it. As for you, Thunderbolt," Leni said coldly, "the Baron claimed you first."

"Long overdue," the Baron agreed. "But of course, half the enjoyment would only come through your knowing that I was the one who pulled the trigger."

James glanced at Lana. There was soft whimpering from the families as the Baron's words set in. He prepared to charge. He knew the Vindico would kill them all anyway. The only way out was to fight.

"You'll get no enjoyment from me," Thunderbolt snarled. "If you think I'll beg, you're sorely mistaken. I'll look you in the eye, coward."

"Good," the Baron said. "I can watch them close."

"And won't that be grand," Hayden commented. "You'll kill a bunch of kids, and all will be well. Makes sense."

James wrapped his arm around Ally's shoulders as she

began to cry. Jen looked like she was unable to move. She sat next to her father, wide-eyed and shaking.

"It'll be okay," James whispered to them. "I'll get us out of this."

He might not have been much of a superhero, but he wouldn't let the Vindico hurt his family.

His father climbed to his feet. "You think we're going to stand here and let you kill our children?" he asked. "You've got something else coming."

"Is that so?" Leni said, looking amused.

All of a sudden, James's father's arms were squeezed against his side and his feet left the floor. His mother shrieked and tried to grasp his legs. James started toward Leni, but Avaria shifted her rifle to aim directly at his head, and he stopped.

"What do you think, James?" Leni said. "Should I kill him first?"

James felt white-hot rage burning inside him as his father was squeezed a little more. He was rapidly losing color.

"Let him go," James snarled.

"Fine," Leni replied casually, and James's father dropped to the floor, his legs twisting underneath him. "Who will go first?"

"I'll decide that," a loud voice said, and the Vindico members all spun toward the front entrance.

Wraiths emerged from everywhere, stepping through the front entrance, pouring out of both hallways, and appearing on the balcony upstairs. There were at least twenty of them, and they all had rifles aimed at the group.

Then the men at the front entrance stepped aside and a strange, dark-skinned man walked through. And, walking stiffly in front of him, was Emily.

"Emily!" James gasped, and he heard similar exclamations around the room.

He felt a surge of hope, but then noticed the gun in the man's hand, pointed squarely at her back. Emily forced a smile. The man said something to her, and she hurried over to join the group. James was nearest, and he enveloped her in a hug.

"You're alive," he said happily.

"For now," she whispered, and released him. "This isn't a rescue."

She went to hug Hayden, and James turned back to the dark-skinned man.

"I wondered when you'd show up," Leni said.

"You should have been more prepared," the man replied. "But overconfidence was always your weakness."

"Who is this?" Avaria asked. She had her rifle trained on the newcomer.

"This is the man who released us," Leni said. "But why, I have yet to figure out."

The man smiled. "That will be explained now. It's time to learn why you're all here and why none of you may leave."

He turned to Avaria. "Hello, Avaria."

The man's discolored skin began to change, softening

into an almond hue. His eyes shrank and turned brown, while the angles of his face shifted, becoming less severe. His muscular tone faded slightly, so that he was a bit thinner and shorter. A few seconds after the transformation began, a totally different man stood in front of them.

Avaria's rifle clattered to the floor. "Derias," she whispered.

34

SAM FELT AN INCREDIBLE WAVE OF CONFUSION, MISERY, AND DESPERATE longing wash out of Avaria. It was so strong that his knees almost buckled under the weight of her emotions, and her voice, which came across in a scream, filled his head with a thousand unanswered questions. Images of this man from years before flashed before his eyes. *Impossible,* Avaria was thinking over and over, *I held your dead body in my hands.* And suddenly she was filled with fear.

Sam quickly blocked her out before she completely overwhelmed him.

"Yes," Derias replied, still holding Avaria's gaze. His lip was curled in derision. "Or I once was. Derias, as you knew him, is long dead."

With that, his skin began to darken again, and soon they were looking at the bizarre, discolored man who had first walked through the door. His yellow eye narrowed, and

Sam could feel his intense anger. It was directly squarely at Avaria.

Derias finally looked around the room. "I'm not even Nimian anymore. He died later, and this man, Dolus, took his place. Hello, Thunderbolt," he said, "it's been a long time."

"How are you alive?" Thunderbolt asked. "Courage told us you were dead."

"He lied to you," Derias said, "about a great deal, actually. That story is intertwined with why we are all here, so I will tell it in full. Some parts you already know. I was deeply in love with my wife, and I was deeply in love with the League. That should have been how it remained, and had it, perhaps I would stand with the League still, with Courage at the helm, and the Vindico would not exist. There would be peace, these protégés would be regular children, and all these events would never have come to pass. But my wife could not let that be. Her greed set off a chain of events that led us to this room."

Dolus turned to Avaria again.

Sam could sense his mother trembling next to him, so he reached out and took her hand. He glanced around the room. The Wraiths were all watching silently, their rifles pointed at the group. *How are we going to get out of this?* he wondered.

"I do not blame you for your desire for powers," Dolus said. "You were surrounded by superpowered individuals—people celebrated by the world. I expect you were also jealous of my love for what the League stood for, of my dedication to their cause. Perhaps you questioned what I loved more. Over time, the solution became obvious to you. You could join the League, and my two affections could be combined.

"For months you asked, screamed at me, whispered it in my ear. But at the time, I agreed with the choice of fate. I recognized the chaos that would ensue if this technology became widely distributed. But you wanted it so badly, Avaria. You finally threatened to leave me, and I folded. You see, had you asked, I would have told you there was no competition. I loved you more."

Avaria looked like she might collapse. Even blocking her off, Sam could feel her pain. But Dolus just stared at her like she was the most sickening thing he'd ever seen.

Be ready for Thunderbolt's signal, Deanna's voice said into his mind. *He's going to wait for an opening.* There was a note of hesitation. *If there's an opening.*

Sam relayed the message to the other protégés. They were all terrified, and Sam knew why. It was different when your families were there. He squeezed his mother's hand a little tighter.

"Over the next few weeks, I prepared the chamber in our basement. Courage grew suspicious of my absence and confronted me several times. I told him, quite truthfully, that I was working on my marriage. When I finally finished, I left headquarters even earlier than usual. I was eager to see if my designs had worked, and I was terrified at the same time, both of the League's response and much more so for my wife's safety.

"I knew the Torturer had already given himself powers, but through an incredibly dangerous, unstable mixture of compounds. He was lucky to survive, as was his protégé. This was to be the first measured chamber transformation in history, since the Baron's attempt had been disrupted, and I wasn't sure it would work. Alas, in my eagerness to get home, I triggered Courage's suspicion again. He hacked into my lab computers and realized what I was doing. He told the Champion, and together they came to arrest me and destroy my work."

Derias's voice lowered and he turned to Avaria again. "I remember kissing you before you went into the chamber. I remember the excitement in your eyes as I began the transformation. It's a process that goes in steps. Ten five-minute sessions, much like you would have had, Lana," he said, staring at her curiously. "The chamber Avaria used on you was an exact replica of mine."

Sam saw Avaria glance at Lana.

"Except she did it the right way for you," Derias continued. "As it turned out, Avaria only got one session. She was about four minutes in when Courage and Champion smashed their way into my lab. Courage just looked at the chamber, and asked me if she was already inside. When I nodded, he told me she had to go to the Perch too. He told me it all had to be destroyed.

"To this day, I don't know what came over me. Perhaps

I just couldn't stand the thought of Avaria being locked away with me in the Perch.

"I fell into a rage. When they went to pull her out of the chamber, I acted. I increased the power input and transformed into the massive brute that I used for some missions. Courage did not intend for what happened next. As we fought in close combat, a few extra support struts lay in the corner, and one of them pierced my chest.

"At that point, Avaria burst from the chamber. She had been in there for too long, at an increased power input. She was already exceptionally powerful."

When the shooting starts, get your family down, Deanna said into Sam's mind. *Lyle and Meirna are going to try and deflect as many shots as they can. Tell Hayden to do the same. And make sure you get down too.*

Sam looked at her. *You too.*

He passed the message to Hayden, and he nodded grimly. His mother was still crying beside him, but Hayden wasn't comforting her. He just turned back to Derias, his fingers curling and uncurling at his sides.

"Courage told me she ripped off the chamber door and swung it at Champion, catching him off guard. He died on impact. Courage refused to fight her, stricken with guilt over my death, and after vainly attempting to calm her down, he flew off.

"Maybe you knelt over me at that point, felt my pulse, and realized I was gone," Derias continued. "Maybe you wept and then realized you had murdered a League member and would be imprisoned for life."

His tone became venomous.

"Courage watched you run away and then returned to the lab. He knew that my powers had a small measure of regenerative abilities, and when he waited long enough, he indeed found a pulse. I was in a coma. But he didn't take me back to headquarters. He said he was too embarrassed."

"He told us Avaria had taken the body," Thunderbolt said.

"Yes, that was his story. In fact, he took me to his own private base, the one he'd had before the League was founded. He had a small medical facility there, and he left me on life support, to be tended by the caretaker. I was in that coma for a year and a half, as my body slowly recovered from what would normally have been fatal wounds.

"When I finally woke up, Courage was there. I was of course delirious and confused, and he explained everything to me, including the last few hours before I was almost killed. As soon as he finished, I demanded to see my wife. I still remember the look in his eyes. He showed me the news reports, told me the names of the League members she'd killed. I didn't believe him until he showed me the surveillance video from one of the League bases, where Avaria and Leni murdered three members. I can still picture her face as she did it. She was smiling.

"My world was in shambles. I realized that I had done this; I had created that monster. I wept as I watched. My own wife had renewed the war and people were dying faster than ever. Courage told me that I was dead to everyone in the world but him. Then he was called to battle again, and he left me alone."

"Why didn't you tell me?" Avaria asked softly.

Derias narrowed his eyes. "I would have, if I'd had the opportunity. But though I was awake, I was still terribly weak. I had months of recovery ahead, and even had I been able, I didn't know where to find you. But after time I heard more and more of the atrocities you were committing, and I no longer had any desire to find you. My wife died the same night she thought I had.

"Months later, Courage told me that he was leaving the League. He had failed again and again to bring Avaria and the others to justice—he wondered if she would continue the fight if he was no longer involved. At the least, he hoped she would spend her time hunting him alone. He was going into exile. And I decided to go with him.

"We spent the next seven years on a tiny island in the South Pacific, with no contact to the outside world. Courage flew in supplies during the night, and we built a house in the jungle. He managed to keep tabs on the war by taking papers from the mainland, and we discovered it had indeed died down and faded into occasional skirmishes. That was partly why we stayed away so long. The other reason was that I didn't want to come back.

"We spoke long and often about the choice of fate, and of Courage's insistence that it was the only way to ensure the right people received powers. But gradually, mostly in the later years, I began to think about things in a different light. I questioned if even the League was not inherently flawed in the same ways as every government and organization on earth. They were poisoned by biases, personal histories, past mistakes, and a million other things that colored the decisions they made. The League was no longer defending the planet—it was just trying to kill the Vindico.

"Eventually, I realized the choice of fate was just an excuse for the League, and people like Courage clung to it because it justified their authority, an authority that was deeply misguided."

"Exactly," the Torturer said.

Derias glanced at him. "And the Vindico were a poison in and of themselves. They needed to be wiped out.

"A plan slowly came to mind, and one day, I asked Courage to fly me back to his long-abandoned base. He consented, though he was disturbed by my change. He left me there and returned to the island. He didn't want to risk restarting the war in full. And that was the last I saw of him. I expect he's still there, living in solitude.

"For myself, a new chapter was beginning. I plunged into several years of research. The caretaker was dead, so I was alone, and I began stealing the materials I needed for a new laboratory. Over time, I constructed new chambers in Courage's base—specially designed chambers that affected both the mind and body. I began to select my first candidates: clear-minded, strong men who wanted more.

"To work properly, my new chambers needed the candidates to agree to the transformation. The process would not work on the unconscious, as their thoughts are too muted and confused, or those desperately trying to escape or fight its effects. I needed clear, willing minds."

He gestured to the men surrounding him.

"You see, my chamber gives them superpowers, much like I did to Avaria, but it also wipes the slate, removes the dangerous individuality, the poisonous biases. It creates a true defender, one who follows orders exactly, one who makes clear, correct decisions. It creates a force of justice such as we have never seen: one that is free of human flaws."

Sam stared at the blank-eyed men and felt a shiver run down his back.

"And who tells them what to do?" Leni asked mockingly. "A poisoned man."

Derias smiled. "You're quite right, Leni. I am no better than the rest of you. When this is finished, my time will be over as well. I just had to ensure that everything was carried out correctly. I have studied the League and the Vindico, looking for any who might indeed be spared. I found none. It was during one of these information raids that I encountered Leni."

Sam watched as Avaria shifted her gaze to Leni, who briefly met her eyes.

"Leni was preparing to attack the base himself. We got the jump on him, several of my soldiers and I. Though I confronted him in a different form, Leni is sharp. We had a brief discussion, and he guessed my identity. We knew each other from the League, of course, and had even been companions of a sort. I showed him my real form, and then I prepared to kill him. But something held me back. Even then, I realized actually killing both groups would be extremely difficult, and in fact, I would need their help.

"I let him go, trusting that he would keep my identity secret. Not because of any sense of decency, but because he loved my wife." Derias looked between the two of them, the disgust evident on his face. "He always has, and he knew that if she found out I was alive, she would never have him."

James was looking around the room now, and Sam knew he was trying to find a weak spot. A way to get his family out. Beside him, Lana was doing the same. They all knew this story couldn't go on forever. At any moment, they had to make their move.

Wait for the signal, Sam reminded them.

"As it was," Derias went on, "it was a while longer before I'd found enough viable candidates and firmly discarded every single member of the League. I was preparing to set events into motion when something very unexpected happened. The Vindico decided to take on protégés."

He turned back to the center of the group.

"I didn't know immediately, of course, though I learned of the disappearances, and after investigating the circumstances, I made a guess. By that time you were already well into your training, and I simply watched as those fascinating events took place."

He smiled at Emily.

"I was very impressed. Despite everything, you found your way to the correct solution. But I had to observe you to test you further. You've been followed ever since you went to your respective homes. Sam almost caught me at the airport, watching him from the form of a young girl, so I had to leave the rest of the observations to my men. They've taken careful reports of every small decision you've made, and I've studied them.

"As this was happening, I was completing my larger plans. I had already kidnapped two members to widen the division in the League. After providing a fake tip, I met with the Flame under a different guise and convinced him that he needed to rebel to save the League. Eager fool that he is, he went right along with my plan.

"By that time, I was already doubting whether these young kids could join my organization. They had no cause, since they already possessed the powers I was offering. As it turned out, Emily was my only true candidate. She was wonderfully pure, but alas, she figured out my identity too quickly and would not agree to undergo the transformation.

"I wish the protégés had never been involved. But we cannot have any survivors telling the world that my new force of justice has this much blood on their hands. For a truly just future, you all must be erased."

"You think you can kill us all?" Leni sneered. "You underestimate us."

"Perhaps," Derias said. "But all those rifles you found in

my ship are rigged." He pressed a small device on his belt. "They no longer work."

Avaria heard Rono click his trigger and curse under his breath.

Get ready, Deanna said into Sam's mind. He passed the message along, and saw the others tense. He sent the same message to Sliver, and saw his former mentor nod in understanding.

Sam knew there was no way they could protect everyone when the shooting started. He gave his mother's hand one last squeeze, smiled reassuringly at her, and prepared to make a charge at the nearest Wraith. He doubted he would make it very far.

Deanna's voice suddenly burst into his mind. *Now—*

"There's one more part to this story," a loud voice said.

An old, sun-weathered man walked through the front door, flanked by Blue, Peregrine, Renda, and Junkit. His face was covered with thick white stubble, and deep lines ran across his forehead. But he wore a familiar navy-blue uniform, and his eyes were still proud.

The original superhero, Captain Courage, walked into the lobby.

Sam couldn't believe it. His idol was standing in front of him.

"It's about an old coward, who realized the man he'd saved had become someone quite different, and who's spent the last year watching him every step of the way. That old coward followed you here, and now, once again, I have to stop you from doing something you'll regret."

"Too late, old friend," Derias replied calmly. "Just a bit too late. I was leaving you for last, with me, but your delusions of grandeur have cost you those last days of peace. There are men all around you, Courage, and even at your best, you could never defeat so many. You'll be gunned down as swiftly as the rest."

Courage nodded grimly. "I'm well removed from my best," he agreed, "and any delusions have long since vanished. I knew I couldn't walk in here and defeat you. You're far too clever. But you forgot about me, old friend, and so you left no one to guard your flank, no one to watch the outside. And so I took all the explosives I found in my former base and placed them all along the roof."

He smiled.

"Heads up, everyone."

Behind him, Blue triggered a device, and the lobby roof exploded.

35

"GET DOWN!" HAYDEN SCREAMED, PROJECTING A WALL OF MENTAL ENERGY.

He felt Lyle, Leni, and Meirna do the same, and the debris and shooting flames crashed against the invisible dome.

Everyone had already thrown themselves onto the lobby floor, and the family members now looked around in terror. Hayden glanced over and saw his mother cowering on the ground beside him, unsure of what was happening. It had been strange waking up to his mother's crying face. He'd felt like he was a little kid again. Hayden was still deeply hurt. Betrayed. But she was his mother, and he had to protect her.

He spotted many Wraiths getting buried in the falling debris, while others were swallowed by the fire. Thick black smoke roiled around the room, and for a moment, it seemed the battle was already over. Then shadowy figures started bursting out of the smoke on all sides, and Hayden turned to meet them.

"Here they come!" he called, and viciously waved his hand toward the nearest attacker.

The man went spinning backward, his rifle flying from his hand. Hayden dropped his section of the protective dome as more and more Wraiths closed in. The debris had stopped falling, but smoke began to pour in the breach.

Projecting a shield in front of him, Hayden plunged into the fray. Four of the Wraiths sprinted toward his end of the circle, and he glanced back to see James and Emily fall in behind him. The Vindico were already engaged on the far side of the circle, while Thunderbolt was leading the rest at the back, including Lana and Sam.

Hayden threw the first man off his feet, and Emily dove toward one of the fallen rifles. She scooped it up and spun onto her back just as another man took aim at Hayden. She fired twice into his chest. The Wraith collapsed to the floor.

James charged another attacker, grabbing his rifle. They fought violently for the gun, each trying to whip the other off his feet. The last of the four Wraiths fired at Hayden, but he narrowly managed to deflect the red blast, and it skimmed right over the heads of the ducking families.

Hayden sent another massive wave of energy at the man, and he went flying into the smoke and rubble. Emily climbed onto one knee and started firing wildly around the outer ring of the lobby.

James finally swung his opponent to the ground and then kicked him across the chin. The man went limp. "We need to go after Nimian!" he said.

"Fine," Hayden replied distractedly, "but maybe we should—"

He stopped when he saw a black metal cylinder sail out of the smoke and bounce past him, heading for the center of the group. Instinctively, he snatched it out of the air on the second bounce and thrust it outward again.

It was about twenty feet away when it went off.

The grenade erupted with concussive force, sending him, Emily, and James flying onto their backs. Hayden skidded right to the feet of James's parents, both of whom grabbed his shoulders and started yelling something nonsensical at him.

Hayden felt his mind spinning. He shook his head and climbed up again.

"Ouch," he muttered.

"Are you okay?" James's mother shrieked.

"I'm fine," Hayden replied, watching as more attackers ran out of the smoke. James was helping Emily up ten feet away. "Now it's my turn."

He raised his hands and sent another invisible blast hurtling toward the attackers.

Sam stuck close to Lana as she and Lyle surged forward, pressing the attack against the strange, unfeeling men. Most of the attackers were now unarmed, having had to pull themselves out of the rubble, and they were forced to close in. Thunderbolt was nearby with Meirna and Jada, but Septer and Sinio were already down.

Sam's family was sprawled out on the floor with their hands over their heads, and he had shouted at them to stay where they were. His mother had tried to grab him as he ran to join the others and then screamed hysterically for him to come back. But Sam had to help, even if he wasn't sure how.

He glanced at Deanna, who was following right behind him.

We're useless here, she said into his mind, and he nodded.

"Look out!" Thunderbolt shouted, and Sam jerked as two more Wraiths emerged from the left hallway and opened fire. Sam cast himself backward, slamming into Deanna. They both crashed to the floor.

But the shots weren't aimed at them. One blast caught Lana in the hip, and she gasped as it burned into her flesh. Another hit Lyle on the top of the arm, and he toppled sideways, his head slamming against the ground. Deanna screamed and crawled to his side.

Thunderbolt roared and sent a blast of energy streaking through the air, striking both assailants at once and sending them careening back down the hall. Lana managed to stay on her feet, but she was bodychecked by another attacker almost immediately. Sam heard frantic screams behind him and looked back to see Lana's father and mother rushing toward the battle.

Stay back, Sam warned them forcefully, and then he

lunged onto the man's back. Lana used the momentary distraction to free her right hand and punch him in the face. He rolled to the floor and Sam spilled off his back.

Lana's father reached the fight and tried to punch the Wraith as he climbed to his feet. In a blur of motion, the man punched Lana's father so fiercely in the stomach that his feet left the ground. Her father landed in a heap. Lana screamed and charged into the Wraith, and they both crashed into the fallen chunks of shingles and drywall.

Deanna was kneeling over her brother, tears streaming down her face, while Lana's mother did the same over her husband. Sam's eyes fell on Septer and Sinio, who both lay unmoving on the floor.

Even if we win, we'll have lost so many, he thought.

Sam saw an attacker running toward Lana as she wrestled with the first.

Without thinking, he charged.

The rifle thudded against Emily's chest as she let loose another round of shots, and the Wraith was at last struck down.

Hayden had another attacker pinned against the wall who was struggling violently against the invisible grip. James walked over, having dispatched his own combatant, and punched the Wraith in the face, collapsing the entire section of the wall.

"We make a good team," Emily said.

Hayden turned around, and she saw that his left pant leg was stained with fresh blood, while the top of his right arm was scorched and blackened. James's entire face was covered with soot, and his left arm was hanging limply by his side.

"Sort of," she corrected.

"And we're not done yet," James said.

Emily turned and a flurry of motion caught her eye. She saw Sam get thrown to the ground and a Wraith walk over to him, ready to bring his foot down.

Emily lifted her rifle, closed one eye, and fired. The shot caught the man right on the side of the head, and he collapsed.

Emily turned around to see Hayden mentally rip a man off of Lana, while James slammed into another Wraith, freeing Thunderbolt to blast a third farther down the hallway.

She scanned the room for Nimian, but he had vanished, as had Avaria, Leni, Courage, and the other captured League members. Despite everything, she pitied Nimian. She now understood how his own twisted sense of guilt had led him to this.

Her eyes fell on the front entrance.

"Stay here!" she called to Hayden and James. "I'm going after Nimian."

Avaria watched as Derias stepped over the fallen body of Junkit, heading for Courage. Peregrine lay on the grass nearby as well, while Renda and Blue stood over her, facing off against the last two black-clad men.

"I didn't think you'd come back," Derias said to Courage.

He held a thin knife in his hand, stained with Junkit's blood.

"When you left, I knew something had changed," Courage replied, and he gestured at Junkit. "The man I know would never murder without cause."

"But you know my cause," Derias said, "and I fear you may now have ruined it. If my men have lost the battle inside, then the rest of the Vindico and League members will be here soon." His eyes went to Avaria. "And it seems that's the case."

"Then surrender," Courage said. "Stop this."

Derias shook his head. "There's no surrender here. My life ended a long time ago. I've been walking in a dead man's shoes."

Avaria stepped toward him, tears streaming down her cheeks.

"Please, Derias," she whispered. "Don't think so poorly of me."

"You murdered them," he spat. "My friends, *your* friends! You murdered innocent people!"

"I only did it to avenge you!" She was racked by a sob. "You should have told me!" She spun on Courage. "You! Why did you never tell me?"

"I regret what happened," Courage said. "I always have. You know I cared for you. But you came out of that chamber a different woman."

"I came out to find my husband dead!" she snarled, and

then turned to Derias. "I'm still here," she whispered. "I never left."

Derias gazed at her for a moment.

"You told me she was a monster," he said quietly.

"She was," Courage said. "I was too. And now, so are you."

"I'm sorry," Avaria told Derias, taking another step toward him. "I should have stayed with you."

He gestured at her. "And I never should have done this to you. We should be living in a house like this watching our children play," he said wistfully. "So many things went wrong."

"It's not too late," Courage said.

"I took so many lives," he murmured. "Those men aren't coming back."

"We all must pay for our mistakes," Courage said. "Myself included."

. Avaria came within a few feet of him. "Derias, please. We'll go to your island. Together."

Derias gazed at her. Finally, the knife fell from his fingers. "It's just too late."

She shook her head. "Let's go now. No one will know."

"I'll take you there," Courage agreed. "Maybe I can give back what I took all those years ago."

Derias put his hand out, and she took it, squeezing his fingers.

"I missed you," he whispered.

"How touching," a mocking voice said, and Avaria

whirled around to find Leni standing behind her, sneering. "But I do not forgive so easily."

Avaria heard a wet thud, and she spun back to find Derias's knife embedded in his chest. Blood spilled out around the hilt.

"No!" she screamed as Derias toppled backward.

"No question this time," Leni said. "Right in the heart."

Courage flew at him, but Leni waved a hand, and he crashed into the grass. Once again, Avaria dropped to her knees beside her fallen husband.

"No," Avaria pleaded. "No!"

He looked up at her, his discolored face betraying no pain.

"At least this time I can say good-bye," he wheezed. "I'm so sorry."

"I can't lose you again," she said, the tears pouring down her face. "I can't."

"I was already gone, Avaria. But it's not so bad. I saw you once more, when I thought I never would." He smiled. "It's not so bad."

Then he closed his eyes, and his skin began to lighten. Soon she was staring at the face of her husband, Derias Tepper, and he was dead.

Avaria turned around and lunged at Leni, but she was stopped in midair. She hovered there, straining every muscle against the invisible grip.

"Murderer," she hissed.

"I did love you, Avaria," Leni said quietly. "He was right.

But you always loved him. I'm sorry, for a great many things. And mostly, for this."

She saw Derias's blood-soaked knife circle around her and then stop, hovering in front of her chest.

"I know you, Avaria. You would hunt me to the end of my days. You already hunted this old fool," he added, gesturing at Courage, "for fifteen years. I have to kill you and end this before it begins. Good-bye, Avaria."

Avaria closed her eyes. She wasn't afraid. She had felt so little for so long, and now she felt only pain, fresh and raw. What was there to fear?

A loud blast split through the air, and Avaria dropped to her knees. She opened her eyes and saw Leni topple forward, crashing into the lawn. Emily stood behind him, slowly lowering her rifle.

Avaria crawled back to Derias. She lay over her dead husband and cried, and no one disturbed her.

36

THUNDERBOLT STARED AT THEM ALL GRAVELY, HIS FACE CAKED WITH BLOOD
and dust. Everyone else looked much the same. Those who had survived the battle were gathered in the center of the mostly destroyed lobby. The dead lay on the far side.

They had labored for the past half hour to collect the bodies, send the injured to the nearest medical facilities, and drag the prisoners to the cells in the basement.

Among the dead lay twelve of Nimian's men, Nimian himself, Junkit, Sinio, Peregrine, and the Baron. James glanced at the Baron, lying peacefully with the others. Thunderbolt had crouched beside the Baron when they first found him and whispered some quiet words. James wondered if it was an apology.

The five protégés now stood beside the remaining seven League members, including Courage. James and Sam's families stood quietly behind them, as well as Hayden's mother, while Lana's family had gone with her father to the hospital.

"We won today," Thunderbolt said, "but at a cost. And again, you five have had to pay for our past mistakes. We have lost more friends. Good people, and ones who didn't need to die today. Even Nimian was a good man once, and I mourn him anew. Courage told me what happened, and it seems he found himself before the end."

His eyes hardened.

"For those who don't know, Leni survived. He wore body armor under his clothing, and it absorbed much of Emily's blast. He is severely wounded, but I have left him alone in a prison cell. He will survive on his own, or not. I know my own preference." He looked at the Baron, and his expression softened again. "Four other Vindico members survived as well. They will be moved back to the Perch soon."

"What about Nimian's men?" Emily asked.

"They will be taken there as well, for now," Thunderbolt replied. "I don't know if the process can be reversed. We'll have to find out."

"I can help with that," Emily said.

He nodded. "That brings me back to you five. Now, more than ever, the future of the League rests on your shoulders. We have lost three members, and some of us grow old and tired. I have formally invited Courage to rejoin the League, and he has agreed to return for a few months to help us transition into this new generation. To see if we can't create something better. After that time, I too may retire from an active role. Nimian was right about one thing: many of us are stained by our histories. I'm one of them. But you five have once again proven yourselves to be more than capable of accepting the torch."

He looked at each of them in turn.

"You have already been inducted into the League of Heroes, and now I formally ask that you take up residence at headquarters and become full-time, active members. You're very young, but you've already been through more than most people ever will. You will still be expected to uphold your studies, but you will be equal members. There will be a state funeral for our fallen in three days, and you will all be introduced to the media soon after."

James glanced at his family. His parents stood with their arms around his younger sisters. His father smiled proudly, and his mother reluctantly did the same. Ally looked positively exuberant. James suspected that she was already planning her first visit to headquarters.

"How big will our rooms be?" Hayden asked. "Can I bring my TV?"

Everyone turned to him.

"What?" he said.

"I'm just going to start ignoring you," Thunderbolt muttered.

"Don't even think about it, Sam!" Sam's mother said, sounding on the verge of tears. "You're only twelve years old!"

"And a member of the League," Sam said firmly. "I wasn't any safer at home. I'm involved now, one way or the other. I might as well be with my friends."

"You can take the Mediator and pack your bags when you drop your families off," Thunderbolt said. "As for the Baron and Nimian, Courage and I have decided to bury them in the League cemetery. It's time we stop ignoring our past mistakes. We'll do that tomorrow."

"I think Avaria should be there," Lana said.

Thunderbolt hesitated. "I agree. All right, the Mediator's in the garage. Take your families home, and be at headquarters by noon tomorrow."

"Can we make it two?" Hayden asked. "We haven't slept in days."

"Fine. Two o'clock. Now get going."

"So, looks like we're all going to be roomies again," Hayden said.

"We better go console your mom, Sam," Lana added, patting Sam's shoulder. Sam looked over to see his mother sobbing into his father's arms.

"We're officially in the League of Heroes," James said slowly.

"Are you all right, Emily?" Sam asked.

They turned to find Emily staring at the line of bodies.

"They spent so much of their lives fighting a war they created themselves," she said. "And they only found peace when it killed them. It had nothing to do with good and bad. None of this. This entire war came from their belief in the choice of fate. They made their own villains."

"We should remember that," Lana said quietly.

They all fell silent, and then James felt a hand on his shoulder.

"James, think we can go home?" his dad asked gruffly.

Ally and Jen appeared behind him.

"I told you he was a superhero," Ally said, almost gloatingly.

Jen shrugged. "I had to see it to believe it. You know, before he's in tights. Then I don't want to see anything."

Ally stepped up and gave him a hug. "You kicked butt."

James looked down at her in surprise. "Was that a compliment?"

"It was," she said, and then smirked. "How about the Weasel for a superhero name?"

"Love it," Hayden said immediately.

James scowled. "No. And yeah, Dad, we can go home. There's just one more thing I have to do. Hayden, can you come with me? I might need backup."

The cell door slid open, revealing the captured Vindico, minus Leni. They were all sitting down, staring forlornly at the walls. The Torturer, Sliver, and Rono sat on one end, each battered and bruised. Avaria sat alone in the far corner, her eyes vacant. She didn't even stir when the door opened.

"Torturer," James said, "can I talk to you?"

The big man looked at him for a moment and then stood up, grimacing with every movement. James and Hayden stepped back to let him through the door, and he limped into the corridor, looking suspicious. Hayden shut the door behind him.

"What do you want?"

James hesitated. "I know you were thinking of helping us before Rono came. I just wanted to say thanks and that I'm going to talk to Thunderbolt to see if I can get your sentence reduced."

The Torturer looked surprised. "I didn't want to kill you," he conceded. "But they won't let me out, ever. What would I do?"

"Maybe you can join the League eventually," James suggested, though he sincerely doubted that would ever happen.

"Yeah, they'll love that," Hayden said, smirking.

The Torturer sighed. "He's right. Too many people hate me already. But there is one thing you could try."

"What?" James asked.

"I just hate the Perch so much," the Torturer said. "I hate it. No sun, no fresh air. They can't free me, I get that, but maybe I could be exiled to one of those islands too, like Courage and Nimian. They could drop me off there, keep people away, and I'd be happy. At least I'd be outside. Can you ask him?"

James nodded. "Definitely. I can try to get Thunderbolt to agree to that."

"Thanks. So are you in the League now or what?"

"Yeah, all of us," James replied.

"I'm glad one of us got in, at least," he said. The Torturer gave him a pat on the shoulder. "If they let me go to an island, maybe you could come by sometime?"

"I'll do that," James said.

Hayden opened the cell door, and the big man traipsed back inside, his footsteps thumping off the metal.

He glanced back. "See you, James."

"See you," James said, and then Hayden shut the door.

"Feel better?" Hayden asked.

"Much. Did you talk to your mom?"

Hayden sighed. "Yeah. She asked if I could ever forgive her."

James glanced at him. "What did you say?"

"Maybe."

James paused. "If you want my advice, give her a chance. You only get one family."

"I guess," Hayden said reluctantly. "You're a good man, James. I like that in a roommate."

"I am not rooming with you."

"Please?"

"No," James said.

"We can get a queen-size bed."

"No."

"But we'd be perfect roomies!" Hayden said, as he started to list the reasons on his hand. "We both like staring at ourselves in the mirror. I could use a personal trainer, and you need help with the ladies. I can clean our room while lying down . . ."

James hurried ahead to get away from him, but he fought back a grin at the same time.

THE RAIN WAS DRIZZLING FROM A GLOOMY, OVERCAST SKY, AND LANA SHIVERED a little in her damp clothes. The five protégés stood silently in the midst of the small group, huddled around two caskets in the far corner of the League's cemetery.

Avaria stood alone in front of the left casket, where Nimian lay. She had no umbrella and her hair and clothes were soaked. Still, she hadn't moved. Thunderbolt stood between the two caskets, letting the silence hold. The water was running down his lined face, and Lana wondered if there were tears mixed with the raindrops.

Finally, he looked up.

"Courage has asked to say a few words," he said, "to honor two old friends."

Courage stepped forward, wearing his League uniform.

"I won't say much. I've found that silence speaks better in times like these. But I do want to say a few things that should have been said a long time ago.

"Two good men lie here: men who were products of our flaws. Before he became our oldest enemy, Martin Benwick was a passionate, brilliant man. Before any of us, he saw that these powers brought hope and gave us the chance to bring peace and justice to the world in a way never before imagined. Some of you may still not know this, but it was Martin who created the League of Heroes."

Lana heard some quiet murmurs around her, and she looked at the Baron's coffin. She had come to understand the man far better after he'd told them his story, and she had always pitied him somewhat, having spent his whole life surrounded by a reminder of what he couldn't be. She was surprised to feel tears in the corners of her eyes.

"He brought us together, he laid the groundwork for our mandate, and he gave four confused individuals a purpose. And for all that, we mistreated him. It was only natural that one day he would try and join us fully, and in our pride, we struck him down. Perhaps we were right to stop it from happening, but we were wrong in how we did it." He turned to the Baron's coffin. "Today, let us remember him as Martin Benwick, a man with a noble dream."

There was a long moment of silence. Lana glanced at the others and saw that they were all somber. It was the Baron that had brought them together, and she knew they all felt a certain sense of gratitude toward the old man, regardless of his intentions.

Finally, Courage turned to Nimian's coffin. He opened his mouth, but closed it again quickly. Then he sighed. "As painful as that mistake was, this one was much worse. Our actions that night destroyed two lives, and for that I apologize again, especially to you, Avaria."

Avaria made no reaction.

"I am only happy that he found you again, as you both once were. We should all be happy that when he died, he was Derias Tepper, a brilliant mind, a good friend, and a loving husband."

Lana felt tears run down her cheeks. She had hated Avaria so deeply for months. Now, she only felt pity for her former mentor, who had suffered for her decisions in a way Lana couldn't even imagine. Avaria seemed to finally crack, and she laid her hand on the coffin and began to weep.

Courage turned back to the group.

"We lay these two men here, a short way from our lost heroes. They have had as great an impact on the League as any. Remember their stories as we strive forward so that we can create a better League than the one that killed these two men." He glanced at each coffin, lingering on Nimian's. "Good-bye, old friends," he said softly, and then walked back to join the others.

Thunderbolt stepped forward. "It's time, Avaria."

For a moment, it seemed she didn't hear him, but then she stepped back from the coffin.

"Hayden," Thunderbolt said.

Hayden raised his hands, and both caskets were slowly lowered into the graves, the Baron's first and then Nimian's. A racking sob escaped Avaria as the casket disappeared from view.

Thunderbolt waited for another minute and then nodded.

"That concludes the service. If you like, pay your respects to these men and the others that lie here. Remember what you are a part of. When you're ready, proceed back to headquarters. Courage and I will meet you there."

Gradually, the small group of League members began to disperse, their quiet conversations filtering across the cemetery.

"Ready?" Hayden asked.

Lana watched Avaria standing motionlessly on the edge of the grave, with Thunderbolt and Courage behind her.

"Yeah," she murmured, "let's leave them alone."

The five former protégés quietly filed out of the cemetery toward the white ships that sat glistening in the rain.

38

"I AM BEAT," HAYDEN GROANED, FALLING ONTO A COUCH IN THE HEADQUARTERS lounge.

They'd spent the last three days moving into their new rooms and helping with the extensive repairs to the building, and they were exhausted.

The state funeral for the three fallen League members had taken place the day before and drawn a huge crowd as the procession drove through the city streets before heading upstate to the cemetery. Many more tears had been shed at that ceremony.

The teens had gotten little sleep that night and had been woken up early to prepare for their official introduction to the media, which they'd just returned from.

James stretched his hands over his head. "Well, that's the end of it."

"They sure had a lot of questions," Emily said. "And all the pictures. I could barely see anything."

"They are journalists, to be fair," James pointed out.

Lana glanced at Sam. "I can't believe they asked if you were in second grade."

Sam scowled. "That guy was a jerk."

"You should have made him take his clothes off and dance on national television," Hayden remarked.

"Thunderbolt would have loved that." James shook his head. "He was already angry that you wore a cape with your suit."

"The cape is going to be my signature," Hayden protested. "I'm incorporating it into my uniform. Speaking of which, have you all thought about yours?"

Lana rolled her eyes. "We all get the same uniforms—"

"I was hoping to do an all-black jumpsuit," Emily cut in, "with shiny black boots and the silver visor and shoulder mount. It's the name I'm having trouble with."

Emily had attracted a lot of questions about her lack of superpowers during the news conference; one reporter had asked if she felt safer staying close to her superpowered friends during the battle. But Hayden had jumped in and said, "Actually, we try to stick close to *her*," and she'd been beaming ever since. Combined with the fact that she was being publicly credited with capturing Leni, Emily was finally feeling like a full member now.

"I have a lot of name ideas," Hayden said, sitting up eagerly. "Sam, you're going to be Kid Kinetic. Lana, you're Lynx. Emily, you're the Black Arrow. And James, you're—"

"I don't want to hear it," James interjected.

"The Gladiator."

James looked up, surprised. "That's not bad."

"And what's your name?" Emily asked.

Hayden got to his feet and swelled his chest. "I am Handsome Hayden, he of the—"

Lana chopped at the back of his knee, and he toppled to the couch.

"Or, I was thinking the Hand," he mumbled, rubbing his knee.

"Do you realize we're all going to live together now?" Emily said, excitedly.

James sighed. "I don't know if I can deal with Hayden every day."

"I was thinking about going out tonight," Hayden said. "We've been working hard for the last two weeks, and we're bound to get free stuff, being superheroes and all—"

The lounge door slid open, and Thunderbolt came in.

"I hope you enjoyed your rest," he said. "We're back to active duty, and we just got a call. There's a hostage situation in the Lower East Side, and they need help. We have to let the world know that the League is back. I'm sending you on your first mission."

"So much for that," Hayden grumbled. He stood up. "I'm on my way, boss. I'll have the bad guys—"

"Sam will be coercing them out of it," Thunderbolt cut in. "The rest of you are the security."

"I see," Hayden said.

Emily jumped up, pulling a white-faced Sam along with her. "We're on our way!"

"Great," Sam added weakly.

Thunderbolt nodded. "Good, take the Mediator. I've already transmitted the coordinates. It's time to become superheroes, kids."

Hayden stuck out his arm. "Hands in?"

Everyone groaned and hurried toward the roof.

"Fine, don't blame me when we come out flat!" Hayden called after them.

"Think we can trim this group to four?" Lana suggested.

"Yes," James agreed emphatically. He pushed open the repaired roof door, and they emerged into the brilliant daylight. A cold wind was whipping in from the river, sending their hair flapping around them. As they walked toward the Mediator, James smiled. He was a superhero. And better yet, he had his closest friends at his side.

They all settled in the cockpit, James in the pilot's seat, Emily beside him, and the others gathered behind. James powered up the ship and heard the engines thrum to life.

"Time to show the world what the Feros can do," Emily said.

James glanced back. "Ready?"

"Ready," they all said confidently.

James nodded and gripped the throttle. "Here we go."

ACKNOWLEDGMENTS

Thanks as always to Brianne Johnson at Writers House, who really does everything but write the first draft. It was a lucky day when you picked up my first manuscript. To my wonderful editor, Shauna (Fay) Rossano at G. P. Putnam's Sons, who brings structure to my world of superheroes. To Jen Besser at Putnam, who continues to give her support and guidance to this series, and who helped give it wings in the first place. To Dana Borowitz at United Talent Agency, who is taking this story to the bright lights of Hollywood to try and find it a home. To Greg Stadnyk for designing these great covers, and to the entire team at Penguin Young Readers Group for helping me get this story to readers.

Thanks to my parents, Tom and Carol King, who continue to give me their unwavering support as I embark on this uncertain adventure. To my brothers, Adam and Eric, who provide me with bitingly intelligent views on the world and no small amount of humor. And to the rest of my extended family and friends who have been there every step of the way and who probably have no idea how much they mean to me: thank you all for everything.